REQUIEM'S PRAYER

REQUIEM'S PRAYER

DAWN OF DRAGONS, BOOK III

DANIEL ARENSON

SLYN

The Widejaw tribe was enjoying the meat of its victims when the demon arrived, offering a deal even sweeter than human flesh.

The raid had begun like any other--with roars, with sharpened bronze, and with the guzzling of hot blood.

"We will slay the men and children, and we will take the women to bear our sons!" Slyn had shouted that morning, voice hoarse. He raised a string of shrunken heads, jangling the lurid trophies. "Widejaws will feast upon human meat!"

Across the camp, his warriors roared--a thousand killers. They beat their bronze *apa* swords against their ring mail, and they stomped their leather boots. Tattoos coiled across their faces and bald heads, a strand for every enemy they had slain; most men sported dozens of the coiling marks. Rings pierced their noses and brows, and bronze disks stretched their earlobes.

Most glorious--more than tattoos, rings, or weapons--were their deformities. Each man of Widejaw, on his thirteenth summer, slashed his own cheeks open from mouth to ears, the wounds then cauterized. As they roared, the men's jaws opened like the jaws of sharks, revealing their teeth down to the molars.

All other tribes flee in terror upon seeing our jaws, Slyn thought. He opened his own wide jaw--he had slashed his cheeks thirty years ago--and shouted for all his men to hear.

"Widejaw will rule the plains from ice to sea!" He pounded his sword against his chest. "Widejaw will be an empire! We will be greater than the all other tribes. We will be greater than the lands across the sea." He shook his sword over his head. "We will be greater than Requiem, the tribe of reptiles!"

His warriors bellowed louder than ever. They had heard of this so-called kingdom in the west, this land of dragons, this Requiem. Slyn feared no other enemy--not the northerners in the lands of ice, not the forest dwellers who skinned their enemies alive, not even the southerners across the sea who built towers of stone. But dragons . . . dragons were worthy adversaries. Dragons were a threat the Widejaw tribe would have to conquer.

But not yet, Slyn thought. *Not yet. First we must grow our power, slay our enemies, capture their women, and eat the flesh of their children. We will grow stronger, strong enough to slay dragons.*

He raised the skull of Chieftain Heltok of the Bearclaw tribe. Blood filled the skull, collected from the children of Bearclaw which he himself, Chieftain Slyn of Widejaw, had slain and consumed only yesterday. He brought the skull to his mouth and drank deeply. Blood trickled down his chin and chest.

"Drink, warriors of Widejaw!" he shouted. "Drink for war."

Every one of his thousand warriors raised a skull and they too drank blood, giving them strength for a new battle. Mouths stained red, the warriors mounted their horses and brandished their swords and spears. Slyn tossed down his empty skull, wiped the blood off his lips, and mounted his own horse--a black stallion that had borne him on many conquests.

"To blood!" Slyn roared. "To meat! To conquest!"

He dug his heels into his mount, and the horse burst into a gallop. Slyn rode south across the plains, and his warriors followed, their cries rising in a storm. They left their camp behind--the tents, the women and children, and the vanquished enemies who roasted upon campfires. They would return with more meals, with more women, with more power for Widejaw.

The grasslands rose and fell around them. Distant forests swayed in the east. Slyn had been driving his tribe south all summer, leaving a wake of bones.

All these lands will be mine, he thought as he led his horde. *All its women will bear our sons, and all its blood will fill our bellies.*

He opened his wide jaws and roared, and behind him, his warriors answered his call.

They rode throughout the morning, and at noon they reached the hills and saw it ahead--the Henge of Bluewood. It crowned the highest hill, its towering boulders engraved with runes. Upon smaller hills rose the homes of the Bluewood tribe. The fools had built wooden huts topped with grass roofs, permanent dwellings so easy to crush and burn. The weaklings emerged from those homes now, pointed toward the advancing Widejaw horde, and shouted in fear.

"Break their bones and drink their blood!" Slyn cried, riding across the hills.

His warriors rode behind him, their battle cries pealing. With flying spears and arrows, with mouths opened from ear to ear, the Widejaw warriors swarmed across the hills.

The enemy mounted only a pathetic defense--a few men firing arrows of sharpened wood that snapped harmlessly against the Widejaws' armor. Slyn grinned as he rode among them, swinging his sword, cutting them down. His bronze blade slashed through a man's neck. Blood spurted. Slyn grinned, licked his red sword, and swung it again, driving the blade into a graybeard's head. The skull cracked, leaking its sweet innards like a melon.

All across the hills, his fellow Widejaw warriors swarmed. Their horses trampled over fleeing children. Their arrows, spears, and blades cut into fur-clad men. Their torches thrust into grassy roofs, and the enemy huts burned.

"Capture the women!" Slyn cried, pointing his blade south. "Bring them to me."

Dozens of Bluewood women were fleeing down the hills.
Slyn licked his lips as he watched them run, savoring the sight of
their tunics swishing against their bodies. Their flight was futile.
Widejaw riders reached them within heartbeats.

One woman spun to face the horde, thrusting a pointed
stick. Her weapon snapped against a rider's armor, and the man
grabbed her, lifted her onto his horse, and laughed as she
floundered. Another woman drew a flint dagger and stabbed
herself in the throat, choosing death over slavery. The others kept
trying to flee, spinning from side to side, trapped within a ring of
horses. Widejaws laughed and plucked them up like falcons
snatching mice.

Slyn grinned as he watched his warriors work. The huts
burned and the enemy corpses piled up. Already Widejaws were
severing heads and stripping them of flesh, collecting the skulls
for their trophies.

Smiling thinly, savoring the scent of death, Slyn rode up the
tallest hill. All around him sprawled fire and blood, and ahead the
great henge rose, its boulders etched with old runes.

A crown of stone, Slyn thought. *A crown for a conqueror.*

He rode between the towering boulders, his dripping sword
held at his side, and saw them there. The Bluewood tribe elders,
bearded druids clad in indigo robes, stood holding scrimshawed
staffs. They prayed to their stone gods, and tears streamed down
their cheeks. They did not flee as Slyn moved between them,
cutting them down one by one, silencing their voices until only
one remained.

The graybeard prayed, the blood of his comrades staining
his robes, as Slyn circled him upon his horse.

"You will live," Slyn said to the druid. "You will flee this
place. You will travel south, and you will tell all those on your
path of the Widejaw empire." Slyn opened his jaw wide, displaying

all his teeth from incisors to molars. "Go and tell them! Go and tell all the land that Slyn of Widejaw rules."

He watched the old man flee across the hills, racing through the devastation and fire. The Widejaw riders jeered as the druid ran by, pelted him with globs of the enemy's flesh, and struck him with the flat of their blades. Blood drenched the man by the time he had cleared the destruction, racing south. Slyn had sent such messengers across the world. Soon all would know of his might and fear him.

"Cut out their skulls!" Slyn shouted from the hilltop. "Take their limbs! Bind their women! Tonight we drink blood from their skulls, cook their flesh on our fires, and plant our seed into their wives and daughters."

He licked his lips, already imagining the evening. The blood would be hot, and the women would quiver beneath him as he mounted them. They would take his seed. They would produce boys, future warriors for Widejaw, or they too would roast upon his cooking fires.

He was about to spur his horse, to lead his men back to his camp, when the demon appeared.

At first the figure was just a silhouette on the horizon. Briefly, Slyn thought the druid was returning, and he tilted his head. But no. This was no man. A darkness clung to the figure, and a chill blasted forth. Frost coated the henge stones and Slyn's blade, and icy fingers seemed to invade him, clutching at his bones, tugging at his veins. His horse neighed beneath him and sidestepped, its fur freezing.

Slyn growled and sucked in a breath. He stared forward, eyes narrowed.

The figure was walking through the devastation, making a beeline to the henge, unperturbed by the surrounding Widejaw warriors. Black smoke enveloped the creature, sending out creeping tendrils. Widejaws hissed and stared, daring not attack. Some stepped back in fear, crying of evil spirits. Others knelt.

"A demon," Slyn hissed. His horse bucked beneath him.

As the creature drew nearer, Slyn gritted his teeth and growled. He had seen beasts before--the great mammoths of the west, the fetid rocs of the Goldtusk tribe, and even a dragon in the distance--but he had never seen a creature this foul. The demon approaching him had the torso and head of a man. The chest was muscular, the head bald, the face hard. The limbs, however, were things of nightmares. One arm was a dripping, twisting tentacle lined with suckers. The other arm was a great, clacking lobster claw. One leg was furred and dank, ending with a hoof. The other was the leg of a bird, ending with a sharp talon.

The demon climbed the hill, his hoof and talon leaving smoking, seared footprints in the grass. The runes upon the henge stones bled, the crimson droplets running down the rock. The iciness left Slyn and now heat bathed him. Sweat soaked him. His hair crackled upon his head, and his armor grew so hot his skin sizzled. Across the hills and valleys below, men knelt and bowed and cried out to the demon.

Slyn refused to bow, refused to flee. His muscles tensed and his veins bulged. He opened his jaw wide, baring all his teeth at the creature.

"I am Slyn, son of Heshok, chieftain of Widejaw." He sneered, holding his sword high. "Name yourself, demon."

The visitor regarded him. His face was calm--the weathered, scarred face of a mortal man, perhaps fifty years of age. The eyes were pale green. Mad eyes. Eyes burning with deep, demonic flame. The stranger tilted his head.

"You burn a village of barbarians." The demon looked around him, lips pursed. "Grass-roofed huts. A few goats. I think I saw the body of an old man holding a stone-tipped spear." He turned back toward Slyn, and his eyes narrowed. "You are the great Widejaw warriors the north speaks of in awe, and you fight humble shepherds and gatherers of berries?"

Slyn took a step closer to the demon, sword raised. The stench of sulfur, burning hair, and worms blasted his nostrils.

"Who are you?" Slyn repeated. "Give me your name or I'll slay you like I slew Kehan the Giant's Bane, Eekar the Serpent Skin, Shenrash the Scarred, and all other chieftains who thought they were mighty, thought they were safe in our territory. I can slay a demon too."

"A demon?" The stranger smiled thinly. "Yes. Yes . . . I suppose I am a demon now. At least parts of me." He raised his arms. The tentacle wriggled, dripping ooze, and the lobster claw clattered. "Most call me Raem Seran, King of Eteer, Lord of the Abyss. To you I will simply be . . . Master."

Slyn roared, jaw stretching as wide as it would go. Master? He--Slyn the Conqueror--serve another?

With a curse, Slyn swung his sword at the demon.

Raem's lobster claw rose, grabbed the bronze blade, and shattered it.

The demon's tentacle stretched out, growing longer and longer, forming an obscene, dripping serpent that wrapped around Slyn. The tentacle's suckers attached to Slyn like lamprey mouths, pinning his arms to his sides, cutting through his armor. Across the hills below, Widejaws howled in rage and fear but dared not approach.

"Release me, demon!" Slyn cried. He tried to free himself, to bite, to kick, but the tentacle squeezed tighter, crushing him. The suckers bit into his flesh, and Slyn roared.

"Release you?" Raem asked calmly. He tilted his head quizzically. "You've named yourself an enemy to me. Almost as deadly an enemy as shepherds and gatherers. Should I not slay you like you slew them?"

Slyn snapped his teeth at the demon. "I serve no master. I serve no gods. I have lived free, and I will die free. Kill me then, Raem." He spat. "I spit upon any man or deity who would call himself my master."

"Kill you . . . to start, yes." Raem nodded. "But you would not remain dead for long, Slyn, son of Heshok. You would wake up in a pit of darkness and fire, and we would change you. Stretch your skin like a sack of wine, pumping you full of blood for demons to drink. You would hang upon our walls, forever screaming, a living sack of sustenance. How you would plead to die! It would please me to hear your screams."

Clutched in the biting, crushing tentacle, staring into the mad eyes of this demon, Slyn felt something he had not felt in many years, not since his father had burned him as a child.

He felt fear.

"I would not scream," he whispered hoarsely; he could speak no louder. His ribs creaked, feeling ready to snap.

"Perhaps not," Raem said. "Some in the Abyss merely weep. You might be a weeper. But I offer you an alternative, Slyn of Widejaw. A chance for glory, for true dominion. I offer you a chance to slay dragons."

The tentacle released him, contracting back to its original size. It twitched, dripping blood and mucus. Slyn had to summon all his will not to collapse. Blood dripped through rents in his armor.

Dragons . . . the only creatures Slyn had not faced in battle. The only creatures he knew could defeat him.

"You speak of Requiem." Slyn spat. "The weredragons rule in the west. They do not fly over my lands, over my territory."

Raem raised his eyebrows. "And yet I see the fear in you. At the mere mention of their name, you grow pale. They frighten you, don't they? They are mightier than you. But see, Slyn, son of Heshok . . . I can make you just as mighty."

The demon's tentacle stretched out, and upon it materialized a golden goblet full of green liquid. Slyn grimaced. Small, strange creatures swam in the drink; they looked like maggots with human faces. Their mouths opened and closed, their eyes spun, and their bodies wriggled as they moved around the murky wine.

"Drink," Raem said. "Drink the elixir. My demons can turn you into a wineskin, or they can give you strength . . . strength to slay dragons. Drink, Slyn of Widejaw, and you will destroy Requiem for me. You will rule the north in my name, and all will know of your might."

Slyn thought back to the dragon he had seen from a distance, a great reptile roaring fire. He had sat upon his horse, staring up, craving the reptile's blood but knowing its fire could easily wash over him. He looked back at the demon--the demon that had almost slain him, that had mocked him, that had made him look weak.

He grabbed the goblet.

He guzzled the drink.

The liquid burned through him, hotter than coals. The tiny demons screeched, scuttled inside him, tore at his throat, raced through his innards. He saw their forms crawl through his veins on his arms. He felt them behind his eyeballs. They scurried inside his face, pushing at the skin.

And Slyn screamed.

"Ah . . ." said Raem. "A screamer after all."

Slyn fell to all fours. He tossed back his head and howled. His body twisted, bulged madly, growing larger, growing stronger. The claws tore through his fingertips. The wings burst out from his back. The fur sprouted across him, dank and stinking.

He rose into the air, cackling, roaring with pain, with fury. His fellow Widejaws knelt in awe before him.

"What am I?" Slyn shouted, his voice deeper than before, a rumble that rolled across the hills. Pain and horror pulsed through him. "What do you see? What have I become?"

His warriors only knelt, crying out, bowing, howling, pounding their swords against their armor.

Below him, the demon Raem turned toward the other Widejaws and shouted for them all to hear. "Drink from my elixir!" He held out the goblet. "Come forth, Widejaws, and drink! Let my blessing fill you."

They drank.

They screamed.

They changed.

They had traveled south as warriors of Widejaw, men of might. They returned north as gods.

JEID

Jeid Blacksmith, now known as King Aeternum, sat upon the Oak Throne of Requiem and gazed upon his realm.

He didn't have to gaze very far.

"A few hills," he said. "A few birch trees. A view of the mountains. Marble columns. That is our kingdom."

Laira stood at his side. The Queen of Requiem placed her small hand upon one of the twisting, polished branches that formed the Oak Throne.

"The mightiest oak grows from a humble sapling," she said. "The tree we planted here will last for eternity."

Jeid looked at his new wife. Whenever he looked at Laira, soothing warmth filled him, her light and goodness holding together the broken shards inside him. He thought back to that night Laira had first come to him. She had been a famished, wounded, dying youth fleeing captivity, bleeding from a dozen wounds, so thin she could barely walk. Today, in his marble hall, Jeid saw a proud queen. She had not grown taller--years of hunger had left her stature short, her bones small--but her skin now showed the rich hue of health, and light shone in her green eyes. Her black hair, once sheared close to her scalp, now hung down to her chin, strewn with wildflowers. Her jaw was still crooked, her mouth still slanted--that old injury would never heal--but those slanted lips were now wont to smile. She wore a rich garment of deerskin trimmed with fox fur, and a circlet of gold topped her head.

"Dorvin carved the throne too small." Jeid reached out and held Laira's arm. "He should have made enough room for the both of us."

She poked him. "The throne *is* large enough for two. It's you who are too large." She smiled--one of those new smiles, the beautiful smiles that always seemed so pure, so hesitant, a ray of sunlight shining through a storm. "I'll find some room."

She hopped onto his lap, so small and light, only half his size, and he kissed the top of her head.

"I think I like the throne this size after all." He wrapped his arms around her. "I want us to stay like this forever. Just like this. This is perfection."

She leaned against him. "Just like this," she whispered.

The columns of Requiem rose around them, a dozen in all, soaring taller than any structure in the known world. Their capitals were shaped as rearing dragons, and they held no roof. The palace of Requiem was not yet complete; it would be many moons, perhaps years, before it stood in full glory. Birches rustled beyond the columns, their leaves orange and gold. Many of those leaves glided down to carpet the hills and to scuttle along the marble tiles of Requiem's hall.

Shadows streamed across those tiles now, and when Jeid looked above him, he saw the dragons of Requiem. Dozens glided in every color, the sun gleaming upon their scales. Many other Vir Requis, these ones in human form, now rested in wooden huts among the trees. Two hundred and seventeen souls lived in Requiem--the genesis of a nation.

Jeid thought back to the days before these columns had stood. Days of death, of fear, of hiding in caves and forests. They had been outcasts, wandering the world, hunted, alone, many unaware that others even existed. So many had died. So much blood still filled his nightmares. This, now, here . . . a hint of peace, a light at last.

Perfection, he had called it. Yet he had lied.

"I wish they were here with us," he said in a low voice. "Tanin and Issari."

Laira's face darkened. She nodded. "I fear for them every day."

Fen, the Eteerian boy who had joined them in the summer, had spoken of an Eteerian exodus, of Issari and Tanin leading the people of that fallen realm into the desert. An urchin with a frail left arm barely larger than a finger, Fin had come to join Requiem, to fly with fellow dragons . . . and to bring news.

"Issari leads Eteer now," the boy had told Jeid. "She is the great Priestess in White. The savior of a lost nation."

The boy had spoken in awe, but those words still wounded Jeid.

And what of us in Requiem? Have you forgotten us, Issari? Tanin, my son--have you too abandoned us, choosing to stay with your beloved?

"If they don't return by winter, I will fly out," Jeid said. "I will seek them across the sea and desert. I will find them."

Laira shook her head. "Even a dragon, flying fast and high, could spend years aflight and explore only a small part of the wilderness south of Eteer." She squeezed Jeid's hand. "Issari sent Fin here with a message for us--a message that she and Tanin are safe, that we're not to worry. I have to trust that message." She sighed. "And yet I miss her deeply, and I worry too, so much that it hurts."

Laira closed her eyes, and Jeid held her close for a long time, silent, as she sat in his lap. The Oak Throne's roots and branches coiled around them, the columns soared, and the dragons flew above--a new kingdom, a new home, a new peace awaiting two missing souls.

"We built this kingdom for the fallen," he finally said. "For the memory of Requiem, my daughter. For the memory of my wife and my parents. For the memory of your mother and brother. For the memory of hundreds slain for their magic. And we built Requiem for those still seeking us, those Vir Requis still lost in the world. I pray to the stars that they all come home."

Laira nodded and whispered, "May they all come home. May--" She stiffened, leaped off his lap, and inhaled sharply.

Jeid growled and rose from his throne. His hands formed fists at his sides. "Who are you? What do you seek here?"

The man emerged from the forest and stepped onto the marble tiles of Requiem's hall--if a man he was. His cheeks were slashed open from mouth to ears, revealing a lurid grin that showed all his teeth right down to the molars. Many rings pierced his nose and brows, and he wore armor of similar rings. Blades hung from his belt, and tattoos coiled across his face and bald head. His smile--the smile of a shark--grew larger as he walked across the hall.

"Hello, King of Reptiles!" The man's voice boomed. "Hello, Queen of Lizards! I am Slyn of Widejaw. I've come to find a new home." He looked around. "I believe this hall will suffice."

Jeid growled and stomped across the hall, moving toward the invader. He let the first tendrils of magic rise inside him, ready to summon. He reached the stranger beneath King's Column, the first pillar of Requiem. Slyn stared at him, eyes cruel and mocking. Jeid recognized such cruelty; his own brother, the dragon-hunter Zerra, had carried the same cruelty in his eyes.

"Leave this place now," Jeid said slowly, "and I will allow you to live."

Jeid was a tall, stocky man--the largest in Requiem--but this stranger stood even taller, closer to seven feet than six. His armor bulged over a bulky chest, and muscles rippled across his bare arms. With his tattoos, many piercings, and split cheeks, Slyn seemed less a man and more a demon.

"You must be the fabled King Aeternum." Slyn smirked. "Men spoke of a great warrior. I see only a weak old man." He looked over Jeid's shoulder at Laira. "Is this your bride? She's uglier than a crone's warts, but she'll be mine, just like your hall. Oh yes, Aeternum. She will bear my sons."

Laira growled and shifted. Golden scales flowed across her back. Fangs grew from her mouth and claws sprouted from her fingers and toes. A golden dragon, she pounced forward and snarled.

"I would rip out your throat before you could touch me." She blasted smoke. "Leave now! Requiem's wars have ended. We crave no more killing. But linger here one breath longer, and I will tear you apart."

Slyn stared at the golden dragon. A thin smile stretched across his lips and split cheeks. "I think, dearest Queen of Reptiles, that you will not find us so easy to kill." He raised his voice to a shout. "Men!"

All across the forest, men emerged from behind the birches, walked between the columns, and entered the hall of Requiem.

Jeid shifted too. A copper dragon, he stood beside Laira, whipping his head from side to side. Hundreds of men were stepping out from the forest, all sporting the same split cheeks, tattooed heads, and pierced faces.

Jeid beat his wings and soared into the sky. An instant later, Laira joined him. The two dragons circled in the air above the invaders. When he looked toward the hills, Jeid saw many more Widejaws--hundreds of them--crawling across the land.

"Dorvin!" Jeid roared. "Maev! To the hall!"

Scales clattered. Fire blazed across the sky. A silver dragon rose from distant trees and flew toward Jeid--Dorvin, his brother in arms. An instant later, a green dragon emerged too--Maev, Jeid's daughter, a princess of Requiem.

Jeid circled above the men below. "Hear me, strangers!" His voice boomed. "We have fought and slain rocs and demons. We can easily slay men. We do not desire more bloodshed. Leave now! Your tribe has wandered into the realm of dragons. Leave now and we will spare your lives." He blasted fire down into the hall; it showered against the marble tiles and splashed against the men's feet. "Leave or burn!"

Dorvin growled, flames sparking between his teeth. "To the Abyss with all these warnings. I say we kill them now."

Slyn stared up at the dragons. His jaw unhinged, and his tongue emerged like a snake from its burrow to lick his lips.

"Warriors of Widejaw!" Slyn shouted, arms stretched out. "See how the dragons are weak! They should have killed our on sight. Their mercy will be their undoing. Show them our strength!"

In the hall and forests, the Widejaw clan shifted.

Their bodies ballooned and sprouted tan fur. Dank feathered wings unfurled from their backs. Their hands and feet sprouted claws. They rose into the air as great lions, as large as dragons, flapping vulture wings. Their faces remained the faces of men, bloated to hideous size as if pumped full of liquid. Those faces leered, the jaws opening wide, the tongues lolling, the eyes burning with hatred.

"Sphinxes," Laira whispered. "Eteerian tales speak of them. Creatures imbued with demon magic."

Jeid roared. "Dragons of Requiem! Rise! Rise! Blow your fire!"

Not waiting for an answer, he blasted flame toward the soaring sphinxes.

The fire crashed against one sphinx, burning the beast's fur. An instant later, a thousand of the creatures swarmed toward Jeid and his companions.

The sky exploded with blood, flame, and smoke.

A sphinx crashed into Jeid, snapping its jaws, tearing at copper scales. Another sphinx grabbed Jeid's tail and yanked. Jeid

roared, clawed, bit, and blew his flames. Around him, his
companions all but vanished into clouds of the creatures.

"Dragons of Requiem!" Jeid called. "Rally here! Slay them!"

Between the sphinxes, he glimpsed flashes of scales. Other
dragons were joining the battle. Blood rained. Scales pattered
down into the forest like hail. Jeid blew flame, torched a sphinx,
and whipped his tail, clubbing another.

"Burn them all!" he cried. "Bur--"

A sphinx ahead of him--it was Slyn, his human head now
bloated and perched upon his lion body like a boil--opened his
mouth and spewed out black smoke that swarmed with flies. The
foul miasma spread across Jeid.

Pain drove down Jeid's nostrils, ears, and jaw. His head
spun. His eyes watered. He couldn't roar; he could barely breathe.
Poison.

The cloud floated around him, and Jeid coughed, struggling
to beat his wings, to stay airborne. With watering, burning eyes, he
saw that these weren't actually flies in the smoke. They were tiny
demons with human faces.

His wings would no longer flap. He fell.

He crashed down against the marble tiles of his hall,
cracking them. It took every last bit of strength to cling to his
magic, to remain a dragon.

Fur and claws flashed. As the battle raged above, Slyn
plunged down like a comet and slammed against Jeid. The sphinx
drove his claws under Jeid's copper scales, and the bloated, wide-
jawed face leaned down and hissed.

"So easy to kill . . ." the sphinx whispered. "No harder than
stepping on a lizard. Die knowing that your wife will live. Die
knowing that she'll bear my sons."

Slyn closed his jaws around Jeid's neck and bit down hard.

Blood spurted. Pain filled Jeid but rage too.

I did not defeat men, rocs, and demons to die in my own hall.

Ignoring the pain, he shoved against the cracked tiles and rose. He swung his tail, driving the spikes into the sphinx.

Slyn opened his jaws to howl, freeing Jeid.

The copper dragon took flight and rained down his fire.

Below, Slyn scuttled along the marble tiles, dodging the flames. Jeid beat his wings and reached out his claws, trying to grab Slyn, only for two more sphinxes to dive down and crash into him.

Golden scales flashed.

Laira swooped, rammed her horns into one sphinx, and knocked it down. Jeid burned the other. Gashes bleeding on his back, Slyn vanished behind smoke and fire.

"Jeid, they're all over Requiem!" Laira shouted. The golden dragon bled from a cut on her forehead. "A thousand or more. They're tearing down the trees and--"

Stones rained and dust flew.

Jeid glanced aside to see a marble column crack and come tumbling down. He grimaced and shoved Laira aside; the column slammed down behind them, missing them by a foot.

A dozen sphinxes roared and flew toward the two dragons, blasting out their foul smoke. The miasma approached, thick with the miniscule demons. Jeid and Laira soared, narrowly dodging the cloud of poison, only to crash into a sky of sphinxes.

"Jeid!" Dorvin cried somewhere above. The silver dragon was battling several of the enemy, blasting out fire and lashing his tail. "These goat-shagging piss-drinkers are everywhere. By the Sky Goddess's teats, there's more of them than boils on a witch's arse."

Jeid roasted one sphinx. Another landed on his back and bit, and Jeid bellowed and shook himself, knocking it off. Another charged toward him; he torched it. Three more advanced, and dragons crashed into them, blowing fire and snapping their teeth.

"Burn them all!" Jeid cried. "Dragons of Requiem, defend your home. Fight them. Burn them--"

He grimaced to see three sphinxes land on a young, white dragon and bite into her neck. Blood sprayed in a fountain. The dragon lost her magic and crashed down to the forest in human form--a thin woman, barely older than a youth. Behind Jeid a cry of pain pierced the air. He turned to see several sphinxes grab a black dragon's limbs and tug, ripping off both hind legs. The dragon yowled and lost his magic, becoming an old man. He fell, crashed against the capital of a column, then tumbled toward the forest floor. With a chill, Jeid saw that dozens of Vir Requis had already died; they covered the marble tiles of his hall, lay upon treetops, and one man even slumped across a column's capital, his head severed.

"Grizzly!" Maev cried. The green dragon flew toward him, bleeding from a dozen gashes. "They're tearing down the eastern huts! More keep swarming in." She blew fire, roasting two sphinxes who flew near. "Dead Vir Requis everywhere. Dead children. Stars . . ."

Jeid lashed his claws, cutting open a sphinx. Another sphinx bit into his flank, and Jeid howled and torched the beast. "Maev, soar with me! Higher!"

The green dragon narrowed her eyes and flew higher. Jeid flew with her. Father and daughter raised two pillars of flame that wove together, clearing a path through the sphinxes. Their claws and tails lashed, cutting into dank fur, knocking the enemy aside. A cloud of poison descended toward them, and the two dragons broke apart, skirted the miasma, and kept ascending. Soon they rose so high the air thinned and frost coated their scales.

Finally Jeid leveled off and stared down at his kingdom.

His heart seemed to freeze like his scales.

Requiem was crumbling.

A thousand sphinxes swarmed over the forest, uprooting trees, toppling homes, and slaying dragons. Corpses of Vir Requis covered the hills, and blood painted the hall.

"They're killing us all," Maev whispered at Jeid's side. "Stars, Grizzly. They're . . . they're killing us all."

Requiem falls. Jeid's throat constricted. *But we won. We won our war. We defeated our demons. How . . .*

"Grizzly!" Laira cried, flying up from below. "They're dragging the children out from the huts! They're slaying everyone!"

Jeid shook his head madly. He swooped.

"Laira, Maev, with me!" he shouted. "Gather whoever you can. We fly north!"

Maev swooped at his side. The wind roared around them. "We can't just flee!"

They crashed through more sphinxes, emerging into the thick of the battle. Blood, fire, and demon smoke swam around them. At Jeid's side, a yellow dragon screamed as sphinxes tore into her. Scales rained and the dragon fell, a woman again, her entrails dangling.

"Dragons of Requiem!" Jeid cried. "Rally here and fly north! Fly to the mountains! Flee!"

Three young dragons--barely larger than horses--tried to fly toward him. Sphinxes blasted them with demonic smoke, then tore the dragons apart. The Vir Requis fell in human form--butchered children, their limbs severed, their chests cracked open. Four more sphinxes slammed into another column. It cracked and crashed down, crushing another dragon.

"Dragons of Requiem, to me!" Jeid roared. "Laira and Maev! Dorvin! Clear us a path."

They blew their fire together. The flaming pillars joined into a blazing inferno. Sphinxes shrieked, burned, and fell. Trees burst into flame. The three dragons began to drive forward, shoving a path through the enemy. Jeid flew above them, roaring for all to hear.

"Dragons of Requiem, follow! We fly north."

A few dragons joined him, flying in his wake. Sphinxes closed in behind them, and Jeid spewed his flames, holding them back. A crowd of other dragons flew toward Jeid, trying to join him; the sphinxes tore them apart, and only three dragons reached Jeid, lacerated and crying out in pain. One dragon held her human babe; the screaming child was too young to shift.

"Blow fire in a ring!" Jeid shouted. "Hold them back and keep flying."

The other dragons flew above, below, at his sides. Some tried to join the ring of fire. Most never made it.

"Fly north!" Jeid bellowed, hoping they heard. Only fifty dragons flew behind him, blowing walls of fire around the group. "Dragons of Requiem, flee! Flee to the mountains! Flee to the forests!"

The dragons flew, a thousand sphinxes flying in pursuit. Some dragons flew behind Jeid; most flew in the distance, hidden behind smoke and flame. The setting sun painted the forests red. When Jeid looked behind him, he saw the bloated faces of the sphinxes, their lion bodies, their dank wings, and beyond them the burning forest and fallen hall of Requiem. Then those columns faded, and all he saw was the nightmare of smoke and blood.

"Slay the dragons!" rose a cry--Slyn's voice. "Keep the golden female alive and slay the others. Bring me their skulls!"

Jeid blasted his fire toward the enemy, but he was down to sparks. The sphinxes laughed, their jaws opening wide, their teeth red with the blood of Requiem.

"Requiem, fly!" Laira cried ahead. "Fly to the mountains."

They flew for hours, flew until the sun vanished beneath the horizon, flew as the sphinxes chased, as the sky burned, as more dragons fell. They left a path of their dead behind them.

Darkness fell but no stars emerged; the smoke hid their glow, and the shrieks of the sphinxes rose everywhere in the night, a song of nightmares, of death, and of a fallen kingdom.

ISSARI

She lay upon tasseled cushions, clad in embroidered silks, painted with henna and kohl, perfumed, pampered . . . and chained.

She was Issari Seran, a queen of Eteer, a priestess of Taal, a princess of Requiem . . . and a slave.

"Smoke some *hintan*!" said Irysa, a young woman with long lashes, gold-painted eyelids, and cascading black hair. "Have some, Issari. It soothes all pain, all fear."

Irysa too wore scanty silks that revealed more than they hid. She too was chained, the bronze links running from her ankle to a bolt in the floor. She took a deep puff on her hookah. Purple liquid bubbled in the glass container, and green smoke rose around the woman. She giggled and passed the mouthpiece to Issari.

The lavender smoke invaded Issari's nostrils, and she coughed and shoved the hookah away. "Don't smoke this! It makes you weak. Makes you woozy. Makes you . . . happy."

She shook her head wildly. The smoke floating through the chamber kept Issari always dizzy, always muzzy, always floating somewhere between wakefulness and dreams. Even without smoking directly from the hookah, the sweet aroma filled her with languor. How long had she been here, lingering in this dream? She did not know. Days? Moons? Years?

She blinked and gazed around her. Dozens of other concubines lounged upon cushions, at the edges of heated pools, and by low tables piled high with golden platters. The scents of wine, honeyed almonds, and sweet pies filled the air alongside the *hintan* smoke. The women were all young and beautiful, their faces painted, their silks revealing most of their powdered skin. Bracelets, necklaces, and rings adorned them. They were treated like queens, and yet all were chained--chained by the bronze links around their ankles, chained by the *hintan* that kept their minds soft.

The chamber swayed around her, the edges fuzzy. Issari blinked and shook her head wildly. She waved her hand, trying to clear the smoke. Her many bracelets chinked, beautiful things of gold and silver inlaid with topaz and sapphire. As the bracelets moved, the gemstones left trails of light. Where was she? She saw columns rising beside her. Was she in Requiem? No; these columns were not austere marble. They were carved of colorful porphyry and ringed with gold. The floor was not tiled but covered with a mosaic. It was a hall of light, of grandeur, of precious metals and precious stones.

I'm in Goshar, she realized. *In the southern city-state, the place where I had sought safety for my people. I'm a prisoner. I'm--*

"Have some, Issari," said another concubine, a golden-haired young woman named Tylal. The beautiful, silk-clad temptress held out a hookah's mouthpiece. "It'll make you laugh!"

A fresh gust of lavender smoke coiled around Issari, tickling her, stroking her like the hands of a lover. Issari sighed deeply. It was so healing, so warm, so sweet.

I was thinking something. I was realizing, remembering. I . . . where am I? She blinked. She did not recognize this place. Where was she? Who was she?

"Girls!" rose a voice. "Girls, feed me. Feed me my precious cakes."

When she squinted and blinked, Issari saw a massive figure at the back of the hall. The man looked like a mountain of melting butter; he must have weighed as much as ten Issaris. He lounged upon many pillows, and he was naked but for a blanket across his lap. Sweat glistened upon his rolls of fat, his bald head, and his jiggling face. A thin, long beard like a rat's tail hung off his chin, and his tufted eyebrows thrust out, dyed green. Each of his fingers sported several gaudy rings.

"Feed me!" he cried out. "Girls! You--Issari. Feed me my cakes, the precious sweetness."

She blinked. Issari? It was her--her name. She was Issari! She rose to her feet. The chamber swayed around her, and the purple smoke wafted. Her fellow concubines giggled, batting their painted eyelashes.

"Feed him, feed him! Feed the Abina Sin-Naharosh. Feed your husband."

Issari narrowed her eyes. Her husband? Yes. Yes, this great man--if a man he truly was, for he looked almost like a demon-- was her husband. She remembered. She had wed him! The serpent had tasted her blood, then tasted his, mingling their souls together. Tanin had tried to stop it, he--

"Tanin," she whispered. Tears stung her eyes. How could she have forgotten her sweet Tanin, the man she loved? Her fellow son of Requiem?

"Requiem," she whispered, and now tears flowed down her cheeks. She had almost forgotten the land of dragons across the sea, her home.

"Eteer." Her lips trembled. Eteer--her first home, the kingdom along the coast, fallen to the nephilim. She had led the Eteerians here! Where were they? How could she have forgotten, abandoned her people, and--

"Feed him, feed him!" chanted the concubines. They danced around Issari, their gilded chains jangling. The smoke puffed out from their lips, stroking Issari. The lights of their jewels blinded her and she laughed. She hovered upon the clouds of *hintan*, and the lights shone, and the gold sparkled.

"I will feed you, my beloved husband." She laughed. "I will feed you your precious cakes, though you are sweeter by far."

She swayed toward one of the low tables, her bracelets chinking. Her gilded chain dragged behind her along the mosaic. Golden platters rose upon the table, full of figs stuffed with almonds, clusters of walnuts and carobs, rolled pastries thick with pistachios and dates, sugared fried breads shaped as swans, and many other delectable sweets. Issari reached for a platter of steaming honey cakes, the abina's favorite. She lifted the golden plate and walked toward her husband.

Seated upon his cushions, the abina licked his lips. His small eyes--they nearly drowned in his puffed face--glittered with hunger. Drool dripped down his chin and onto his naked, powdered chest.

"Here, my sweetness." Issari held out one of the small cakes. "Eat."

He opened his mouth, and she placed the cake inside. He chewed greedily and opened his mouth again, ready for more. She kept feeding him cake after cake, cleaning up the drool and crumbs. It felt like feeding a giant, thousand-pound baby.

"Mmm, they are as sweet as you, my wife." Abina Sin-Naharosh licked his lips. "Will you stroke my head and sing me a song?"

"Of course, my husband." She kissed his cheek, stroked his head, and sang to him. She sang the only songs she knew--the old songs of Eteer, her home upon the coast.

Eteer!

The memory returned to her.

Eteer--a land of white towers, of hanging gardens, of a canal full of many ships. Eteer--the land where she'd lived as a princess. The memories flooded her: the smell of the carob trees below her balcony, her brother's smile, and her father's cruelty . . . a father who would strike her, who had tossed her to the demons.

Those demons destroyed Eteer. She kept singing, but inside she trembled. *I led my people across the desert, but now I'm here, chained, trapped in a dream state.*

Clouds of *hintan* smoke coiled before her, all but obscuring the abina's many concubines. But here, where Issari stood, the smoke had cleared; the abina did not smoke his hookah while feasting. Slowly her thoughts coalesced.

I am Issari Seran, the Priestess in White, she thought as she sang. *Tanin needs my love. The people of Eteer need my leadership. Requiem, far in the north, needs my wings.*

Her wings! Of course! She could become a dragon! She had that magic. How had she ever forgotten?

"Sing louder!" Sin-Naharosh demanded. He struggled to lift his arm, but it was too heavy; his hand only rose an inch, then slapped back against his thigh. "Sing, my wife."

She nodded and sang louder, but all the while her mind worked feverishly. She had been lingering here far too long, too muzzy to track the passage of time.

As she sang those old songs of Eteer, she found the tune changing on her lips, and new words flowed from her. She had heard this song only once, but she had never forgotten it. Dizzy, weak with the smoke, she sang the song of Requiem in the hall of Goshar.

"As the leaves fall upon our marble tiles, as the breeze rustles the birches beyond our columns, as the sun gilds the mountains above our halls--know, young child of the woods, you are home, you are home." Tears stung Issari's eyes at the memory of dragon wings. "Requiem! May our wings forever find your sky."

The giggles died across the hall.

Sin-Naharosh stopped chewing, letting saliva thick with crumbs slide down his chins.

Issari froze.

"Requiem," the obese abina whispered. His face reddened. "The land of dragons." He swung his massive arm with a burst of strength, knocking over the platter of cakes. "The kingdom of reptiles!"

What have I done? Issari stopped singing. "My lord, I'm sorry. I--"

He roared, spraying spittle on her. "How dare you mention the dragons to me? Do you think I don't know that your paramour, that creature you call Tanin, is a weredragon? Do you think I don't know how he lusts for you?" The abina spat. "Yes, I have heard him scream in the dungeons. As my guards' whips tear into his flesh, he cries out your name." Sin-Naharosh laughed mirthlessly. "Oh, the boy tries to shift into a dragon. Tries again and again, only for the chains to dig deep, to keep him in his human form . . . a form so easy to hurt. Should you meet him again, you would not recognize him. I've made your weredragon lover ugly. You are mine, Issari." Through some feat of will, the abina managed to raise his arm; it must have weighed more than Issari's entire body. "You are my wife. Only mine! You will sing to me. You will pleasure me. And you will feed me. Feed me!"

The palace guards, standing between the columns, shifted uneasily and reached for the hilts of their khopeshes. Issari stood frozen, the fallen honey cakes lying around her bare feet.

Tanin.

Her eyes stung with tears.

My sweet Tanin . . .

She thought back to the first time she had met him, a tall northern boy with brown hair and kind eyes. He had flown south to Eteer to free her brother. She had ridden his dragon form, had fought demons from his back. She had learned to become a dragon herself and flown at his side. She had made love to him in the sand, had traveled with him into exile, had seen him grow from boy to man, from juggler to warrior. She had grown to love him.

Now you scream for me. Her tears flowed. *You scream in a dungeon while I linger here, eating sweets, clad in silk.*

"Feed me!" the abina demanded. "Fetch more cakes and feed me, whore!" He reached for the whip that always lay by his side. He was too weak to cut her skin, but the lashes still stung, leaving red marks. "Feed me!"

Issari nodded. Numb, she took a few steps back toward the table. Her chain jangled behind her. She reached across the table, feeling so hollow, so hurt.

"Feed me!" the abina's voice rose behind.

She lifted a golden platter of honeyed almond cakes and stepped back toward her husband. The obese abina smacked his lips, and his tongue darted greedily. His hands opened and closed.

"Mmm, good. Feed them to me. Feed me my sweets."

She stepped closer, her fingers tingling. His mouth opened like a baby bird's beak. She placed a cake inside.

"I will feed you," she whispered. Her eyes burned. "Sweets for my sweetling."

She placed another cake in his mouth. He chewed lustfully, crumbs and drool dripping down his naked chest. She placed a third cake into his waiting jaws.

For Tanin.

She placed another cake in the king's mouth.

For Eteer.

"Wh-- Iss-- sto--" The abina sputtered, crumbs falling from his mouth.

For Requiem.

She lifted three cakes and shoved them into her husband's mouth.

He began to choke. He tried to spit them out.

"I will feed you," she repeated. She shoved more cakes in, ramming them down his throat. Her eyes burned with tears, and rage exploded through her. Her limbs trembled. She kept shoving cakes in. "Eat! Eat them!" Her voice rose to a shout. "Eat them all!"

She grabbed his jaw with one hand, forcing it open, and stuffed more cakes in, driving them down his throat as he sputtered. His hands flapped uselessly; he was too weak now to raise his massive arms. His legs twitched under his blanket, too heavy to kick. His face reddened, then began to turn blue.

"Eat them and choke, my dearest, beloved husband," Issari whispered and shoved the last cake in.

Three palace guards rushed forward. Their long, curled beards swayed, and they reached for their swords. They stared at her, eyes filling with rage. Issari faced them, allowing her anger to flow away. She let concern wash her face.

"He's choking!" she cried to them. "My dear husband is choking! Help him! Help him!"

If the guards had suspected her, that suspicion now vanished. They raced toward their king. The obese man had fallen over, his rolls of fat splayed out around him. His limbs twitched, and his face turned deep purple. He tried to speak but he could utter only choking sounds. The guards began to pound his chest and reach into his throat, desperate to revive him.

The guards' backs faced her. Issari tightened her lips, reached to one guard's belt, and grabbed his khopesh. She scurried backward, holding the sickle-shaped sword.

The guard spun toward her, eyes widening.

Issari raced across the hall, chain jangling behind her, and leaped into a cloud of *hintan* smoke. She held her breath. The purple haze hid her, and she swung her sword down hard. The blade slammed against the bronze shackle surrounding her ankle, nicking the metal.

"Concubine!" shouted the guard. He raced into the cloud, breathed in a mouthful of the spice, and shook his head wildly.

Issari swung her sword at him. The blade sliced through his throat and emerged bloody. Before he even hit the floor, Issari swung her blade down again. Again. Each swing chipped her anklet further. She forced herself to keep holding her breath, daring not breathe the *hintan*. Her lungs ached for air. She swung again. Guards shouted behind her.

Her sword slammed again into the anklet.

The metal snapped and the blade sliced her skin

Ten guards raced into the cloud.

Issari snarled, grabbed her magic, and shifted.

Her fire roared across the men. They burned and fell.

A white dragon, she stepped forward, her fire shrieking in an inferno, blazing across the hall. The flames crashed forward, knocking down the other guards that raced toward her, spraying across the columns, and washing over the choking abina. The hall became a fiery oven. Issari--finally freed from her chains, finally a dragon, finally a warrior--tossed back her scaly head, and she roared. It was a roar of rage, of pain, of anguish--a roar for the long moons she had lingered here, half-alive; a roar for the man she loved, a man who suffered; a roar for her two homes. The cry shook the chamber, deafening. She knew all the city could hear.

When her howl and her flames died, she spun around to see the concubines.

Twenty filled the hall. They had fled as far as their chains would allow; they now cowered at the back of the hall, hugging one another. Their eyes were wide, their mouths agape. A few wept. All trembled.

The white dragon stared at them, smoke pluming from her nostrils. With a growl, Issari took a step closer. The concubines shrieked and hugged one another more tightly. But Issari ignored them for now. She stepped toward the strewn hookahs of *hintan*;

the vessels lay among the cushions and upon the poolsides. One by one, Issari stomped upon them, shattering each glass vessel and letting its liquid spill.

"You are free from the chains of *hintan*," Issari said, her voice rumbling through the hall.

She stepped closer. The concubines crowded together, shivering. The chains ran from their ankles to columns across the hall; near the huddle of women, the chains had braided into a single strand. Issari stepped closer, ignoring the women's whimpers and screams. She lashed down her claws, cutting through the chains. They snapped.

"And you are now free from your chains of metal," the white dragon said. "Go. Leave this place. And tell all whom you pass that Issari Seran, the White Dragon of Requiem, the Queen of Eteer, will free all those enslaved, all those in darkness."

She whipped her tail over the concubine's heads, incurring screams. Her tail slammed into the hall doors, knocking them open. Fresh air and daylight flooded the hall. Issari inhaled deeply, breathing the free air for the first time in many days.

The concubines stared at one another. For a moment they were frozen, hesitant, staring from side to side. A few shed tears. One reached toward the shattered hookahs and wailed. A few tried to step back into the hall.

Issari slammed down her tail, blocking their access. She stared at them one by one, meeting their gazes, silent. Slowly, as she stared at them, the women's fear seemed to ease. They dried their tears. One concubine stepped forward and gingerly placed a hand upon Issari's snout, then stroked her gently again and again. Another concubine stepped forward too and stroked Issari's neck. Others approached, caressing her, hugging her, weeping onto her scales.

"Thank you," they whispered. "Thank you, Issari, the white dragon, the savior of concubines."

They left the hall slowly, blinking, holding one another's hands.

Issari stepped outside and beat her wings.

She soared.

She flew from the Gosharian palace and glided over the city-state. Temples, streets, and thousands of brick homes rolled around her, a painting in tan, brown, and yellow, a dry city nestled among the mountains. She rose higher, letting the wind fill her nostrils, and she roared again. Her cry echoed across Goshar and the desert beyond.

Where are you, Tanin? Where are you, people of Eteer?

She flew across the sun, sounding her cry, a free dragon.

LAIRA

They huddled behind the roots and vines, two shivering women caked in mud. The sphinxes shrieked above.

"That does it." Maev clenched her fists and made to leap from their cover. "I'll burn them! I'll cut them apart. I'll--"

"Maev, hush!" Laira grabbed the woman and tugged her back. "Please. Please be quiet and still."

Maev grumbled--far too loud of a grumble, Laira thought-- but stayed put. The maple's roots rose above them like a cage, thick with moss and vines. Grass and reeds rose beyond the hideout, further obscuring the two women. Laira--small and fragile as a child--easily fit in the burrow. Maev--a tall warrior--had to bend and twist and dig into the dirt. Deeper in the den hid its original inhabitant: a skunk Laira was very, very careful not to disturb.

Its spray won't be deadly like that foul smoke the sphinxes spew, she thought, glancing back at the skunk. *But please contain your stench a little longer, my friend.*

Outside in the forest, the sphinxes still shrieked. Some flew above, while others seemed to be moving between the aspens and elms, calling out.

"Come to us, dragons!" rose a cry. "Come now and we will kill you quickly. Hide from us, and when we find you, your death will be a lot slower."

Maev sneered and made to leap out again, to challenge the enemy. Laira grabbed the woman's shoulder and held her back.

"Don't listen to them," Laira whispered. "Please, Maev. Trust me. Hide with me."

Maev trembled with rage, and her fists pressed deep into the mud, but she obeyed.

Laira huddled deeper into the burrow. After a long night of fleeing through the forest, they had found this place to hide. The sun now shone overhead, and she dared not emerge, but once darkness fell again, Laira would wander the forest. She would seek the others. If they lived, she would find them.

She closed her eyes.

Did any other Vir Requis even live in this world? Had the sphinxes slain them all? She tried to think back to last night, to the pain and blood and fire. The sphinxes had torn into the group of fleeing dragons, had ripped so many from the sky. Laira had cried out to her husband, tried to reach him, but the sphinxes had swarmed. Claws had scratched her. The dragons had scattered, fled to forests and hills, and now . . .

Now only Maev and I are here, she thought. *Maybe the last two in the world.*

The sounds of sphinxes slowly faded, their cries moving farther away. Laira allowed herself a shaky breath of relief. At her side, Maev relaxed, her tense muscles deflating. Only a distant roar now sounded outside, moving south.

"Are they gone?" Laira whispered. "I don't hea--"

A boot stomped down right outside the burrow of roots and vines, only several inches away from Laira's face. She froze and bit down on her words. At her side, Maev bared her teeth, and her hand reached to the dagger at her belt. Laira had to clasp Maev's wrist, halting her from drawing the weapon and attacking.

"The two whores are here somewhere," rose a deep voice outside. The man hawked and spat. "The little one with the black hair and the tall yellow-haired beast. I saw them running this way, I did."

A second voice answered; this one was raspier and higher-pitched. "I see no damn tracks. No tracks for almost a mark. Ain't

no women here for you, Ktar. We got women back in our camp.
Bed them and forget about these reptile scum."

The first voice, low and gruff, answered. "Shut your mouth,
Ferish! I got enough women to bed anytime I like. But you heard
what Master Raem said. We're to kill every last dragon other than
this Laira one, the little girl with the black hair. The demon's got
his own plans for her, and he'll pay great treasures to those what
find her. And I saw her! Saw her running here."

Hidden in the burrow, Laira winced and her heart leaped
into a gallop. Raem. Her father. So this Widejaw tribe was
working for him. Her innards trembled, though she was not
surprised. Raem had hired the Goldtusk tribe to hunt her last year;
why not hire another tribe, an even more vicious one?

"But there's no tracks--" rose the raspy voice--Ferish's
voice.

Ktar grumbled. "Of course there ain't no tracks. Damn
things can turn into dragons, same what we can turn into
sphinxes. They must have flown off to hide somewhere." He
sniffed. "I think I can smell something." His boots, barely visible
through the burrow's curtain of roots and grass, turned toward
the hideout. "I do. I smell something hidden in the brush." More
sniffs and snorts sounded. "Smells like . . . like women. Yes! They
flew here somewhere. I smell them hiding."

Maev sneered. Laira shot her a glare and shook her head.
Outside the burrow, the boots stamped about the forest. When
Laira peered between the roots and parted the grass, she could see
the pair. They were two muscular men in ring mail, swords at their
sides. Their cheeks were split open--Widejaws. Widejaws who
could become sphinxes. Even if Laira and Maev slew them, they
would raise the alarm before they died, calling hundreds more of
their kind.

"I smell nothing," said Ferish, the older of the two.

Ktar kept moving about. "I do. I could smell me women a mark away. They're . . . here! Look. A burrow!" He came stomping toward the roots and grass beneath which Laira and Maev hid.

Before Maev could leap out--the woman was already growling and tensing her muscles--Laira reached behind her, grabbed the skunk, and pulled it forward. She shoved the animal out of the burrow, letting it race toward the two Widejaws.

The tribesmen froze.

Their eyes widened.

The skunk scurried forward, spun around, and raised its tail.

"Shagging goat-herders!" Ktar shouted. "Run!"

The two men spun on their heel and raced away.

"Smelled something, did you?" Ferish roared as they ran among the trees. "You and your maggoty nose!"

Within moments, the two men were gone, their cries distant.

Laira waited a few moments longer, heard no more Widejaws, and finally crawled out of the burrow. She rose to her feet and kicked her legs about, loosening her muscles. Maev crawled out next with a string of curses so foul Laira was surprised the trees didn't wilt. The skunk, meanwhile, lowered its tail--spray still unreleased--and crawled back into its home.

"Stars damn it!" The tall, golden-haired warrior spat. "We're bloody Vir Requis. We're warriors." She pounded her fist into her palm. "We could have slain those sheep-shagging sons of shite-eating whores."

Laira nodded. "Perhaps. And their cries would have alerted the others." She glanced up at the sky. "They're still flying somewhere up there, seeking us. A thousand of them. Maybe more. With that smoke they can spit out, they're probably even deadlier than demons."

"And we're deadlier still." Maev drew her sword and swung the blade around. "I could crush a thousand of them. I'll slice them to ribbons. I--"

"Maev!" Laira grabbed the woman's wrist and pulled down her sword. "These are enemies we cannot fight. Not just the two of us. You saw what they did to Requiem." Laira winced, remembering the bloodshed. Her voice dropped to a whisper. "You saw how many they killed. Maybe . . . maybe they killed everyone else. Maybe we're alone."

Maev's eyes softened and she sheathed her sword. She held Laira's shoulder awkwardly, keeping two feet of air between them. "I don't believe that. They couldn't have killed King Aeternum. My father is the greatest warrior I know. They couldn't have killed Dorvin, that fool of a boy. He's tougher than he looks, that pup. They're still alive, maybe many of them, somewhere in this forest, or in the mountains, or the plains, or . . ." Maev sighed. "They could be anywhere. But I believe they live, Laira. I will not believe that we're the only two left."

Dry leaves glided around them. Oaks, maples, birches, and pines spread as far as the eye could see. Laira lowered her head and clasped her hands behind her back.

I miss you, Jeid, she thought, eyes stinging. *My husband. My beloved.*

Laira had loved few people in her life; this life of hardship had presented her with few opportunities to love. She loved her mother; the woman had burned upon the stake. She loved her brother; he had taken his life, too fearful of their father. She loved her sister; now Issari was missing in the south. And as much as anyone, Laira loved her husband, her dear Jeid. She thought of the tall, gruff man with his bushy beard and brown eyes, with the kindness she saw in him, the strength in his wide arms and his soul. He was a lumbering bear of a man, so strong and frightening to many, but to her he was a gentle soul, a pillar of strength and a warm cloak of comfort.

Please, stars of Requiem, don't let me lose Jeid too.

Maev hawked--a ridiculously loud and long sound--and spat. "Come on. Let's go find the others." She began to shift, green scales emerging upon her.

Laira grabbed the young woman in mid-transformation, tugging her back into human form. "No flying! Too many sphinxes in the sky."

Maev's eyes widened. "No flying? Bloody stars!"

"I mean it." Laira glared. "Trust me. I used to hide in the southern forests from the rocs. Sneaky and small--this is how we survive now."

"I'm neither sneaky nor small, even in human form."

"Smaller and sneakier than a dragon! Please, Maev. I was right about the burrow. I've spent my life slinking and hiding. I know how to remain unseen. And I know you never thought much of me, never thought I'm a warrior or a strong queen or . . ." She let her words fade away. No, this was not the time to bring up that pain. She sighed. "Let's just walk for a while, seeking tracks, seeking the others. Maybe they're not far."

Yet as the two walked through the forest, stepping over fallen boles and twisting roots and mossy boulders, Laira couldn't help but dig up that pain. She glanced at Maev as she walked. The young woman, once a wrestler and now a princess of Requiem, grumbled and cursed under her breath with every step. Beside Maev, Laira always felt inferior.

I'm short and weak beside her, Laira thought. *The top of my head barely reaches her shoulders. I'm ugly beside her, my jaw crooked, my mouth tilted. I'm not strong, not beautiful, not tall . . . and yet I'm her queen. Her stepmother.*

After marrying Jeid, Laira had wanted to become friends with Maev. She would bring wildflowers to Maev's hut among the birches, only for the woman to nod and toss them into a bowl, forgotten. She had tried to speak to Maev over meals, to ask about her dreams and hopes, only for Maev to drink deeply of her ale and sing raucously, ignoring Laira's attempts at conversation.

I want to be close to you, Laira thought, *but you push me away.*

She sighed. Of course Maev would push her away. Not only was Laira different in every way, she was three years younger than Maev. Few women wanted a stepmother, and what woman wanted a *younger* stepmother?

I'm too young, too weak, too different, Laira thought. *Will she ever respect me?*

"I reckon Dorvin must be singing now," Laira said. "He always sings, probably even when hiding from sphinxes. Maybe we'll hear him. Don't you hate his songs?"

Maev gave Laira a cold stare, then looked back ahead. "I don't feel like talking. Makes too much noise."

As they kept walking in silence, Laira lowered her head. Even this was more than Maev had said to her all autumn.

"If we keep our voices low," Laira said, "we--"

Maev glared. "I don't feel like talking to *you*. All right, Laira? I don't want to talk about Dorvin or about anything. Stars!" Maev clutched her head. "When will you stop? You keep trying to start these damn conversations when nobody wants to talk. I wish I'd been stuck here with somebody else, even Dorvin and his songs, just not you, not my damn stepmoth--" Maev bit down on her words, and her cheeks reddened. She stared down at her feet. "Never mind. Forget I said anything. I'm sorry."

Laira nodded silently, her eyes stinging. She said no more.

They kept walking, seeking tracks, hiding whenever sphinxes shrieked above. Hours went by, and many enemies flew overhead, sending Maev and Laira into bushes and burrows. But no dragons. No sign of Jeid and the others. The sun began to set and shadows stretched across the forest floor. When the first stars emerged, Laira dared speak again.

"We'll need a place to hide for the night."

Maev grunted and said nothing.

Cold wind gusted and rain began to fall. Laira looked around, seeing nobody in the darkness, and dared to shift. A golden dragon, she dug under a boulder, creating a burrow just large enough for her and Maev. She hid the entrance behind branches and vines, then released her magic. A human again, she crawled through the leafy curtain and entered the clammy tunnel.

Maev followed. The wrestler stared around at the earthen walls and said nothing.

"It's a bit small," Laira said, "but it'll keep us warm and dry for the night. And at least there are no skunks. We'll keep searching tomorrow."

With only a grunt, Maev lay down, turned her back to Laira, and did not move. Laira lay down too. The burrow was narrow, forcing her body to press against Maev's, and she wished she had dug it wider.

At least it'll keep us warm, she thought. *Even if her heart remains cold.*

"Goodnight, Maev," she whispered. There was no reply.

Laira lay awake for a long time, worry gnawing on her. After all she had gone through, she was fleeing again, an outcast, afraid. This time it felt even worse. When fleeing the Goldtusk tribe, she had only her life to worry about. Now she worried about so much more: about people she loved and about Requiem.

Requiem . . . A tear fled her eye. The beacon of her soul. The light of her heart. The kingdom she had killed for, bled for, prayed for. It was more than a kingdom to Laira; it was a symbol of hope, of home, of starlight. Only moons after gaining its independence, Requiem had fallen--just like that, within moments.

I swear to you, Requiem, I will fight for you. I will not forget you. My wings will forever find your sky.

Along with her worry for her family and her kingdom, another worry--deeper, colder--filled her.

The Widejaws had spoken of Raem. *Of my father.* Laira shivered. *He's alive.*

How could he live? Laira had bitten off his arms. Jeid had bitten off his legs. How could anyone survive such an injury? And yet those words returned to her, the words the Widejaw had spoken: *. . . you heard what Lord Raem said. We're to kill every last dragon other than this Laira.*

The fear clutched her like sphinx claws. *Raem lives.*

She couldn't sleep, and the thoughts kept racing through her mind, and it seemed like half the night had passed when Laira heard Maev whisper.

"I'm so sorry." Maev trembled. "I'm so sorry, Laira."

Laira stiffened, sure that Maev was talking to her, but no-- Maev kept whispering to herself.

She thinks I'm still asleep.

"I'm sorry." Maev's voice was choked with tears. "I'm so scared. Please be safe, Dorvin. Please be safe, Grizzly. Please forgive me, Laira. I'm so scared."

Laira felt something warm melt inside her like tallow over a fire. She waited until Maev's voice faded to a whisper and was gone. Then Laira wriggled a little closer, letting her body warm Maev. She hesitated for a moment, then slung an arm across Maev, holding her close.

Maev stiffened. "Laira, are you awake?" she whispered.

Laira said nothing. Maev's words had been spoken in secret; she knew that.

But I can still soothe her, give her some comfort, some warmth. She's taller than me, older than me, stronger than me, but I'm still married to her father. She's still my daughter.

Maev's tense muscles relaxed, and soon she slept, breathing deeply. Laira smiled and let her worries flow away for one night, and she welcomed the deep embrace of sleep.

Daniel Arenson

TANIN

He languished in shadows.

All was darkness, screams, and blood.

He huddled in the corner of his cell, shivering. It was a small cell, too small for him to lie down; he slept seated, knees pulled to his chest. A single torch flickered in the hallway, its light falling between the bars of his door, illuminating craggy bricks, cobwebs, and bloodstains. Shadows fell whenever the guards walked by; five or six patrolled the hallway, clad in ring mail, their beards long and curled.

"Come to me, friend," Tanin whispered. He reached out a frail, trembling hand toward the spider. "Come to me."

The thin, long-legged arachnid crept across the floor, moving toward him.

"That's it," Tanin whispered.

The spider reached him and Tanin lowered his hand, letting it crawl onto his finger. He lifted his hand, admiring his little companion.

"Hello there, friend. So nice of you to visit. I've been lonely. I've been so alone."

The spider seemed to regard him in the flickering shadows. Tanin closed his eyes, shoved the animal into his mouth, and quickly swallowed. He tried to ignore the feeling of the spider sliding down his throat.

I've killed a friend.

Yet the hunger--the hunger was all consuming, maybe even worse than the welts across his back. The guards had whipped him several times by now, and the chains chafed his ankles, and the bricks hurt his skin, but the hunger was perhaps the worst. Every spider was a blessing.

One of these days, Tanin hoped, he would catch a rat. The rats scurried outside sometimes. He saw them in the hallway, yet none had yet come to visit. None were his friends.

I wonder if rats ever visited Sena as he languished in his prison, Tanin thought.

He thought back to the prince of Eteer, Issari's brother. The young man had always seemed odd, too quiet, too hurt. The memory of Sena hanging from the oak visited Tanin sometimes, a waking dream, a warning.

He lost his sanity while imprisoned, Tanin thought. *I have to cling to mine. I have to.* He clenched his fists, though he was so weak his fingers could barely bend. *For Requiem. And for Issari.*

At the thought of her, something swollen and wet filled his throat. His eyes stung and ice and fire filled his belly.

"Issari," he whispered.

She needed him. She was imprisoned too, held high above in the ziggurat, enslaved to the abina of Goshar. He had to find her, to save her. His fists shook. He would burn down this entire city to see her again.

He thought of her large green eyes, her determined mouth, her raven braid, her strength, her wisdom, her courage--an innocent princess who had become a queen, a priestess, a great leader. The thought gave him the strength to struggle to his feet. The chains binding his wrists and ankles jangled.

"I have to find you, Issari." He stumbled toward the door. "I have to . . ."

His head spun. He was too weak, too dizzy, but he tightened his lips and summoned his magic.

Red scales flowed across him.

And he screamed.

As his body grew, the chains cut into his wrists, ankles, and torso. Blood spilled. Tanin roared with pain, and his magic left him. He collapsed onto his knees, lowered his head, and trembled.

Boots stomped outside.

Tanin cringed.

Several guards approached the cell. They stood outside the bars, glaring in at Tanin. Each man wore rusty old ring mail, and their beards mimicked the armor, curled into tight rings. Whips and daggers hung at their hips.

One man shoved a torch between the bars. The flames crackled, spewed smoke and sparks, and forced Tanin back against the wall.

"What are you screaming about, weredragon?" the guard demanded. He spat on Tanin. "Shut your mouth or I'll bash in every last one of your teeth."

Cringing away from the flames--they felt hot enough to melt his eyeballs--Tanin spoke in a hoarse whisper. "Let me see her. Let me see Issari."

The guards burst out laughing. "The abina is taking good care of her," one said. "Keeping her nice and satisfied. Bedding her right now, I reckon." The guard licked his lips. "Bet she's nice and soft. Bet she's hurting."

Tanin winced. He did not understand every word these guards spoke--he had been studying the southern languages for only several moons--but he could piece together the sentences well enough from the man's tone, darting tongue, and cruel eyes.

She's hurt. She needs me.

"Let me see her," he repeated.

One guard drew his whip and lashed it through the bars. The bronze-tipped thong slammed into Tanin's shoulder, tearing through skin. The guards laughed as he bled.

Along with his pain, rage flared in Tanin.

I am a Prince of Requiem. I can become a dragon. He bared his teeth. *I will slay these men.*

He struggled to his feet as the guards laughed. Another whip tore skin off his chest, but he did not fall.

I will shift here in this cell, he thought. *Even if the chains tear off my hands and feet.* He growled. *I will burn these men, and I will fly out, and I will free Issari, even if I bleed to death while I fight. I will die knowing she's free.*

As the guards raised their whips again, prepared to strike him down, Tanin reached deep inside for the magic of dragons.

Before his scales could appear, shouts rose from down the hall.

"A dragon!" a man cried. "A dragon flies! A dragon in Goshar!"

Tanin froze. He wasn't a dragon yet. Why did they--

"A dragon flies!"

Tanin sucked in his breath.

"Issari," he whispered. His eyes dampened, he leaped, and he shouted, "Issari!"

Cursing, the guards raced down the hall, leaving his cell. All across the dungeon, screams of fear rose from the other prison cells, echoing madly.

Tanin slammed himself against the bars, trying to peer outside into the hall. He glimpsed the guards racing away, crying of a dragon in the sky. Tanin's heart pounded.

Issari is free.

Across the torchlit hallway, the other prisoners moaned, screamed, or wept in their cells. A few hopped about like mad frogs, their eyes buggy. Others simply lay still, too weak to rise. Only one guard remained in the dungeon--the large, lumbering one the other men called Halfhead.

Tanin reached between the bars and whispered urgently, "Halfhead! Halfhead, to me!"

The jailor turned around. He was a massive man, standing seven feet tall. He shoulders thrust out like the beams of ships, and his belly wobbled before him like a bale of hay. He was easily the largest man Tanin had ever seen; he was almost twice Jeid's size, and that old grizzly bear was something of a giant himself.

"Halfhead!" Tanin whispered, thrusting his face between the bars.

Unlike the other jailors, Halfhead sported no long, curly black beard; his beard was wispy and pale, his eyes blue. He was a northerner like Tanin, perhaps once a hunter or gatherer, possibly sold overseas by his old masters. His most distinguishing feature was not even his prodigious girth but his head. A large chunk of that head was missing; the cranium caved in, forming a declivity like a crater, perhaps the result of some old wound. Whatever had caused the deformity must have left Halfhead half-witted; the giant drooled and often mumbled incoherently, seeming no more mature than toddler.

"What you want?" Drool slid down Halfhead's chin and clung to his rusty ring mail. "You no talk. Dragon! Dragon flies up above." The giant shivered. "Halfhead no like dragons."

Tanin clutched the bars. If there had ever been a chance to escape this cell, it was now.

"Open my cell, Halfhead," Tanin said. "Open it so I can help you fight the dragon."

Halfhead's eyes widened. He took a step backward, banging against the opposite cell. "Dragon . . . coming here?" He fumbled for his club and raised the weapon. "Halfhead no like dragons!" His bottom lip trembled. "Dragons scary. Dragons once hurt Halfhead." He caressed the declivity on his head. "Dragon once lift Halfhead, drop him, hurt him. Halfhead scared. Please send dragon away."

As the giant trembled, Tanin couldn't help but feel sorry for the poor thing. But right now he would have to scare Halfhead a little more.

"Halfhead, if you open my cell door, I can help you fight the dragon. I've slain dragons before."

Halfhead sniffed and wiped mucus off his face. He growled, lolloped forward, and swung his club. Tanin leaped back and the club banged against the bars.

"You can't go out!" Halfhead wagged his finger. "You can't. Can't go out! Masters told Halfhead. Halfhead is never to let anyone out again. Ever."

Tanin grimaced to think that right now, archers might be firing at Issari as she flew above the city, seeking him.

"But the dragon might come here!" Tanin said. "Dragons love dungeons. If it flies down this tunnel, I can help you."

Halfhead roared even as tears streamed down his cheeks. He swung his club through the bars, forcing Tanin to leap back against the wall. "Halfhead will fight! Halfhead will have revenge. He will kill dragon." He growled and spun in circles in the hall, swinging his club, as prisoners hooted and wailed in their cells. "Dragons hurt Halfhead. Now Halfhead hurt dragon!"

The giant jailor paced the hallway, swinging his club through the air, blubbering about how the dragon had hurt him, how his head still ached, how revenge would be his. Tanin sighed.

Poor fellow, he thought. He wondered if the story were true. Had some Vir Requis in the north truly wounded this man? A flow of shame filled Tanin. Every man like Halfhead, hurt by dragons, was another reason for the world to hate Requiem.

"Halfhead," Tanin said, deciding to change his approach. "Halfhead, listen to me. That dragon outside? I summoned it. I created it."

The giant froze, club in mid-swing, and turned back toward Tanin. His boots thundered across the floor. "What you mean?"

Tanin raised his chin and tried to appear ominous--at least, as ominous as a haggard, tied-up prisoner could appear. "I have an old magic, Halfhead. A magic that can turn people . . . into dragons."

Halfhead gasped and stepped back. "Halfhead scared of magic. Magic evil!"

"Very evil. Look."

Tanin took a deep breath and summoned his magic. Red scales flowed across him. Horns began to bud upon his head. Fangs lengthened in his mouth. Just as his body began to grow larger, Tanin froze the transformation. He lingered between human and dragon, small enough to keep the chains from tearing him apart. Holding the magic halfway inside him felt like keeping food halfway down his throat; it ached to go one way or the other.

"Do you see my magic?" he rumbled. "Do you see, Halfhead?"

Halfhead gasped, whimpered, and covered his eyes. "No . . . please. Don't hurt Halfhead."

Tanin released his magic, returning to human form. He stepped closer to the bars. "I have the magic to turn man into dragon. I created the dragon outside. I can create many more; I can turn every prisoner in these cells into dragons! Would you like that, Halfhead?"

The giant blubbered, fear of dragons and fear of his masters battling across his face. "Halfhead fight them all!" He swung his club. "Halfhead fight all the dragons."

Tanin narrowed his eyes and smiled thinly. "Would you fight even yourself?"

Halfhead froze and sucked in air. "What . . . what you mean?"

I'm sorry, Halfhead, Tanin thought. *You have to let me out, even if it means I'll terrify you half to death.*

"If you don't release me, Halfhead, I will turn *you* into a dragon." He snarled. "Open these bars and unchain me, or you will suffer this curse."

Halfhead whimpered. A stain spread across his pants as he wet himself. With trembling fingers, he pulled his ring of keys off his belt. He fumbled and dropped them twice before he found the right one. The barred door creaked open. For the first time in what felt like years, Tanin stumbled out into the hallway.

"And the chains," Tanin said.

Halfhead mewled and thrust his key into the chains' padlock. The bonds clattered to the floor, freeing Tanin at last.

Tanin placed his thin, pale hand against Halfhead's arm. "Thank you, my friend."

His legs were weak, his head spun, and his belly ached for food. But Tanin ran. On bare feet, clad in rags, he raced down the tunnel and found a staircase. All the guards were gone to fight the dragon, to fight Issari. Tanin stumbled up the stairs, wheezing and weak, and for the first time in many days he emerged into the sunlight.

He found himself standing in a cobbled courtyard. Walls rose around him, topped with battlements and archers. A single cypress tree swayed in the wind, a tower rose into blue sky, and through an archway, Tanin glimpsed city streets full of racing soldiers.

He inhaled deeply, eyes stinging. Air. Light. Freedom.

The archers upon the walls were firing arrows skyward. A distant roar sounded above. One archer noticed Tanin and spun toward him, calling to his comrades. Soon ten archers tugged back their bowstrings and fired.

Tanin rose as a dragon, roaring, beating his wings. The arrows clattered harmlessly against his scales. He blew fire, a shrieking inferno. The guards fell, screaming, comets of fire, and thudded against the courtyard below.

Tanin was weakened and thin, but he felt so heavy. He could barely beat his wings. With a few mighty strokes, he cleared the walls and rose higher. He strained, eyes narrowed, grinning and shedding tears as he kept flapping, ascending past the tower top and into the sky.

Goshar spread around him, a tapestry of yellows and browns: the coiling ziggurat like a mollusk shell, many streets lined with brick homes, domed temples, swaying palm trees, towering walls, and beyond them the mountains and the desert. Soldiers were racing along the streets, and archers were firing from roofs.

A cry rose behind him. "Tanin!"

He turned around. He saw her there.

The white dragon flew across the sky, the sunlight gleaming upon her scales. Her green eyes shone with tears. She appeared to him like a deity of starlight.

"Issari," he whispered.

Arrows arched around them. The two dragons flew toward each other and soared higher above the city.

"I was trying to find you," Issari said. "Thank the stars. Thank the stars, Tanin."

He nodded, his own eyes damp. "Now let's fly out of here. Let's fly north. Back to Requiem."

They glided upon the wind, too high for arrows. The city spread below them, nestled among the mountains. To the north spread the desert, and lush green lands spread to the south, lined with three rivers.

"My people, Tanin," Issari said. "The people of Eteer."

She pointed her claws. Tanin looked down. Beyond the city walls, the Eteerian exiles--myriads of them--labored in chains. They toiled upon the mountainside, chiseling stone, bustling across scaffolding, and crying under the whips of armored masters. They were carving a great statue into the mountain, he saw--a statue larger than any palace. Still crude, the statue was shaped as a man with the head of a serpent, the eyes large as dragons.

"The goddess Shahazar," Tanin whispered.

Issari nodded. "They're slaves." She looked at him. "I will free them, Tanin. Eteer has fallen; their home is gone." She bared her fangs. "But I will lead them through this city--to green, good lands. To hope. To freedom. To a new home." She reached out and touched him with her wing. "I'm a princess of Requiem, but I am Queen of Eteer. You may fly north. I will not ask you to join me here. I--"

But Tanin was already diving toward the mountainside. "Come on, Issari! Less speeches and more dragonfire." He growled. "It's time to shatter more chains."

Daniel Arenson

JEID

He stood inside the cave, his snout thrust out the opening, and roared his fire across the mountainside. A hundred sphinxes shrieked, trying to fly near, but his flames kept them at bay. Jeid could barely see them past his showering dragonfire; he only glimpsed their furry lion bodies, their rank wings, and their bloated human heads. A few of the creatures blew their foul miasma toward him, the smoke rustling with demonic maggots. The dragonfire roasted the tiny creatures, blocking the attack.

"You cannot blow fire forever, dragons!" roared one of the sphinxes. "We will enter your caves, and we will sew pelts from your hides."

The beast flew near. Jeid blew fire with all his might. The roaring jet sprayed forth, forcing the sphinx back.

They will not enter, Jeid swore. *We will hold them back.*

Soon his flames began to weaken, the fire depleting inside him. The sphinxes grew more brazen, flying closer, desperate to enter the cave. A few landed on the mountainside and shifted back into human form--warriors of Widejaw, their mouths opening wide in lurid grins, their bodies clad in armor. They drew their swords and began to climb, prepared to enter. Jeid tried to roast them, but he was down to sparks.

"Bryn!" he grumbled between blasts of fire. Where was the damn woman?

He felt a tap on his tail. *Good.*

With a last blast of fire, he pulled his snout back into the cave. He released his magic, returning to human form. Bryn stood in the cave, a young woman with a mane of red hair, her body

58

clad in leather and fur. Within an instant, she shifted into an orange dragon and thrust her snout through the cave opening. Her fresh fire roared across the mountainside, and Widejaws screamed.

Standing behind the orange dragon's tail, Jeid took ragged breaths. He had never felt so weary. His shoulders slumped, his eyelids felt heavier than boulders, and queasiness filled his belly. He felt like he could collapse and sleep for weeks. He dared not rest even for a moment.

Requiem needs me.

Leaving Bryn to guard the cave entrance, he shuffled deeper into the darkness. The cave narrowed, tapering from a wide chamber into a tunnel barely large enough to let him walk through. The sounds of Bryn and the sphinxes faded behind as Jeid trudged deeper into the darkness.

In the cold tunnels beneath the mountains, they hid--the survivors of Requiem.

As Jeid reached them, he forced himself to square his shoulders, to raise his chin, to hide all signs of weariness and fear. He had been their king back in Requiem; he would be their king here too.

From a marble hall to walls of granite, he thought. *From splendor to ruin. From a palace to a tomb.* The pain clawed inside him. *Does Requiem end here in darkness, far from the light of our stars?*

The caves were long, narrow, and winding, a labyrinth twisting under the mountains. Back at the cave entrance there was room enough for a dragon. Here the tunnels were too small for shifting. The Vir Requis huddled in human form, resting against walls, perched in alcoves, or lying on the floor.

"My king," whispered an elderly woman. She sat against a wall, reaching out to him.

He nodded at her. "May the stars bless you, Grandmama."

He walked past her, moving deeper into the mountain. A young man shivered, slumped in the shadows, clutching the stump of his severed arm. Sweat beaded on his brow.

"My king," he whispered.

Jeid stroked the boy's head. "May the stars heal you, my son."

He kept moving, passing by every one of his people--the fearful, the brave, the wounded, the grieving. Everyone here had lost a soul in the attack on Requiem. Two hundred Vir Requis had lived among the birches; only a hundred now hid in this cave, the others lost or fallen to the enemy's claws and poison.

The caves twisted and formed, branching off into many paths, each only two or three feet wide. Jeid kept walking deeper into the cold darkness. Almost no light filled this place. A few clay lamps rested in alcoves, their wicks flickering in their oil; the light was barely brighter than stars on a cold, moonless night.

There are no stars here in the mountain, he thought. *Only fading light. Fading hope.*

Jeid kept walking, passing by more people until he reached Dorvin. The young man leaned against a wall, jaw tight, fists clenched at his sides.

"Dorvin." Jeid placed a hand on the young man's shoulder. "Why are you here? It's almost your shift. Go replace Bryn at the entrance."

The black-haired young man raised his eyes. A dark fire blazed in them. "There's no word of her yet?" His lips twitched. "No word of Maev?"

Jeid felt his belly tighten, the fear stretching inside him like a growing demon. "No word. Not from Maev. Not from Laira." He clutched Dorvin's arm. "But we have to believe they're alive out there. We have to."

Despite his words, Jeid noticed that his hand was trembling around Dorvin's arm. His teeth knocked together, and even breathing became a struggle.

Maev, his daughter, and Laira, his wife--the two women he loved most in this world--missing.

A thousand times since arriving in these caves, Jeid had summoned the memory, seeking clues. The sphinxes had crashed into them two marks south of here. Fire and blood had stormed over the trees. The enemy had flown among them, plowed through their lines, tore the dragons apart.

"Laira!" Jeid had howled. "Maev!"

He had caught only glimpses of their scales, and then sphinxes had slammed into him. The dragons had fled into the caves in a mad route, a chaos of screams and wails.

I thought you were behind us. I thought I'd find you here among the others. Now you're gone.

"Let us fly out," Dorvin said. He bared his teeth. "Let us fly out in glory and find them. And if they're fallen, let us avenge them."

A year ago, I would have flown with you, Dorvin, he thought. *A year ago I didn't care for my life. But today the people of Requiem need me. They need us. They need leaders. They need warriors.*

He shook his head. "Dorvin, go replace Bryn. Now. We will not fly out, not until our very last breath. Not while there is life here to protect."

Dorvin's eyes flashed. "And we hide here--for what? To die of starvation, of thirst? There is no hope here!" His eyes reddened. "At least I would die a warrior, crashing against the enemy. I--"

"So long as the sphinxes are besieging these caves, they're not hunting Laira and Maev. If nothing else, our presence here--even if we have no hope--keeps the enemy off their tails. But I believe there is hope, Dorvin. There is always hope, even in the shadows, even when all light seems lost. Go. Relieve Bryn. Protect the cave."

Dorvin gnashed his teeth and clenched his fists. Thoughts seemed to be racing through his mind. Finally, with a grunt, the young man nodded and stormed off.

Jeid watched him leave. *He is young and fiery and loves my daughter. Please, stars of Requiem, if you can hear my prayers, shine upon Maev and Laira. Shine upon us all.*

Soon his shift at the cave entrance would begin again, and he'd blow fire at the sphinxes, holding them back until Bryn replaced him and another cycle began. Only fifty Vir Requis here were well enough to shift and blow fire, and each could only produce flames for several moments. The others--half the survivors--were too young, too old, too hurt.

Jeid kept walking among them. He smiled at children, trying to cheer them in the shadows. He prayed for the wounded. He embraced those who grieved for the fallen or trembled with worries for the missing. He kept traveling through the labyrinth of tunnels, passing by each of his people. He could not remember when last he had slept. Since arriving here--it had been at least two days, maybe three--he had alternated between blowing fire and consoling his people.

I need sleep. I need food and drink. I need Maev and Laira here with me.

He was talking to a trembling mother, her son fallen, when the scream echoed through the caves.

Jeid froze. He spun toward the sound. He began to run.

He raced down the tunnel, passing by pale, trembling people. The smell of blood guided him. He rushed around a corner, froze, and nearly gagged.

Stars . . .

One of his people lay slumped against the wall, his chest cracked open. The ribs had been tugged outward like swinging doors. The innards had been scooped out--the heart, the lungs, all missing--leaving a hollowed cavity. Splatters of blood covered the wall. It took Jeid a moment to realize: those were no random splatters but rather a painting. The blood formed the shape of the Draco constellation.

Bryn came walking down the tunnel, mumbling to herself, her shoulders stooped with weariness. When the young woman saw the corpse, she stepped back and covered her mouth, stifling a scream.

"Who did this?" she whispered, pale and trembling.

Jeid stared down at the corpse. His chest constricted. He looked at Bryn and forced the words from his mouth: "We are not alone in these caves."

RAEM

Raem Seran, King of Eteer, stepped into the halls of the Abyss with his demon bride.

Today I sink into the very depths of the underworld, he thought. *Today I rise to my greatest heights.*

A tunnel stretched before him, its walls formed of skin and veins. As Raem walked upon his hoof and talon, the floor bended and bled beneath him. It felt like walking through the vein of a giant. Prisoners were sewn into the walls, floor, and ceiling--some were humans, some were demons, and some were something in between. Their mouths smacked. Their eyes shed tears. Those who could speak begged for death; those that could not simply whimpered or screamed. Raem smiled at the poor creatures.

"They are witness to the marriage march of a king and queen," he said to his bride. "They weep for our glory."

Angel--daughter of Taal, Queen of the Abyss--crawled at his side. Since consuming human flesh, she had grown to monstrous size. Her stone body was still shapely, her waist narrow, her hips full, but her limbs had stretched out, too long to let her stand upright in this tunnel. She crawled on all fours. Drool dripped between her sharp teeth, and cracks glowed upon her craggy body, revealing the lava within.

"All in the Abyss and the worlds above will see our love." Angel licked her lips. "Our love will burn the world."

Raem draped his left arm, the squirming tentacle, across her back. His right arm, the lobster claw, clanked at his side. His hoof stepped on a gaping face in the floor, crushing the poor soul's teeth. His talon drove into blinking eyes. They kept walking, accompanied by the chorus of screams.

After walking for what felt like eras, the tunnel opened up into a great chasm--the throne room of the Abyss.

Here was a sister to the throne room of Eteer, a dark mimic buried marks underground. Festering ribs, hundreds of feet tall, formed its foundations. Craggy rocks grew between them like boils. Many creatures hung from the walls and ceiling, bloated to obscene size, their bellies distended and threatening to burst; here were the living blood-sacks of the abyss, creatures to feed the warriors of the underworld.

A throne rose ahead, taller than three men, made of many tongues woven together. The severed muscles twisted, licking, drooling, coiling together, stolen from humans whose words were forever silenced. That great throne now cried out with thousands of voices, unintelligible, laughing, slobbering, wailing, smacking together.

Creatures scuttled around this throne, danced across the floor, clung to the ceiling, and flew through the air. The dragons of Requiem had slain a thousand demons, but many still filled these halls. Blobs of slime dragged themselves along the walls, leaving glistening trails. Furry balls with red faces tore the limbs off feathered men, crunching the bones and sucking the marrow. Horned, hoofed creatures with bearded faces copulated on the floor, thrusting into shrieking red swine with vulture beaks. Centipedes the size of men flew on translucent wings. Lanky giants lumbered across the room on many-jointed legs, their bodies turned inside out, organs pulsing and dripping.

"My hall of nightmares," said Angel. After crawling through the tunnel for so long, she finally unfurled to her full height. The stone woman towered over Raem; his head only reached her hips.

"*Our* hall," Raem said. He stroked her. "My bride."

Several demons rolled forth, balls of metal, and unfurled into tall beetles. They raised bone horns and blew out clarion calls. All across the hall, the demons hissed and howled and knelt. Bones creaked and saliva spilled. Smoke wafted from nostrils. All the demons gazed as the bride and groom walked through the hall.

"My queen!" piped a little demon, no larger than a cat, fluttering toward her with bat wings. "Hail Angel, Queen of the Abyss, and hail--"

Angel grabbed the little creature and stuffed it into her mouth. She chewed. Blood dripped down her chin like gravy.

They reached the throne of fluttering tongues. A child stood beside it--a beautiful, noble child, his skin covered in boils, his jaw hanging halfway down his chest, his eyes green and curious.

Raem reached out to him. Already his son was taller than him.

"Ishnafel," Raem said, clasping the boy's shoulder. He kissed the warty cheek. "My precious son."

Angel stood with her back to the throne. She raised her arms, and fire burst out from her, forming wings of flame. Smoke rose from her mouth, and lava leaked from her eyes. The cracks on her body blazed with red light.

"I've chosen a husband!" she shouted, her voice high-pitched, a storm like thousands of boiling seas. "I've chosen a mate, a male whose seed has quickened in my womb. No longer is Angel, Queen of the Abyss, barren. I have brought forth a son!" She lifted Ishnafel and displayed the twisted creature to the crowd. "For the first time in thousands of years, Angel, daughter of Taal, has created true life." She tossed back her head and laughed, the sound so loud it shattered several of the living sacks upon the ceiling. Blood rained. "And Raem will give me many more spawn. Step forth, Priest of the Abyss! Step forth and join two into one."

Fleshy doors opened in the wall like a cervix ready for birth. The priest emerged, stepping forth on black talons. His body was lanky and black, and his head flared out in a crown of spikes. A vertical mouth split the head from chin to forehead, filled with metal hooks, and eight spiderlike eyes stared from its sides. Chains of iron--metal unknown to the mortals aboveground--hung around the priest's neck, holding amulets infused with the blood of Taal, blood Angel herself had shed centuries ago.

Raem smiled. *And thus I rise--from the king of a mere city-state to the lord of the underworld.* He laughed. *Oh, but if only my mortal children could see me now! If only the dragons knew of the power I gain!*

The priest reached them, so tall its head nearly brushed the ceiling; it had to bend down, creaking and raining dust, to stare at Raem and even at the towering Angel. Its mouth opened wide, red and raw, and its words oozed out like pus from a wound.

"Two shall be joined. In the name of fear, of pain, of the unholy, of those cast from Taal's light, I will join your souls eternally like twins conjoined in the womb. I--"

A voice tore across the hall, interrupting the priest. "You will not! They will not join. I refuse it! You will not."

The crowd of demons hissed and screeched and pointed. The crowd parted, and a man came walking down the hall.

Raem narrowed his eyes.

The man is me.

At least, the figure approaching was the man he had been-- Raem Seran before the war, clad in bronze, his original limbs still attached. The demons across the hall, from the smallest fluttering insects to the largest lumbering beasts, cowered as the doppelganger walked toward the throne.

Angel hissed and shoved Ishnafel behind her back,
protecting her spawn. Raem stared, his tentacle twitching and his
claw clattering.

"Who are you, imposter?" he called out.

His doppelganger reached him and smiled thinly. Crow's
feet spread out from the green eyes across the tanned skin. Black,
coiling strands emanated from the man, and he began to melt, to
twist, to *change*. The smoke spread out, then pulled back inward,
coalescing. The man twitched madly, then with a single pulse took
a new form. While before the creature had looked like Raem, now
it was Issari who stood before him.

It was a mirror image--the large green eyes, the smooth
olive-toned skin, the raven braid, the white tunic fringed with
gold. Raem couldn't help it. A twinge of sadness stung him, of
memory, of love.

You were my youngest child, the purest thing in my world, he
thought, staring at his daughter. His old life thudded back into
him: the smell of fig and date trees in the courtyards, his palace of
blue columns capped with gold, the good and warm sunlight, the
whispers of the sea, the love of his family. Of Issari. Of his
dearest child.

"Hello, Raem Seran of Eteer," the creature who looked like
Issari said. Even her voice was the same--high and pure and
musical. "Hello, Father."

Now rage filled Raem, replacing the bittersweet memories.
He snarled and raised his lobster claw.

"How dare you take the form of my daughter?" He took a
step closer to the imposter. "Show your true form! Reveal and
name yourself!"

Smoke rose from the creature and it shifted again. This time
it took the form of Prince Sena, a noose around his neck. The
eyes bulged out. The tongue hung loosely. The face was gray and
bloated with death, rustling with flies.

"Do you like this form better, Raem?" the corpse asked. A centipede fled from its mouth. "This is what happened to your son."

Angel stepped forward. Her feet slammed down, shaking the hall. "Enough of this! Sharael, leave this place. I have forbidden you from entering my hall. Leave now or I will tear out your lying tongue and add it to my throne. Leave now or your bones will crunch between my jaws, and your blood will feed my wedding guests. You are not welcome here, Deceiver."

The corpse smiled thinly, lips flecked with blood. Ignoring Angel, he stared at Raem. "Oh, but this *is* my true form, mortal. I am pain. I am memory. I am deceit. I am Sharael, the Deceiver, the cold terror that lurks inside every soul. Before you drift off to sleep, when the seed of awareness rises inside you, the realization of the great pits of agony that lie beneath your safe world--that is me. When in a moment of silence fear strikes, true understanding, true sight of the enormity of agony--that is my whisper. I am worlds untold, undiscovered, waiting, sharpening my blades, nurturing my darkness. I am the dark hills beneath the mind where no life grows, where souls shatter, where vast spaces expand beyond all that mortals can know, beyond all that minds can comprehend. My true form?" He cackled. "Upon seeing my true form, your eyeballs would shatter, and your mind would shriek. A man cannot comprehend great numbers of multitudes, great sizes like the space between worlds, or minute universes within grains of sand. The minds of both mortals and demons are limited. But I am unlimited. If you saw my true form, it would engulf this hall, the Abyss itself, the world above, and you would beg me. You would beg me to take the form of your dead child again, Raem Seran."

A chill ran through Raem. His tentacle twitched. Angel, however, growled at the shapeshifter.

"Your skull is worth less than a pot to piss in," the Demon Queen said. She reached out her claws. "I've banished you from this hall and you've returned. And now your pain begins."

She leaped toward the demon.

Sharael changed again.

He grew taller, slimmer, brighter. Silver light flowed from him. His body became smooth and naked, formed of liquid silver. He lowered his bald head, and his palms opened at his sides, facing outward. His light, pale like the moon, grew brighter than the sun.

"Taal," Raem whispered.

The light fell upon Angel, and the Demon Queen shrieked in pain. Cracks widened across her body.

"Deceiver!" she shouted.

Sharael laughed. "You still cower at the sight of your father! I am mightier than Taal, mightier than you, mightier than this mortal you seek to wed. I will be your husband. I will be the King of the Abyss. I am more than a demon. I am a god. I will rule this underworld, and you will be my wife. You will be my slave, my whore." The shapeshifter turned toward Raem. "And you, mortal. I will find your precious Issari, the girl you still love. Oh yes, I saw your love for her when I took her form. I will find her . . . and I will make her suffer. I will twist her."

Raem had heard enough. Angel perhaps feared the light of Taal--even the fake light of an imposter--but Raem had always served the silver god. He thrust his lobster claw into the light, grabbed Sharael's throat, and sliced through his neck.

The silver head clattered to the floor.

Sharael shrieked. He shifted again. The silver head bloated and melted, took the form of Issari, of Sena, of Laira, of a waterlogged boar, of a rotting dragon, of a skull caked with charred skin. The headless body convulsed, changing from woman to man to animal to demon.

"Grab him!" Angel cried to the demons across the hall. "Add him to the walls. Pump him with blood."

A thousand demons screamed and flew toward the fallen Sharael, reaching for the head and body.

Sharael still lived. Smoke blasted out from the demon, and he shifted again. The body became that of a great dark bird, feathers oily, talons serrated. The headless bird grabbed the severed head--it was still changing forms, the transformations so quick they blurred into one another. With a great shriek, the towering vulture flew across the hall. Demons tried to reach it, but the bird's wings and talons held them back. With a last, echoing screech, Sharael flew through the doors and vanished. Only the demon's final cry lingered in the hall: "You will break, Raem Seran! The Throne of Tongues will be mine!"

"Find him!" Angel shouted. "Bring him to me! Break him!"

A thousand demons cried out, scuttled, leaped, wept, screamed, and drained through the doorway in pursuit. Globs of saliva, pus, and fat remained behind them. The demons' cries echoed in the hall, a last reminder of their presence.

Angel trembled with rage. She tossed back her head and screamed so loudly that more living sacks burst upon the ceiling. The red rain showered. Flames burst out from Angel in rings, searing the demons stitched into the walls and floor. The Demon Queen spun toward the priest, the only demon remaining.

"Wed us!" Angel screeched. "Wed us now!"

The priest bowed its great, thorny head. Its eight eyes blinked with sucking sounds.

"Angel of the Abyss. Raem the Half-Mortal. You are now joined in unholy matrimony, and may you--"

With a scream, Angel swiped her arm, knocking the priest aside. She spun toward Raem, grabbed his shoulders, and leaned down above him. Her eyes burned, blasting out white light. Her jaw unhinged, and her tongue unfurled to lick him from navel to forehead.

"Now give me another child," she hissed.

Face dripping, Raem smiled. He wrapped his tentacle around her and pulled her close. "Let us find a chamber to--"

She knocked him down. "Now!"

With blasts of smoke, a twitching tentacle, and leaking lava, they copulated beneath the Throne of Tongues. All around them, faces leered and the screams echoed.

Raem smiled as he consummated his marriage, as the heat of the Abyss flowed through him.

I was a prince, then a king of a city. He laughed as Angel's claws dug into his back. *Now I am a Demon King. Now the worlds above and below will fear my might. Now Requiem will truly burn.*

LAIRA

She knelt and lifted the fallen copper scale. Blood dulled its shine. She hefted it in her hand; it was heavy and thick like a plate forged of true metal. Laira felt something tight and cold inside her, constricting her breath.

"Jeid's scale," she whispered.

The autumn forest spread around them: oaks with rustling yellow leaves, birches with peeling white bark, maples whose red leaves glided in the wind, and many boulders and fallen boles green with moss. Geese flew above, honking, but no more dragons. The wings of Requiem no longer filled the sky.

Maev took the scale from Laira's hand. She stared at it, jaw clenched and bottom lip thrust out in defiance. Her fingers tightened around the scale, and her other hand formed a fist.

"He's still alive," Maev said, forcing the words past stiff lips. "Dead dragons return to human form. They wounded him. They tore off a scale. But he's still alive." She looked at Laira, her eyes blazing with rage and haunting fear. "I know it."

Laira touched the scale again. It was cold and very smooth like mother of pearl. Her eyes stung and she wanted to caress the real Jeid, to hold him close, to know her husband was safe.

"We'll keep searching." Laira nodded. "We're going the right way. We know that now. Grizzly flew here, and maybe the others too." She touched Maev's arm. "Maybe Dorvin too."

Maev took a step back, her expression hardening. She turned and kept walking through the forest, not waiting for Laira to catch up.

Laira sighed. *Whenever I see some warmth to her, her ice returns. Whenever we get close, she pushes me away.* Laira feared the sphinxes, feared losing her husband, feared losing all of Requiem. Perhaps Maev feared showing that she was more than a dragon, that she was human too.

"Maev, wait." Laira struggled to keep up on her shorter legs; Maev was walking quickly, and Laira had to take two steps for every one of Maev's. "Wait for me. Let's not get lost ourselves. I--"

Howls sounded above. Wings beat. A stench like burning hair and sulfur flared.

"Sphinxes." Laira clenched her jaw and leaped under a bush.

Maev, however, remained standing in the forest. She still held the copper scale. She refused to budge, only stared at the sky, her eyes hard.

"Maev!" Laira whispered urgently, gesturing for her from under the bush. "Come. Hide!"

Maev looked at Laira, expressionless, then back at the sky. Her hands formed fists. Her muscles coiled, making her dragon tattoos dance. Her lip peeled back.

"No," the warrior whispered. "I'm done running."

Sphinx wings hid the sun. Their drool rained from their maws. One cried out, "Below! A weredragon below!"

Maev growled, tossed the copper scale aside, and shifted into a green dragon. She soared and blew her fire.

Three sphinxes dived through the treetops and slammed into Maev, knocking the green dragon onto the forest floor. The beasts roared, their massive jaws splitting their bloated human heads down to the ears. Their lion bodies bristled, and their feathered wings beat madly, raising a cloud of fallen leaves. Their claws scratched at Maev, and the green dragon roared.

"Stars damn it!" Laira leaped from under the bush, shifted into a golden dragon, and leaped toward the fray.

One of the sphinxes spun toward her, growling. Its human head leered, covered in tattoos, stretched to several times the normal size as if pumped with water. The beast's feline body crouched and bristled, and its mouth opened. It spewed a cloud of smoke thick with small, bustling demons; each looked like a grub with a human face.

Laira hissed and beat her wings. She soared above the smoke, hit the treetops, and swooped. Her claws drove into the sphinx's back, through fur and skin and into stringy flesh.

The creature howled and bucked. Its tail lashed, covered in spikes, and slammed into Laira's back. She roared, scales cracking, and clung to the beast. She leaned down, grabbed a fold of its flesh between her jaws, and bit deep. Acidic blood flooded her mouth.

At her side, Laira glimpsed Maev fighting two of the creatures. The green dragon rolled on the ground, clawing and lashing her tail. One of the sphinxes pinned her down, and the other blew a cloud of its demon-infested smoke. Maev shut her eyes and her mouth, and even her nostrils pinched shut as the cloud spread over her.

Beneath Laira, the sphinx she had grabbed bucked madly, tossing her about. Clinging, Laira turned her head and blasted fire against the sphinxes attacking Maev, trying to keep the flames off the green dragon.

The sphinx below Laira thrashed, bleeding but still alive. It tossed Laira off its back and against a maple. The tree shattered and branches rained. An instant later, the wounded sphinx pounced on Laira, jaw biting into her chest. Laira fell backward, slamming into an oak. The tree cracked and fell.

The sphinx stood before her, grinning, its claws red with her blood. It blasted its unholy miasma her way.

Laira blew her dragonfire.

The two jets crashed together, fire and smoke.

Trees burst into flame. Grass burned. The weapons roared, and Laira sneered as she blew her fire. She stepped forward, foot by foot, shoving her pillar of flame against the smoke until it drove through the cloud and crashed into the sphinx.

The creature burned.

Its magic vanished, and it returned to human form--a blazing, screaming man.

Laira stepped closer and stomped down her foot. Her claws passed through flames and into the man's chest. She yanked back, tearing out ribs and meat.

Shaking the gore off her claws, Laira turned to see Maev standing over the corpses of two Widejaws, both back in human form. The green dragon stared at Laira, smoke rising from her nostrils.

"That," said Maev, "is how we treat the enemies of Requiem."

"That," said Laira, "almost got us killed."

The green dragon advanced toward Laira, eyes narrowed and nostrils puffing out smoke. The dragon's every movement spoke of menace. "We're alive. They're dead." Maev snarled. "I'm a warrior. You are too; your claws and fangs are drenched in blood. I will no longer cower."

Laira was a smaller dragon, but she refused to back away. She glared at her stepdaughter and hissed, puffing smoke against the green dragon's snout.

"Next time, Maev, you will listen to me and hide. I am your queen, and I am your stepmother, and--"

"You are nothing to me!" Maev shouted. She tossed back her head and roared.

"Hush!" Laira ground her teeth. "You'll alert the other sphinxes to--"

"Good!" Maev blasted flame skyward. "Let them hear! Let them see my beacon. Let them come and die! You cannot stop

me, Laira. You cannot! Things were fine before you joined us."
Tears filled Maev's eyes, but she still growled and her claws dug
into the earth. "We lived in the escarpment. We were safe. Then
you drew the rocs toward us. Then your father sent demons to
slay us. Now the sphinxes tore Requiem apart, and they might
have killed everyone else, and it's your fault again, Laira. Your
fault!" Maev blasted more flame, hitting a tree. The forest burned
around them. "And to make things worse, you took my father
from me. And now he could be dead." Tears flowed down Maev's
scaly cheeks. "Queen? Mother? You are only a menace. You
destroyed my family."

Laira's anger flowed away. She felt deflated. As scattered
flames flickered around her, she released her magic.

The green dragon snorted before her, chest heaving, smoke
rising. Laira stepped forward in human form, embraced Maev's
snout, and laid her head against the dragon's scales.

"I'm sorry, Maev," Laira whispered. "I'm sorry. I love you. I
love you very much."

The green dragon trembled. More hot smoke blasted out.
And then suddenly Maev was in human form again, embracing
Laira, crushing her in her arms. Maev's tears fell, dampening
Laira's hair.

"I'm sorry too, Laira." Maev squeezed her desperately like a
drowning woman clinging to a floating log. "I didn't mean it. I
didn't mean what I said. Forgive me."

Laira smiled tremulously and touched Maev's cheek. "You
meant it. And I'm glad you said it. It's out of you now. Just know
that I'm sorry, that I never meant to bring evil to your doorstep,
and I understand how you feel. But I love you and I hope we can
be like a true family--not like a stepmother and daughter, but
more like sisters. Sisters of Requiem."

Maev nodded and wiped tears from her eyes. "I'd like that.
Now let's keep walking. The smoke and fire are a beacon, and we

have to find the others." She squeezed Laira's hand. "Let's walk and if more sphinxes arrive, we'll hide. We'll--"

A voice rose behind them. "You will come with us, dragons."

Laira and Maev spun around, gasping.

A dozen men emerged from between the trees, clad in green cloaks and hoods. Each man held a bow, arrows pointing forward. Instead of a flint or bronze head, each arrow was tipped with a bundle of rolled up leaves and vines.

With only a glance at each other, Laira and Maev shifted back into dragons.

The arrows flew and slammed into them.

The two dragons screamed.

Upon impact, the leafy bundles unfurled. Green strands spread across Laira like vines clutching a boulder. They squeezed. They spread stinging pain through her. She yowled as invisible hands seemed to grab her magic, to yank it out, to shatter the starlight inside her. Her scales vanished. Her wings and claws retracted. She fell onto the forest floor in human form, the green strands still racing across her, rustling with leaves, stabbing her with thorns. Maev thrashed on the ground beside her, clutched in similar green bonds, her magic also gone.

"Lift them up," said one of the archers, a tall man with an auburn beard. "Toss them across the horses." He smiled thinly. "Two more cursed ones for the Green Lord."

Laira tried to shift again, to rise, to fly, to burn them. The robed men grabbed her, tugged her to her feet, and shoved a sack over her head. Darkness spread across her and she screamed.

JEID

The young man's voice echoed through the tunnels, hoarse and far too loud, singing a bawdy song.

"The girl went to the sea
And got stung there by a bee
And the bee got her right on the bottom!
And she took off her clothes
From her chin down to her toes
And--"

Jeid stomped forward. "Dorvin!"

He rounded the corner and saw the black-haired hunter there. Dorvin sat slumped against the wall, legs splayed out. He held a tin bottle and Jeid smelled spirits.

"'ello, old grizzly bear!" Dorvin said, waving weakly. He raised his drink. "Want a sip?"

"I want you to shut your mouth." Jeid glared down at the young man. "There are people sleeping in these tunnels, people praying, people--"

"--who could use a good song!" Dorvin said. He struggled to his feet, a little wobbly, and held the cave wall for support. With a deep breath, he began to sing again. "And she jumped into the water, where a giant squid caught her, and a fish began to nibble her--"

"Enough!" Jeid grabbed the younger man's collar, then winced. "You stink. What's that you're drinking?"

Dorvin grinned. "It don't stink!" He raised the bottle. "This is special stuff. Not just regular wine and ale like they brew in the north. This stuff's from across the sea. Distilled. Powerful. Like a whole cup of wine with every sip. Want some?"

Surprisingly, Jeid did.

With a sigh, he released Dorvin, and the two men sat side by side and leaned against the tunnel wall. In the distance to their right, rose the sound of prayer from survivors deeper in the tunnels. To their left, Jeid could hear dragonfire roaring as Vir Requis guarded the entrance, taking shifts.

"Pass me that bottle," Jeid said. When he sipped, the drink shot through his throat and stung his nostrils, blazing hot and bitter.

"Good?" Dorvin said.

Jeid nodded. "Good."

For long moments, they sat passing the bottle back and forth--a grizzled, burly king and a wiry, fiery hunter half his age. Jeid looked at the young man--Dorvin's sharp eyebrows, his black hair that always fell across his brow at a jaunty angle, and his cheeks which even here in the caves he kept clean-shaven. A vain boy. A stupid, hot-tempered, rude, useless lump.

The man my daughter fancies, he thought.

He had seen Dorvin and Maev walking alone through the woods. He had seen them sneak together into huts, emerging flustered, their clothes in disarray.

"Do you sing these rude songs around my daughter?" Jeid asked.

Dorvin snorted. "Stars no. Maev clobbers me whenever I sing around her. Damn mammoth arse got fists like two boulders." He rubbed his cheek.

Jeid raised his own fist. "Don't call her that. Show her respect. Especially with her missing, maybe--"

Maybe dead, he thought. He could not speak those words.

Dorvin nodded solemnly. "I meant to say 'Maev.'" He drank deeply and screwed up his face at the flavor. "I respect her, Grizzly. I love the mamm-- I love Maev." Suddenly the young man's eyes dampened. "If she's alive, and if we ever get out of here, I'll let her know that. I'd never sing around her again, or call her a bad name, or annoy her, or anything. I'd just love her. Always." He lowered his head and rubbed his eyes. "Stars damn it! Damn drink always gets into my eyes."

Jeid grumbled and patted the younger man's back. "I miss them too. Maev. Laira. Tanin and Issari." He took the bottle and drank deeply, the liquid racing through him like fire. "I wonder if they're under the sky now, watching the stars, thinking of us . . . maybe flying as dragons."

"I hope they're alive," Dorvin whispered, "but I'm scared. I'm scared they fell like my sister." He looked at Jeid, his eyes red. "Do you know what Alina used to say? She said that when a Vir Requis dies, his or her soul rises to the stars. She said that the halls of Requiem stand there, already built, all woven of starlight--an image we must build here in the world. She believed that all who fell now live up there, drinking wine and singing."

"Not singing your songs, I hope." Jeid took another sip. "And drinking something more proper than this too, if there's any justice in the heavens." He squeezed Dorvin's shoulder. "I don't know if it's true. I don't know if celestial halls rise above us, home to our fallen. But I know this: the stars gave us our magic, and they blessed our column."

Dorvin stared up at the ceiling. "But they don't shine here. If we die here underground, will we find our way to them?" He lowered his voice to a whisper. "To Alina? I miss her, Grizzly." His voice cracked. "I miss her so badly. And I miss Maev and Laira and everyone else, but with my sister it's even worse. I was such a damn fool." He spat, his eyes still damp. "I never showed them that I love them. Never. Not until it was too late. But if I see

Maev again, I swear to the stars--I'm going to be the best damn man I can for her." He looked at Jeid. "I'd like to marry her, if you approve. I promise you, my king, that I would treat her like a princess."

"She *is* a princess. She's the king's daughter after all."

Dorvin nodded. "You know, I used to sit like this under the stars. Would find a nice boulder or fallen log to sit on, stare up, and drink whatever I could get--ale, wine, cider, anything I could trade salted meat or furs for. And I'd just stare up, watching the stars, trying to imagine what they were. We were wanderers, in my tribe. Called ourselves Stonespear. Old name. We'd travel from the southern sea to the northern hinterlands, from the western mountains to the eastern grasslands, and wherever we'd travel, those stars would be the same. I used to think it so strange! How babes were born, elders died, how the earth changed from rock to grass to water . . . but those stars kept shining, traveling across the sky but always coming back home. I used to think I was so small, so lowly, nothing compared to those lights in the sky, those celestial warriors." He thumped his chest. "But maybe there's a little starlight inside me after all. Inside all Vir Requis." He looked at Jeid, and his voice was hoarse. "Grizzly, how do you feel light and joy when you're in darkness, when there's so much pain and death, when you miss people so much, when you feel so alone?"

Jeid sighed. He slung his arm around the younger man. "You don't. Not always. I don't always feel the light of the sun or stars, the warmth, the beauty of the world. Often all is dark within me. But darkness passes. Loss, grief, fear . . . we cannot always heal these things, but we can find light too. Even in darkness. Even in grief. Even when alone. Hope is like a candle in a dark forest; it doesn't banish all shadows, but it gives you enough light to walk by. And there is always some hope, some light, some joy. You are not alone, Dorvin. No Vir Requis will ever be alone so long as our column stands. And it still stands--out there in our forest."

Dorvin nodded, rubbed his eyes, and rose to his feet. "We will find our column again. We will find our sky." He emptied his bottle. "And we'll find more of this damn magnificent stuff."

Jeid rose to his feet, joints creaking. "Now go guard the entrance. It's your shift."

As the young man walked off, Jeid remained in the dark tunnel, alone.

He'd be a good man for you, Maev, he thought. *And maybe I gave him some hope.* He throat tightened. *But why can't I feel the same hope within me?*

Jeid clenched his fists and lowered his head, feeling lost in the shadows.

ISSARI

The white dragon flew over the mountain, staring down at the ruin of her people.

The children of Eteer, exiled from their home upon the coast, wailed under the whips of their Gosharian masters. Clad in rags, their backs striped, the slaves climbed the mountainside, some moving across scaffolding, others clinging to the bare rock. Their picks and chisels worked at the stone, forming the shape of a great statue five hundred feet tall--the goddess Shahazar, her breasts bare, her navel shining with jewels, her head that of a serpent.

At the feet of the statue, more Eteerian slaves toiled. They were digging a tunnel between the statue's feet, raising columns to flank it, and carving a great staircase that led from the desert to the entrance. This was more than a statue, Issari realized; the granite Shahazar was guarding a temple being dug into the mountain.

All across the work site, the Gosharian masters patrolled. They whipped Eteerians, laughing as they bloodied the slaves. One old woman collapsed, spilling the basket of rocks she carried. The masters kicked her and snickered as she wailed. A child pleaded for mercy; the masters beat him, lashing his chest, his arms, his face. The cries of Eteer rolled across the mountainside, cries of agony and of hope.

"Issari! Issari! The white dragon rises!"

"You cry to me," Issari whispered, gliding above. "And I hear your cry, Eteer."

Tanin flew up to glide at her side. "What's the plan?"

She gave him a wry smile. "To show Goshar the might of dragons."

And then fly home, she thought. *To Requiem. To Laira.* Her eyes stung, for she missed her family, and she missed her home in the north, but she would not abandon the children of Eteer, not while blood still pumped in her veins and her wings still found her sky.

Across the mountainside, the Gosharian masters shouted and pointed at the approaching dragons. Some fired arrows. Others fled. Issari and Tanin glided closer.

"The overseer is there." Issari pointed a claw. "He stands upon the head of the statue."

Tanin nodded. "Right. We burn him, then get everyone out."

Issari shook her head, scales clattering. "We speak to him. We will speak reason. We might not need to burn anyone; enough have died today."

She cringed inwardly to remember those guards she had burned in the palace. She felt no guilt for slaying the obese abina, but what of his men? Had the palace guards truly held her any animosity? And yet she had shifted into a dragon, and she had burned them dead, as Tanin had burned soldiers upon the walls outside his prison. Issari liked to think of herself as a creature of starlight, pure and good, yet perhaps she was more a creature of fire and blood. Perhaps dragons were creatures both noble and terrible, and for the first time, Issari thought she understood why so many feared the children of Requiem.

The two dragons, white and red, flew over the work site as masters wailed and slaves chanted. The head of Shahazar stared from the mountain, carved of granite, larger than a dragon--the head of a great cobra, the eyes fitted with copper plates that caught the sun. Issari landed upon the head with a clatter of claws, and her tail whipped, sending scaffolds crashing down the mountainside. An instant later, Tanin landed at her side. The red dragon sneered, raised his tail like a scorpion, and blasted out smoke.

Upon the great stone head, the Gosharian overseer took several steps backward until his back slammed against the mountainside. He was a portly man, clad in bronze ring mail. His beard was black and long, his eyebrows thick, his head bald. He drew a curved blade and held it before him.

"Stand back, reptiles!" Spittle flew from his mouth. "I am but a mortal, but the goddess Shahazar protects me. Leave this place, foul creatures. Leave or the goddess's curse will wilt your wings."

Issari sneered and raised her paw. The light of Taal burst out from the amulet in a beam. The Gosharian wailed and covered his eyes.

Issari released her magic. A human again, she stood upon the statue's head, facing the overseer. Without her magic, she was only a slim young woman, still clad in the silks of the harem. But she spoke with the gravity of a queen.

"You will order your men to lower their whips and blades." She took a step closer to the man. "You will secure Eteer's passage through the city of Goshar and into the fertile lands of the south. But before the children of Eteer depart, you will pay every man, woman, and child a coin of gold." She clenched her fists. "And you will beg each one for forgiveness, and all shall know that Shahazar is powerless to resist the might of Queen Issari."

The overseer howled, cheeks red, and swung his blade toward her.

Tanin sucked in his breath.

Issari ducked and the blade whistled over her head. She opened her palm and slammed her amulet into the overseer's chest.

Light blazed out and the overseer screamed. His sword clattered to the ground. He fell back against the mountainside.

"I forgot to add one thing," Issari whispered, her amulet blazing. "If you disobey me, I will show you no mercy."

The overseer roared, drew a dagger, and raced back toward her. Issari sidestepped, dodging the blade, and let the man keep running. He tried to halt upon the edge of the statue. A shove from Issari kept him on his way. The overseer teetered for a moment on the ledge, then tumbled. He fell, screaming, hundreds of feet down the mountainside. Slaves below scattered as their master slammed into the earth.

"You were right," Tanin said. The red dragon whistled appreciatively. "Didn't need to burn anyone."

Issari walked to the edge of the serpent's head. She gazed down upon the land--the mountainside where the slaves labored, the city of Goshar beyond, the scorching northern desert of her exile, and far in the south the fertile grasslands to which she would lead her people. She raised her arms high.

"Hear me, children of Eteer!" she called out. "I am Issari Seran, the Priestess in White, the Queen of Eteer, a dragon of Requiem. I've heard your cry and I will lead you to freedom, to safety, to a new home!"

The children of Eteer chanted her name. The Gosharian masters fled.

Issari smiled and leaped off the statue. Wings burst out from her back. White scales rose across her. She dived down the mountainside.

"Follow, children of Eteer! Follow me to freedom."

She landed at the base of the statue and resumed human form. The slaves crowded around her, reaching out to to touch her, to seek a blessing. She walked among them, smiling softly, and she held her hand high. The light rose from her amulet, a pillar reaching into the sky.

"Issari! Issari!" they chanted. "The Priestess in White!"

Tanin soared overhead, a red dragon roaring fire. Issari walked upon the earth, her light shining. A pillar of fire and a pillar of light led the children of Eteer from slavery and into the city of Goshar.

Between stone houses and columned temples, soldiers of the city raced forth to stop the children of Eteer. They wore armor and carried curved blades and round shields, and their faces twisted with fear and rage. Chariots rolled between them along the cobbled streets, their wheels scythed.

"Turn back, slaves!" their captain shouted. "You cannot pass. Goshar is forbidden to you."

Issari, walking at the lead of a great flock, smiled thinly. She wore a white cloak across her shoulders, a gift from a young slave boy, a raiment to hide the silks of the harem.

"We shall pass," she said. "And we will not dwell in Goshar but in the fertile lands beyond her walls. I have promised those lands to my people, to a people exiled and hurt, a people I have freed from the tyranny of Raem, from the devilry of the Demon Queen, and from the whips of Goshar. If you seek to stop us, I will free my people from your yoke too, soldiers of the city. Step aside and let us pass, or the light of Eteer and the fire of Requiem will flow across you. I've slain your lord, the Abina Sin-Naharosh. Step aside and I will show you mercy, for I am merciful."

She raised her hand high, and the pillar of light crackled.

And the soldiers of Goshar turned and fled before her.

"Issari! Issari!" her people chanted, tears in their eyes. Their voices rose in song. She walked at the head of the column, leading them through the city, as above the red dragon flew and roared.

They walked by many homes and halls, through many courtyards and squares, until they reached the southern walls of Goshar. A gateway rose here, flanked with granite statues, and through it Issari saw the green lands she sought. A place of freedom, of plenty, of peace.

"A new home for Eteer," she whispered. "From fire and blood into green lands and blue skies."

She had taken one step through the archway, had placed one foot into the lands beyond, when she heard the shrieks behind her and smelled the stench of rot.

She turned around.

She felt the blood drain from her face.

They flew above the city like a cloud of locust, hundreds strong, their wings buzzing, their eyes blazing, their maws dripping, their shrieks echoing.

Issari trembled, her eyes dampened, and her heart thrashed against her ribs.

"Nephilim," she whispered.

JEID

The scream echoed through the tunnels.

Jeid cursed and ran.

"Again!" Dorvin shouted, running behind him. "Stars damn it! What in the Abyss?"

All along the tunnel walls, the exiled Vir Requis huddled in human form, faces dour. Some whimpered and others wept. Some simply stared sternly, clenching their fists. A few lay on the cave floor, clutching wounds from the battle at Requiem: the stumps of limbs, gaping gashes, and flesh wilted by the sphinx smoke.

But right now we face a new enemy, Jeid thought, racing by them. *An unknown shadow in the dark.*

The scream rose once more, then faded. Jeid took several wrong turns through the labyrinth in the mountain, backtracked, and finally smelled the stench of death. He followed his nose and there, in a narrow tunnel far from the cave entrance, he saw it-- another corpse.

The woman lay on the ground, glassy eyes staring, mouth frozen in anguish. Like all the others, her chest had been cracked, the ribs tugged open like swinging doors, and the innards scooped out.

"Gutted like a fish," Dorvin said. He came to stand at Jeid's side, chest heaving, and wiped sweat off his brow. "Fifth damn one. Grizzly, what's doing this?" The young, dark-haired man spun around and shouted, "Show yourself! Whoever you are, come here and fight me like a man."

Jeid stared down at the corpse, feeling just as hollow. The slain woman was named Serra, a pale gatherer of berries with short black hair and dark eyes. She had been so young, not yet twenty, all her life still awaiting her.

She should have lived to see Requiem flourish, Jeid thought. *She should have married, raised a family, lived in peace and died in old age in the light of our halls . . . not here. Not like this.*

"Come on!" Dorvin was screaming, spinning his arms around. Spittle flew from his mouth. "Come on and face us, damn it! Come and--"

"Dorvin." Jeid pointed at the ceiling. "Look."

One of the survivors, a lamp-maker, had fled Requiem with three clay lamps in her pack. Jeid now raised one of those small lamps. The oil was low, and the wick flickered; they had enough oil for only another day or two of light. The orange glow revealed a hole--perhaps a foot wide--in the granite ceiling. Blood stained its rim.

"What in the Abyss?" Dorvin frowned. "That hole's barely wide enough to piss through. You think whatever killed Serra came through there?"

Jeid wove his fingers together. "Go take a look. I'll give you a boost."

The young man's eyes widened. "I'd sooner bugger a dead bloated whale."

"Shut your mouth and look."

Dorvin grimaced. "And if whatever's in there chews my face off?"

"Then at least I won't have to look at your ugly mug anymore."

Grumbling under his breath, Dorvin placed a foot in Jeid's hands. Jeid shoved, boosting Dorvin up toward the ceiling. The young hunter winced, cursed, but dutifully peered into the hole.

"Emptier than Maev's skull," Dorvin said. "And stinkier than your backside, Grizzly. Whatever got Serra was here all right. There's damn blood and mucus all over." He hopped down onto the floor and shuddered. "By the Sky Goddess's teats, if there were room to shift in here, I'd claw that hole open and tear apart whatever's living in there."

Jeid grunted. "Even if we had room to shift in here, the walls are mostly granite. Harder than marble. We'd be chipping away an inch at a time; could take years. But something dug this hole, something with sharper claws than dragons. Stay here, Dorvin. You're guarding this hole from now on."

Dorvin's eyes grew so wide his eyeballs looked ready to pop out. "Warthog's shite I am!" He gestured down at the hollowed-out body. "You saw what that creature did to Serra."

"I did. And I don't want it doing that to anyone else. So draw your sword, boy, and guard this hole." Jeid smiled wryly. "Whatever's in there, it's no deadlier than the army of sphinxes outside."

As if to answer his thoughts, screams rose from far above in the caves. Jeid tensed.

The sphinxes.

He cursed and ran.

He whipped around bends in the labyrinth, racing past the other survivors until he burst into the wide chamber near the mountainside.

Jeid had positioned Verin, an old man with a long white beard, to guard the entrance in dragon form. When Jeid had left this place, Verin had been blowing fire out the exit, a gray dragon with cracked horns. Verin now lay dead upon the cave floor, a human again. Two sphinxes stood above him, ripping into his flesh and guzzling it down. Three Widejaws were walking across the cave in human form, approaching the tunnel, bronze-tipped spears in their hands.

Jeid roared, drew his sword, and ran to meet them.

The Widejaws grinned, their cheeks split to the ears, revealing shark-like maws. One man thrust his spear. Jeid knocked the weapon aside, ducked under another spear, and kicked. He hit one man in the shin, swung his sword, and cut into another man's arm. A spear thrust and scratched along Jeid's shoulder, and he roared. Silhouetted by the sunlight at the entrance, several sphinxes hissed and took human form; they too entered the cave and advanced toward him.

"Jeid!" rose a voice behind him.

An instant later, Koren raced forward and thrust his spear. The gaunt man--once a fisherman of the River Ranin--screamed in rage, and his flint-tipped weapon drove into a Widejaw's neck. Jeid stabbed another Widejaw in the chest; his bronze sword crashed through the man's mail, scattering metal rings across the floor.

Jeid sneered and drove forward, sword waving madly, relying on his size to shove the enemy back. Another spear drove into his thigh, and he howled but kept shoving the enemy back.

"Stand back, Koren!" Jeid cried and shifted.

He ballooned into a dragon. An instant before he could be crushed, Koren leaped backwards. A copper dragon, Jeid slammed against the walls, filling the cave like a lemon stuck in a man's throat.

He blasted out his flames.

The Widejaws burned and fell.

Jeid shoved himself forward, clawing at the fallen bodies. Sphinxes still flew outside; one reached the entrance and blasted in a cloud of demon smoke. Jeid roared his fire, roasting the small demons floating in the cloud and the sphinx behind them. With a few more steps, Jeid reached the entrance and roared out dragonfire in a great fountain. Hundreds of sphinxes still flew outside, shrieking and fluttering away from the inferno.

We can't keep doing this much longer. The flames roared and the fear twisted inside him. *Danger lurks outside and within. Too many lost.*

Fewer than a hundred Vir Requis now hid in the tunnels, and more were falling every day--to the sphinxes outside and the creature within. As Jeid blasted his fire, he knew that the fallen had been the lucky ones. Their deaths had been quick.

When his flames ran low, he pulled back into the cave, and Koren replaced him at the entrance, taking the form of a blue dragon.

Leaving Koren to guard the cave, Jeid walked back toward the tunnels, bleeding, dizzy. His wounds left a red trail behind him. He wanted to collapse. Pain flared and he fell to his knees, lowered his head, and breathed raggedly

I can't do this anymore.

He wanted to join the dead, to see them again: little Requiem, his parents, his fallen wife--

Laira is my wife now.

He clenched his fists, and his chest heaved.

"Laira," he whispered.

So many years after losing Keyla, his first wife, he had met a new woman to love--a woman who brought him new light, new hope, new joy.

I have to live. I have to find you again, Laira.

He summoned Laira in his memory: her large green eyes, her mouth trembling with a hesitant smile, her warm body wrapped in his arms, the courage and strength of her soul, the love and pride in her wings and golden scales.

For you I will keep fighting. Always. If you are alive, Laira, I will find you. If you are fallen, I will burn down the world in revenge.

"Jeid!"

He raised his head. Bryn came running toward him from the depths. The red-haired woman stared at him with wide eyes.

"I'm all right, Bryn," he managed to rasp.

She reached him, knelt, and examined his wounds. "You are not! By the stars." She looked over her shoulder. "We need a druid! The king is hu--"

"Bryn!" Jeid grabbed her arm. "They cannot know I'm hurt. They must think their king is strong. Do you understand?"

Her brown eyes dampened, but she tightened her lips and nodded. She drew a granite dagger from her boot and sliced off strips from her cloak. Her fingers steady and her lips pursed, she bound his wounds as best she could.

When her work was done, Jeid sat down and leaned against the wall. He knew he should be walking along the tunnels, comforting the others, showing them his strength, assuring them of survival. But he felt too weak to rise, too hopeless to fight. Byrn, silently understanding, sat at his side and leaned her head against his shoulder. She stroked his chest, passing her hand up and down his fur tunic.

"I'm here for you, my king," she whispered, her breath soft against him. "Should you need me for anything--if only to whisper of your pain, to feel my warmth, to know that I love you--I'm here. I will always fight for King Aeternum of Requiem."

He turned his head toward Bryn and found her face near his; their lips were only an inch or two apart. Her warm brown eyes stared into his, full of love for her king, full of warmth, comfort. She caressed his cheek and whispered softly, "I'm always here for you."

Jeid looked away. His jaw clenched and his belly felt tight. "Bryn, we cannot survive here. All our food is gone. The rivulet of water in the lower tunnel has all but run dry. How much longer can we survive on worms and beetles and whatever else we find in the darkness?" He looked back at her. "Dorvin wants us to fly out, to face the sphinxes head-on, to die in a great battle. We are fewer than a hundred, and they cover the sky. We can choose between a slow death in darkness and a hot death in fire and blood. And I don't know what to choose."

She shook her head wildly, her orange curls swaying. "I do not abandon hope. Not yet. You taught me that. You taught me that there's always hope, even in the pit of despair, even in the greatest darkness where no light shines." She squeezed his hand. "And so I still hope. Perhaps it's blind hope, a fool's hope, but it's better than despair. Whatever you choose, my king, I will follow you. I will fight at your side or die at your side. But until then I'll believe that we will live, that we will see Requiem again." She raised her chin, and her eyes shone. "Requiem! May our wings forever find your sky."

Jeid looked up above him. He saw only the dark stone ceiling of the cave, but somewhere above all the rock waited the sky. The sky of Requiem. No, he would not abandon that sky, would never forget the wind beneath his wings, the glow of the stars, or the pale columns of their lost hall.

If we fly out, we will die in the sphinx's smoke. If we stay here, we will starve or fall to the creature in the holes. Jeid kept racking his mind, seeking some solution. Even if he could become a dragon in the narrow tunnels, his claws would be unable to dig in these mountains, not with the walls formed of granite. Death beyond. Death within. How could--

Again screams echoed across the tunnels. Above them rose an inhuman shriek.

Jeid and Bryn leaped to their feet.

They ran deeper into the cave, following the sound.

They raced past other survivors, around a corner, and found a woman trembling and pointing.

"There!" she cried. "There, I saw it!"

Jeid grimaced and ran. He reached a fork in the tunnel, heard another scream, ran down a slope, and he saw it there.

"Stars damn it."

A long black leg shone ahead. Another shriek sounded, too high-pitched for a human or animal. White eyes blazed, perfectly round. A shadow loomed over a hollowed-out body. Smooth legs scuttled and leaped up.

Jeid leaped toward the creature and swung his sword. The blade sliced through air. When he looked above him, he saw many legs folding together and pulling into a hole in the ceiling--a different hole than the one Dorvin was guarding farther down the tunnels. Jeid leaped into the air and swung the sword again. He hit a leg, and the creature screeched and vanished into the burrow.

Jeid's feet slammed back onto the floor. The creature was gone. He looked at his sword and found the blade covered with steaming black blood.

Bryn raced up to his side, panting. "What was it?" she asked. "I saw something. I saw eyes. Spider legs. What was it?"

Jeid stared up at the hole, then back at the blood on his blade.

"Our way out."

SLYN

He sat on the Oak Throne, gazed at the ruin of Requiem, and drank hot blood from the weredragon skull.

Three of Requiem's columns had shattered in the battle; they now lay fallen across the hall. Beyond the standing columns, most of the birches had burned; they now rose like charred skeletons, their leaves gone, their branches black. Blood still stained the marble tiles, and the scent of smoke still filled the air.

Hundreds of Widejaw warriors lounged across the hall. They sat upon the fallen columns, drinking from skulls. Mud stained their fur cloaks and tattooed faces, and the blood of their enemies stained their augmented mouths. Campfires burned upon the marble tiles of Requiem's hall, and upon them roasted the flesh of the enemy. Limbs and torsos of dead weredragons crackled and dripped their juices. In death, the creatures were like any other men and women--savory and delicious.

"Bring me meat!" Slyn roared. "You, the dark one. Fetch me a leg."

The dark-haired weredragon knelt by a campfire, a chain running from her ankle to a column. Bruises darkened her face. The chains would keep the wench from shifting. Three other women knelt at the feet of his throne, similarly chained.

"Meat, whore!" Slyn said, pointing at the raven-haired woman.

The weredragon nodded, too fearful to resist. She had tasted his fist the last time she had disobeyed him; her two missing front teeth served as a reminder. She stepped toward a campfire, her chain jangling. Her face was dead, expressionless, too hurt to show any more pain. She lifted one of the roasting weredragon legs--the leg of a child, small and soft--and carried it back toward the Oak Throne.

Slyn grabbed the meat from her. With his other hand, he backhanded the woman. "Now get back on your knees. You are a weredragon. You will kneel before your king." He stared at the rest of them. "That goes for all of you! You will remain kneeling in the presence of Slyn, King of Requiem." He stared at them one by one, savoring the sight of their cuts and bruises. "Aye . . . I know what you're thinking, you whores. You're craving the magic. Craving to shift into dragons, to burn me, to burn my men, to fly off to find your husbands." He barked a laugh. "I am your husband now. I am your only king. You are mine, and you will serve me, or I take more teeth."

He unslung the pouch that hung around his neck and tossed it toward the chained women. Teeth spilled out across the marble tiles--their teeth. The weredragons lowered their heads, shivering, struggling not to weep. They had learned that weeping meant more pain.

Slyn burst out laughing. All across the hall, his fellow Widejaws also laughed. Above in the sky, a dozen sphinxes flew in patrol, and their voices too boomed down with cruel mirth.

"You heard me!" Slyn rose to his feet and held the roasted leg above his head. "I am the King of Requiem! I sit upon the Oak Throne!" He snorted. "Kneel before your king."

His fellow Widejaws laughed. Trembling, the captive weredragons knelt and bowed before him.

Slyn sat back down and stretched out his legs. He took a deep bite from the roasted weredragon leg. Juices flowed through his mouth, and he shut his eyes and sighed with pleasure. Divine. Simply divine.

"There is no taste better than human flesh, do you know?" he said. "Even the flesh of a weredragon's human form." He grabbed one chain and yanked a golden-haired weredragon toward him. "It tastes like wild game, but softer . . . richer." He licked his lips. "Fatty and tender."

The golden-haired weredragon lowered her eyes. Her lip trembled. Slyn stroked her cheek.

"You are tender too," he whispered. "You are also rich . . . soft." He tugged her closer and licked her cheek. "You too are delicious. You taste like fear and sweat and blueberries."

She trembled. "Please, my lord."

"Please?" Slyn laughed and clutched her cheeks, squeezing them. "Are you begging too for a taste? I'll let you taste it." He held the meat up to her mouth. "Eat it. Take a bite." He laughed. "You were holding a child in the battle, weren't you? Yes . . . I saw you protecting the boy. Perhaps this is him, this roasted meat before you. Perhaps this is your son." Slyn grinned and licked his chops. "Taste him. Feed upon him. Savor the flavor."

She looked away, grimacing. A tear flowed from her eye. Slyn pressed his fingers into her jaw, forcing her mouth open. He brought the meat closer.

"Slyn of Widejaw!"

The voice boomed across the hall.

Slyn raised his eyes and cursed. He shoved the woman aside. She fell onto the tiles and scuttled away, chain clanking.

"Maggoty bones," Slyn cursed.

The demon Raem stood across the hall of Requiem, wreathed in black smoke. The creature spread out black wings, soared across the hall, and landed before the throne. Those wings were woven of human skin; Slyn had flayed enough enemies to recognize human leather.

"Welcome, mighty demon," Slyn said, meeting the creature's eyes. He leaned back in his throne. "Will you feed with us?"

Slyn would not bow, not lower his eyes, not call this demon "lord." He was King of Requiem now; he had no gods nor masters. But he would welcome Raem into his hall. He would show him respect. Because of Raem he had his kingdom; he would not forget that, and he would show the demon hospitality.

Raem stared at the campfires. He stared at the human leg clutched in Slyn's hand. He stared up at Slyn's eyes.

And he shouted.

His voice tore across the hall, cracking a column.

"Where is Laira?" The demon's eyes burned with red light. "Where is my daughter?"

Slyn gritted his teeth, struggling against the urge to cover his ears. Slowly he rose to his feet.

"The whore fled us." He spat. "So did a few of the others. My men are chasing them. They--"

"Did you slay their king?" Raem stretched out his tentacle and grabbed Slyn's arm. "Did you slay King Aeternum?"

The demon's tentacle dug into Slyn's arm, tearing the skin, sucking up blood. Slyn could see the crimson liquid flowing through the tentacle's veins.

"The king escaped into a labyrinth of stone," Slyn said. "Five hundred of my sphinxes are besieging him. Laira is lost. I have three hundred sphinxes scouring the forests for--"

"You will find them!" Raem shouted. "You will find the king and shatter him. You will find Laira and bring her to me. You will not sit here, drinking and feasting, while weredragons still live. You will not keep weredragons as slaves for your base pleasures."

The demon turned toward the weredragon women who cowered on the floor, chained and beaten. Raem sniffed and his face reddened.

"Those slaves are mine!" Slyn said, stepped forward. "I captured them in battle. I--"

Raem grabbed one woman in his tentacle, closed his lobster claw around her neck, and severed her head.

Slyn hissed and froze. The other women screamed and tried to flee, but their chains only let them run for several feet. Raem moved between them methodically, decapitating one after another. One of the women shifted into a dragon. Her chain tore through her ankle, ripping off her foot. The dragon beat her wings, rose several feet in the air, and wailed as Raem's tentacle grabbed her tail and yanked her down. The demon thrust his claw through the beast's back, and the dragon returned to human form and twitched on the floor, then fell still.

Covered in blood, Raem turned back toward Slyn. "You will keep only Laira alive," he said. "And she will be mine, Slyn. Do you understand? I gave you your magic. I gave you your kingdom. I can take both away. I give you one more chance. Next time I return, if you've not accomplished your mission, it will be your flesh roasting upon these fires."

With that, the demon stretched out his wings and soared. Within an instant, Raem vanished into the clouds, leaving only the stench of sulfur and acid.

Slyn remained standing at the base of his throne. He fumed. His men all stared at him, awaiting his reaction.

How dare he enter this hall? How dare the demon humiliate me in front of my men? The fires blazed through Slyn, and he ground his teeth. He tossed his meat aside.

"You heard him!" Slyn shouted. "Why are you lounging here like useless lumps? Charan, gather your men, fly out, tear up every tree until you find the missing girl. Herosh! Join the others at the mountain. Shatter the entire mountain if you must, but bring me the king's body. Go! Fly!"

The Widejaws grunted and shifted, becoming sphinxes. They beat their wings and rose past the columns. They vanished into the clouds. Only a hundred men, the women, and the children remained behind, standing upon the bloodstained tiles and between the charred birches.

Slyn walked toward a campfire, grabbed a roast rib, and returned to his throne. He sat down among the coiling oak roots and branches, sniffed at the meat, and tossed is aside. His appetite was gone.

LAIRA

She struggled against the leafy vines that bound her to the boulder, unable to free herself. She tried to shift, only for the vines to bind her magic as securely they bound her body.

"Druids, free us!" Laira cried. "You cannot do this."

At her side, Maev was similarly strapped to the same boulder; the rock rose from the grass, large as a hut. The druids' arrows had cast a web of leafy, sticky tendrils around them, and that web now secured them to the stone. Maev looked like some thrashing insect wrapped in green cobwebs. Like Laira, she fought and kicked, unable to free herself.

"Stars damn it!" Maev shouted, face flushed. "Release me and fight me like men. Cowards! I'll tear your limbs off. I'll crack open your heads, scoop out your brains, and piss into your skulls." She spat, trying to reach the druids, but her spit only landed a foot away. "Unbind me or I swear I will burn you all. I will rip your bones out of your living flesh and play them as flutes as you die."

Laira relaxed in her bonds and sighed. She looked at Maev. "I don't think that'll convince them to release us, Maev."

The tattooed, golden-haired woman growled, spat again, and tugged mightily at the leafy strands. "Those cowards. Those sons of whores. I'll burn down this whole village."

With another sigh, Laira looked back at their surroundings. The boulder they were tied to rose from a grassy valley beneath an overcast sky. Hills strewn with jagged dark stones circled the valley like walls, shrouded in mist. Four towering inuksuks rose upon the hilltops, surrounding the dale--statues roughly resembling human shape, constructed of massive boulders larger than men. Mist floated around their jagged stone legs, and deep green runes appeared upon their sandstone chests, one per inuksuk: a barren tree, a tree sprouting young leaves, a tree in full summer growth, and a tree whose leaves were falling.

Below in the valley, guarded by these giants of stone, rose mounds of earth and stone. Small archways, constructed of many small rocks, led into these homes. Grass grew upon the mounds; if not for the doors, they would have seemed like hillocks rather than dwellings.

Druids moved across the valley, dressed in dark green robes, bearing staffs formed of tree roots. Pewter amulets hung around their necks on leather throngs, and heavy hoods shadowed their faces. Hearing the two prisoners shout, the druids turned their heads toward them. One druid stepped forward, the wind beating his cloak. He was an old man of perhaps sixty years--few men lived that long in a world of wild beasts, wars, and harsh winters--and white streaked his long auburn beard. His eyes were deep green flecked with blue, gleaming beneath tufted red eyebrows. His face was weathered and deeply lined, the nose large, the jaw wide, the brow weary and creased.

"The anger burns through you." The old druid stood before Laira and Maev. Sadness filled those deep, moss-colored eyes. "Your fire forever screams for release. You crave the dragonfire, desperate to let it sear your pain away." He nodded and his eyes dampened. "I know of such anger, of such pain. I know why you thrash in your bonds, why you scream. But my children . . . dragonfire is not the answer, not a cure for loneliness. Dragonfire cannot burn your pain away, only make it flare."

Tied to the boulder, Maev and Laira glanced at each other, then back at the druid.

Laira spoke carefully. "Why do you think us lonely?"

Maev was less diplomatic. "If you don't release us, old man, my dragonfire will burn the flesh off your bones, torch every hut here, and make you all scream so loudly your pretty stone statues will crumble." She howled with rage. "Release us!"

The old druid nodded. "I am Auberon of the Cured Druids. I was once like you. I was once . . . a weredragon." He reached out and stroked Maev's face, pulling his hand back when she tried to bite him. "I too was once so angry, so afraid, so lonely, so full of dragonfire. I found a cure." His eyes dampened. "And now I cure others. I can cure you too. I can heal you."

Laira's eyes widened. She gasped. Another Vir Requis! Her heart leaped, and she tugged at the vines binding her to the boulder. Despite being tied in this valley, hope leaped inside her. More Vir Requis lived!

"Auberon!" Laira said. "Auberon, it's not a curse. It's not a disease. I thought so myself once. But . . ." Her eyes stung with tears. "But we have a kingdom now. We have a king. And we know that our magic is pure, a gift from the stars, not a disease. Not--"

Auberon's face changed. All his piety seemed to vanish, and rage burned in his eyes. His mouth twisted into a sneer. "It is a filthy shame! It is an impurity! A cruel curse, a--" He caught himself and forced a few deep breaths. He bowed his head. "Forgive me. Though I've been cured, some of the old anger still fills me." He shuddered, closed his eyes, and breathed deeply until his face calmed. "Perhaps some dragonfire still courses through my veins, though I strive daily to expel it. Watch, Laira and Maev. You have come here on the right day. Today is a Day of Redemption."

Farther back in the valley, the other druids--Laira counted fifty of them--lifted their staffs, and their voices rose as one. "Day of Redemption!"

Auberon walked toward them, leaving the boulder behind. He too raised his staff. Pewter charms, hanging from the shaft on leather throngs, chinked as he walked. "The Cured Druids welcome another to our order! Today a soul is redeemed."

The druids formed a ring in the misty valley. Around them, the inuksuks stared down from the rocky hills, four gods of the seasons. The veil of gray clouds swirled above, letting in only a single ray of light. As if summoned by the druids' call, the sunbeam fell within the ring, illuminating a flat stone on the grass.

Auberon raised his spear overhead. His voice boomed out across the valley. "Step forth, Eeras of the Mossoak Tribe. Step forth and be cured."

A man emerged from one of the grassy mounds. He wore a simple canvas tunic over leather britches. His feet were bare, his face unshaven, his hair scraggly and muddy. His eyes darted and his fists clenched and unclenched at his sides.

"Step forth, Eeras," said Auberon.

"Step forth!" repeated the other druids, reaching out welcoming hands.

Glancing from side to side, the man shuffled forward. He walked with a limp, and he whispered feverishly under his breath. Tied to the boulder outside the ring of druids, Laira only caught snippets of his words: "I will be brave . . . I will . . . cured . . . for her . . ."

Finally, eyes damp, Eeras stepped onto the flat stone within the ring of druids. The sunbeam fell upon him, washing him with golden light. Tears flowed down the man's cheeks.

The druids passed around a pewter mug full of green liquid, and each took a sip in turn. When the mug reached Auberon, the old druid stepped toward the beam of light.

"Tell us of your sins, my son." The old druid smiled at the young man. "Tell us of your hurts."

Eeras's body shook as his tears fell. "I . . . I am a weredragon."

The druids all chanted, voices rising in song, their amulets rattling.

Laira glanced at Maev. The golden-haired warrior was still straining against her bonds. Her dragon tattoos coiled across her arms as her muscles bulged, and veins rose upon her neck, but she couldn't free herself. Her own hope of escape long gone, Laira looked back toward the ceremony.

"Show us, son," Auberon said softly to the young man. "Show us your curse, so we may see the evil before driving it away."

Eeras nodded, closed his eyes, and shifted.

Silvery blue scales flowed across him. Azure wings rose from his back. He stood in the valley as a dragon, his horns long and white, his eyes gleaming like pale crystals. Then, with a shudder, the dragon returned to human form. Eeras, a man again, hugged himself and trembled.

He spoke again, tears hanging off his nose. "I . . . I used to fly as a dragon at night, in secret, in shame. I blew my fire in the darkness. And once . . . oh by the gods . . . once I flew too low. I blew too much fire. Our village burned." Sobs racked his body. "My sister was hurt. She ran from me. She called me a monster. And I am one." His voice tore in agony. "I am a monster."

The druids chanted louder. Auberon reached out and stroked the man's hair. "We will cure you. We will drive the curse away from your blood. With the drink of the gods, we will heal you, and you will be purified." He kissed Eeras's forehead. "You will be forgiven."

Eeras shook as he wept. "Thank you, Auberon. Thank you."

The old druid held out the pewter goblet to Eeras. "Drink, my child, and be cured. Drink and the tillvine will drive the dragon magic away."

Laira squinted. From the distance of the boulder she was tied to, it was hard to see into the goblet, but she glimpsed a green potion thick with crumpled leaves. Was this the same plant that the priests had balled up and attached to their arrows? The same plant that had knocked the dragon magic out of Laira and Maev, that now bound them to the boulder?

"Tillvine," she whispered. "It undoes dragon magic."

She remembered that feeling: the tillvine strands wrapping around her, digging through her, tugging her magic free. She had crashed onto the forest floor as a human, her dragon form yanked away, at only the touch of this plant. But to actually drink tillvine juice?

"Drink," Auberon repeated. "Drink and the dragon magic will forever leave you, my son."

Hands shaking, Eeras accepted the goblet.

"Wait!" Laira shouted. "Eeras, stop! Don't drink!"

The man looked up. He stared at her, and a tear streamed down his cheek.

"I will never hurt anyone again," he whispered. He raised the goblet to his lips and drank deeply.

"No!" Laira screamed, tugging at the bonds. "Damn you, Auberon!"

Eeras's neck bobbed as he drank, emptying the goblet. When he lowered the cup, he stood still, pale, silent.

For long moments, nothing happened. The druids sang. Eeras even smiled tremulously.

Then he gasped.

He clutched at his throat.

His skin turned a sickly green color, and tendrils ran across him like the vines that bound Laira and Maev to the boulder. He fell to his knees, tossed back his head, and screamed.

Scales rose and vanished upon his body. Horns grew from his head, then cracked and fell to the ground. Smoke blasted from him. Claws grew and detached. He fell over, writhing, twisting, screaming in agony.

"You're killing him!" Laira said.

"Auberon, damn you, I'm going to crush your bones into powder!" Maev shouted.

The druids ignored the two prisoners. They chanted out to their gods, spears raised high. The inuksuks upon the hills seemed to lean in, and the runes upon their stone chests burst into light. They glowed green like the tillvine, a sickly color of disease.

"Help him!" Laira cried out. "He's dying."

The druids ignored her. Eeras began convulsing. Green foam rose from his mouth and leaked from his eyes. He screamed again, a sound that curdled Laira's blood, then lay still.

Maev stared with wide eyes. "The bastards killed him. By the stars, they killed him."

"No, look," Laira whispered.

Wisps of light began to rise from the fallen Eeras. This light was not green like tillvine, not golden like the sun, but silver as starlight. It rose in strands, coiling skyward, and took the shape of a dragon. Laira gasped and her eyes watered. The astral dragon rose higher, spread its wings, and let out a keen, a cry so sad and beautiful that Laira wept. Then it dispersed in the wind and was gone.

"They killed his dragon soul," Laira whispered.

Silence fell. The druids lowered their staffs. Eeras let out a gasp, sucked in air, and finally rose to his feet. He rubbed his eyes, and a tremulous smile touched his lips.

"Am I cured?" he whispered.

Auberon only smiled thinly. "Try to shift, my son. Become the dragon."

Eeshan screwed his eyes shut, clenched his fists, and gasped. He opened his eyes. "I can't. It's gone. The curse is gone." He fell to his knees and embraced Auberon's legs. "Thank you, Auberon. Thank you. Thank you . . ."

Laira shook her head slowly, a hollowness in her chest.

It's worse than murder, she thought. *To steal a man's magic, to remove the dragon from inside him . . .*

"Auberon, what have you done?" she whispered.

The bearded druid walked toward her, a small smile on his face, and his eyes were sad.

"Only what has been done to me." The old druid reached into his robes. He pulled out a single green scale which hung around his neck on a leather string. "This was my scale once. I was a sinner. I was lonely, afraid, ill . . . until the Cured Druids found me and healed me." He turned back toward his comrades. "My friends! Show me your scales."

They reached into their robes and pulled out their own scale amulets, all in different colors. Eeras, still pale, reached down to the flat stone and raised a single blue scale that lay upon it. He held his own last remnant of magic.

"You too will be cured," Auberon said, looking at Laira and Maev in turn. "You too will drink the tillvine essence and joined the Cured."

Maev spat. "Like the Abyss we will. I'd sooner eat mammoth shite."

Laira raised her chin. "We will never join you, Auberon. You are false. You are cruel. Your piety masks your hatred. I know men like you. My father is one. We refuse to join your order. Free us now."

The old druid sighed, and his shoulders slumped. "Sometimes we see others like you . . . consumed, stubborn, blind

to their own disease. But they all turn. They all accept the tillvine.
You will stay here upon the boulder, watching the skies, feeling
the wind and rain, reflecting, dreaming . . . until you drink of our
juice. And if you do not drink, you will drink nothing at all."
Auberon stroked Laira's hair. "Sweet child, do you not
understand? You will abandon your magic, or you will abandon
your life."

With that, the druids turned and crossed the valley and
entered their grassy huts.

Laira and Maev remained outside upon the boulder.

The clouds thickened and rain fell. Laira kept struggling but
the bonds were too strong. The sun set and the storm grew,
leaving her wet, in shadows, and crying out in rage.

ISSARI

The nephil swarm descended upon the city of Goshar like flies upon a carcass.

Issari stood at the southern gates in human form, staring up at the unholy host.

"But we were almost free," she whispered. Her fingers tingled. "We were almost home."

The nephilim hid the sky. The children of demons and mortal women, they were shaped as men, as tall as dragons were long. Their frames were skeletal, their flesh mummified, their eyes red and their teeth long as swords. They seemed like corpses, gaunt and reeking, and they flew on insect wings. They laughed as they landed upon roofs and walls, tearing into the people of Goshar. Their claws tore into flesh and dug out innards to feast upon. Their cries rolled over the city.

Fire blazed above and a roar tore across the sky--Tanin flying overhead. A lone dragon, he charged toward the nephil army.

Issari looked at her people. The children of Eteer filled the streets, thousands of them, awaiting salvation. Now they cried and pointed at the nephilim. A few of the creatures descended into the crowd, snatched up Eteerians, and tore them apart. One nephil ripped the limbs off a screaming boy and scattered them. Another dug the entrails out of a woman, laughing as he stuffed them into his mouth.

There is no salvation, Issari thought, numb, frozen. *After all we've traveled through, we die here.*

"Issari!" Tanin cried above, blowing his dragonfire. Nephilim crashed into him, tearing at his red scales. Blood rained.

A droplet of Tanin's blood hit Issari's head, snapping her out of her paralysis.

She soared as a dragon.

She blew her fire.

"Hide, children of Eteer!" Issari cried. "Into homes! Into cellars! Into--"

The nephilim crashed against her.

Their claws grabbed at her scales. Their fangs bit into her. Their laughter rang and their eyes mocked her.

Issari screamed and roared her fire. Her flames washed over the nephilim, but their hard, mummified flesh would not burn. Her claws, her fangs, and the spikes on her tail cut into them, shedding their black blood. They flew everywhere, and Issari wept as she slew them, for they were half-Eteerian, born from human wombs. She knew that slaying them was a mercy, though with every one that fell, she wept for her people.

"We can't fight them all!" Tanin cried at her side. He blew fire in rings and whipped his tail, trying to hold them off.

The creatures surrounded the two dragons, a sea of rot. As Issari fought, she saw more nephilim scuttling over the city. They shattered roofs, pulled humans out from within, and sucked the meat off the bones. They shattered columns and sent temples crumbling. They knocked down statues of Shahazar; the goddess seemed helpless to stop them. Blood stained the streets, buildings collapsed, and dust rose in clouds.

Like Eteer before it, the city-state of Goshar fell to the rot of the half-demons.

We are lost, Issari thought. She swiped her claws and tail and blew fire, holding the enemy off, but she knew she could not win this battle.

Thousands of soldiers raced across walls and roofs below, shouting and firing arrows. A few arrows sank into nephil flesh. Most shattered uselessly against the creatures' leathery hides. The nephilim kept swooping, lifting archers off roofs, and tearing them apart. Shreds of ring mail, severed limbs, and gobbets of flesh fell upon the city, vanishing into the crumbling ruins.

Goshar falls. Issari stared below, and through clouds of dust, she glimpsed a hundred nephilim trundling down the streets, towering over the children of Eteer, clawing them apart. *Eteer falls.* She looked up at Tanin. A dozen of the creatures were landing upon him, clawing at his scales. *We fall. We cannot win. Not only two dragons.* Her eyes stung. *We need Requiem. We need armies of dragons. We--*

She blinked.

She blew fire, roasting a nephil who flew toward her. She clubbed another with her tail.

"Requiem," she whispered.

A screeching nephil soared toward her from a collapsing dome. Its mouth opened wide, full of yellow teeth as long as swords. She roasted it with dragonfire, then swiped her claws across its neck. Maggots fled the wound and the creature crashed down.

Issari flew higher. "Requiem!" she cried out. "Dragons of Requiem!" Her eyes stung. They had to be here too. They had hidden in the north in caves and forests. They had hidden in Eteer in brick homes. Surely the stars blessed Goshar too. "Dragons of Goshar, hear me! I am Issari, a Princess of Requiem, a kingdom of dragons. You are not cursed!"

The battle raged below, thousands of people dying, thousands of buildings collapsing. Several nephilim flew toward her, reaching out their claws, cackling and licking their maws. Tanin flew somewhere below, engulfed in a cloud of the creatures.

"Hear me, dragons of Goshar!" Issari cried. She zipped across the sky, dodging nephilim. "I have freed the dragons of Eteer! I have fought with the dragons of the north. A kingdom of dragons rises. You need not be ashamed. You need not hide your magic, for it is blessed by the stars. Arise, dragons of Goshar! Fly with me! Blow your fire with mine! You are dragons of Requiem." She roared out her cry. "Requiem! May our wings forever find your sky."

A nephil landed upon her back and dug its claws into her. She yowled. Another nephil slammed into her belly and bit her chest. She could barely stay aflight. A third nephil grabbed her left wing and tugged.

"Dragons of Goshar!" she cried. Her blood spilled. "Fly with me. For Requiem. For Requiem . . ."

She tumbled through the sky toward the falling city. Below her, the palace of Goshar collapsed, raining bricks and dust across the ruins.

Goodbye, Requiem, she thought. *I rise now to your stars. I rise to your celestial columns. To--*

Firelight rose in a dozen pillars. A temple of flame rose from the ruins.

Roars pierced the air.

Issari wept.

Requiem lives.

A dozen dragons rose from the rubble, roaring. Their fire washed across the nephilim around Issari. She thrashed and shook herself free from the beasts grabbing her.

"Dragons of Goshar!" she cried. "Arise! Fly with me. Fly for starlight, for freedom, for Requiem! Requiem lives!"

The dozen dragons rose around her. A hundred more soon took flight from the ruins, soaring, blowing their fire, lashing their claws.

"Bloody stars!" Tanin said, flying toward Issari. Several of his scales were missing, and blood dripped from the wounds. "Where did they come from?"

"From the stars that bless the world. They were always here, hiding, ashamed." Issari laughed. "We freed them."

The dragons of Goshar rallied around her--red dragons, blue dragons, metallic dragons, dragons small and large, all blowing fire, all roaring.

"Issari!" they cried. "Fight for the white dragon."

"For Requiem!" Issari shouted. "Burn the enemy."

Soon two hundred dragons roared. Two hundred pillars of fire blazed across the city.

The nephilim shrieked in fear.

Some of the creatures tried to attack; they fell, burnt and lacerated. Others turned to flee; dragons chased them across the desert and burned them down. Corpses of the mummified, reeking
beasts tumbled down to crash against the ruins.

The last walls of Goshar fell; so did the last of the nephilim. Death and scattered stones spread where once a proud city had stood. Issari soared higher, and the dragons of Goshar--now the dragons of Requiem--rose around her. They formed a great pillar in the sky, a typhoon of scales and dragonfire.

With fire, blood, and dust, Requiem rises, Issari thought. *With the ruin of cities and nations, our kingdom is forged.*

JEID

He stood in the deepest, coldest tunnel in this labyrinth of stone, staring down at the body.

"May your soul rise to the stars," he said, head bowed. "You will forever shine among them."

He lowered the little body--only a boy, not even ten years old--and placed him among the others. Like the other dead, the boy's chest had been cracked open, his innards scooped out and consumed by the creature in the mountain. Jeid's throat felt tight, his eyes close to tears, as he draped the boy's fur cloak over his body. They nestled together here in the darkness--seven dead, seven souls lost to the beast of shadows.

"Grizzly." Dorvin placed a hand on his shoulder. "Grizzly, we can't keep them here forever. It's cold and dark in this tunnel, but the bodies are going to start to stink soon." Dorvin covered his nose. "Stars! I can already smell them. What do we do when they rot?"

Bryn stood further back; the tunnel was so narrow they had to stand in single file. The red-haired woman glared at Dorvin, her eyes flashing. "Show some respect! These are children of Requiem. They--"

"--are going to rot and stink," Dorvin finished. "Like the rest of us, sooner or later. Have you ever seen a rotting body, Bryn? I have. They spread disease. They'll kill us as surely as whatever killed them." The young hunter sighed. "Sphinxes outside. A demon in the walls. Thirst and hunger. Now the threat of disease. All that's left to do is guess what'll kill us first."

Jeid stared down at the bodies. His fists clenched at his sides.

"No. We no longer wait." He spun toward Dorvin and Bryn. His voice shook, the anger replacing his grief. "I hid in a cave once before. With my children and father. For years we hid in the canyon, waiting for our enemies to hunt us. And then we built a kingdom among the trees, and we raised a column of marble blessed by the stars, and we flew freely under the sky. It's time we found our sky again."

Dorvin bared his teeth and pounded his fist into his palm. "Yes! We fly out. We face the sphinxes. We--"

"No." Jeid shook his head. "We will not charge rashly into death."

"But you said we'd--"

"We will find another way out," Jeid said. "We'll dig our way out."

Dorvin and Bryn stared at him, eyes wide.

"Dig?" said Bryn. "The walls are mostly granite. Our blades can't cut them. Even if we had room to shift into dragons, our claws would be too weak." She tapped one wall with her sword; the bronze clanged against the stone. "How will we dig?"

Jeid walked around them, motioning for them to follow. They walked through the coiling labyrinth, moving past other survivors, until Jeid stopped at a curve where blood stained the walls and floor. He pointed at the ceiling.

"A hole," he said. "This is where the creature emerged. This is where it slew the boy." He drew his sword, reached up, and tapped the hole's rim. "Solid granite, yet whatever that creature is, it dug through it like a groundhog through soil. Its claws are sharper than our blades, sharper even than dragon claws. It can dig a way out for us."

Dorvin blew out his breath, fluttering his lips. "Grizzly! By the stars. First of all, that hole's smaller than your head. Secondly, even if the creature could dig us a tunnel out, how are you going to convince it? Invite it for a drink of wine, give it a few kisses, and then ask to borrow its claws? Don't think that'll work."

Jeid tapped the hole again. "It'll work or it won't." He looked back at Dorvin and smiled thinly. "It's worth trying; we have nothing to lose. Now let's hunt a demon."

They got to work.

There was no day or night in the tunnels, but Jeid felt like they labored for most of a day. Bryn moved through the tunnels, collecting belts, spears, leather straps, ropes, and axes. She returned the items to Jeid and Dorvin, who sat on the floor, snapping the shafts off axes and spears, tying them together into long sticks, and weaving belts into harnesses.

"Do you really think this can work?" Dorvin said. He thrust out his tongue as he tied two wooden shafts together.

"Probably not." Jeid tested a leather noose, tugging it between his hands, unable to break it. "Almost certainly not, in fact." He smiled up at Dorvin. "But when has Requiem ever had more hope?"

Finally their work was done. Jeid stared down at the contraptions--long wooden shafts, each ending with a leather harness.

"You do realize the creature can dig through granite," Dorvin said. He bit his lip. "It'll smash through leather and wood like dragonfire tearing through mist."

Jeid thought back to his only sighting of the creature. Long black legs, spiderlike, tipped with claws. Red eyes. A bristly, soft abdomen. "Only its claws are sharp. It's those claws we want to avoid. If we grab the rest of it, we can secure it. Subdue it. We'll lasso its neck--if it has a neck." Jeid rubbed the back of his own neck. "I'm not sure it has one, but we'll find out. I--"

The patter of feet interrupted him. Bryn came racing around a corner, blood staining her face and fur pelts. "Grizzly! Two more sphinxes broke in. They killed Perin." She grimaced. "And they wounded Celani; bit off her hand. I have the Redtooth twins guarding the entrance now, but . . . oh stars, Grizzly. We're falling fast."

Jeid grimaced and that old terror rose inside him again, threatening to engulf him. Perin--a kindly, bald man who used to whittle toys for the children. Celani--a shy woman, a weaver of cloth and rope.

Jeid clenched his jaw. "We have no more time." He tossed Bryn one of the traps, another to Dorvin. "We go hunting a demon."

They carried their gear through the caves to the deep, craggy tunnel where the creature had snatched its last victim. Blood still stained the stone, the stench of death still lingered, and the hole still gaped above. Jeid raised his lamp toward the hole but saw nothing, only darkness inside.

"How do we know the bastard will show up here again?" Dorvin asked. "The damn sheep-shagger keeps popping out of different holes each time." He spat. "Damn thing moves about faster than a cock in a hen house."

Jeid gazed up into the darkness of the hole.

Who are you? he thought. *What are you hiding?*

"There is method to its killings," Jeid said. "It went after the wounded. It hasn't attacked me, you, Bryn, or any of the other strong Vir Requis. Its first victim was recovering from a gash along her leg. The last victim had only just hurt himself, stumbling in the dark and bloodying his nose." Jeid looked around him at the bloodstains on the floor. "Maybe the smell of fresh blood attracts it. It can smell it through the walls. Dorvin, go stand behind that corner with the gear. Bryn, you walk the other way and hide. Keep your harnesses ready."

The two young Vir Requis glanced at each other. Dorvin muttered curses. Bryn raised her chin and tightened her lips. The two hefted their makeshift traps and each stepped around another corner, hiding in the shadows.

Jeid propped his own harness against the wall, drew his sword, and etched a cut along his palm. His blood dripped. He lifted the harness with his good hand, then raised the bleeding hand toward the hole.

"Come on, you bastard," he whispered.

He waited, hand raised.

Nothing happened.

"Come on . . ." he muttered. "Where are you?"

His blood dripped down his arm. The tunnel was silent.

Dorvin's head thrust around the corner. "Grizzly, anything yet?"

Jeid glared at the young man. "Do you see a demon?"

Dorvin squinted. "That beard of yours might qualify. I'm pretty sure it's possessed."

Jeid grunted. "Get back."

With a smirk, Dorvin pulled back behind the corner. Jeid stared up into the hole, seeing nothing but shadows. In the silence, he could hear the cries of sphinxes at the distant cave opening, the roar of dragonfire holding them back. But no scuttling of demons. No screams of dying.

"Grizzly!" Dorvin stuck his head around the corner again. "Any damn demon yet? I gotta piss, for stars' sake."

"Get back!"

Dorvin cursed. "Bloody bollocks." His head vanished behind the corner again.

Grumbling, Jeid raised his hand, stood on his toes, and smeared blood around the hole. The wound on his palm stung, but worse was his fear.

"Come drink," he whispered into the darkness. "Smell it. Come to us."

The moments passed by.

Jeid waited.

He paced.

Time stretched on.

Finally he sat down with a sigh, leaned against the wall, and stared up into the darkness.

It won't work, he thought. *The creature is sleeping, or the creature knows it's a trap. It'll strike again, somewhere else, and more will die.*

As he sat here, he wondered what he was fighting for. So many were gone already. The halls of Requiem had fallen to the enemy. Every day, another Vir Requis died. Perhaps worst of all were the three holes inside him, as dark and real as the hole above.

"Laira," he whispered. "Tanin. Maev."

His family--the only family he had left--was gone. He had already lost so many others: his daughter Requiem, his first wife, his parents. Was he alone now? Were the others dead like the bodies in the tunnels?

Why do I fight? he wondered. *Why do I keep going when there is so much darkness in the world?*

It would be easy to close his eyes, to wait for the demon to emerge and devour him. It would be easy to fly out into the sky and face the sphinxes, to die in battle. Why did he keep going, year by year, when the pain, the loss, the fear never ended?

"For Requiem," he whispered. "For hope. Maybe for nothing but the fight."

Fighting for a lost cause is better than giving up. We all must die someday. Some sooner, some later. If I must, I will die fighting. But I pray to the stars . . . I pray that I see you again, my wife, my children, my kingdom.

A scratch sounded above.

Jeid inhaled sharply and stared up at the hole.

A shadow stirred. A single claw, large as a dagger, emerged from the hole and scratched along the rim, collecting the droplets of blood.

Silently, Jeid rose to his feet and readied his harness. He clenched and unclenched his fist, opening the cut, and raised his hand above.

"Smell it. Smell the blood . . . Come on . . . Come--"

With a shriek, the creature burst out from the hole.

Jeid gasped and nearly stumbled back.

The hole was perhaps no larger than his head, but the creature that emerged unfolded into a massive size. Eight long black legs--each tipped with a claw--spread open like blooming petals around a red center. In this center gaped a round mouth containing a ring of teeth. A tongue unfurled, enclosed in a black shell and tipped with clacking, fast-moving blades. White eyes gleamed upon the creature's bloated head like boils ready to burst.

Jeid thrust his harness up against the creature.

The demon snatched the shaft in its mouth and tugged. Its claws slammed down, wrapping around Jeid. He roared as they cut into him.

"Dorvin! Bryn!"

The two raced into the tunnel and thrust their own harnesses.

"Come on, you bastard!" Dorvin shouted, struggling to wrap his leather noose around a leg. Bryn screamed at the other side, trying to lasso the creature.

"Where do we grab it?" she cried out.

"Anywhere!" Jeid shouted. The claws wrapped around him. One drove into his thigh. The creature's tongue thrust down, lined with moving blades, and Jeid roared and grabbed the writhing strand, holding it inches away from his face. Saliva dripped onto him, and the creature's mouth opened and shut, teeth snapping.

"Get its claws off me!" Jeid roared.

Dorvin and Bryn struggled at his sides, thrusting their harnesses.

"Got him!" Dorvin finally cried. He tugged back, tightening a noose around one of the creature's legs. Dorvin yanked the shaft back, pulling the creature's leg outward.

The demon screeched. It was a horrible sound, too loud for human ears. Pain washed over Jeid. His ears rang, numb, feeling full of water or perhaps blood. He gripped the creature's lashing tongue in one hand, the harness in another.

"I got another leg!" Bryn said. She lassoed one of the long, clawed digits and hauled back.

But the creature had many other legs, and they were still stabbing at Jeid, tearing through his thick fur and leather.

The creature was laughing. A bubbling, deep voice emerged from it.

"I will feast upon your innards, King of Reptiles." Its saliva dripped. "I know your name. I am Golgoloth, a Digger of the Abyss. I serve the Demon Queen. I will drink your--"

Jeid slammed his harness upward, wrapped the lasso around the creature's mouth, and yanked back, tightening the noose. The leather strand squeezed the demon's mouth shut like a string wrapped around a newborn's umbilical cord.

The tongue dangled, twitching. Jeid yanked it like a rope, stepped between the legs, and tugged the demon's head down onto the floor.

Golgoloth, this digger of darkness, lay on the ground, thrashing, lashing out its legs. The Vir Requis stepped back, gripping their shafts, pinning the creature down.

"Yeah, how do you like that?" Dorvin laughed and kicked the creature. "Not so fun when you're the one hunted, is it?" He kicked again, driving his boot into one of the demon's eyes. The eyeball popped and leaked white fluid.

"Dorvin!" Jeid roared. "Stars damn it. Don't hurt the beast. We need it to dig."

But Dorvin was still kicking, driving his boot again and again against the creature. Its abdomen, previously hidden in the hole, was large and soft and covered in small hairs; it twitched and jiggled whenever Dorvin kicked it.

"Yeah, feel the pain!" Dorvin shouted, but now his laughter was gone, and red rimmed his eyes. "Just like the people you hurt. Scream! Just like they screamed." Dorvin let out his own hoarse cry. "Just like you demons killed my sister. You're mine now, you puke-drinking son of a--"

"Dorvin!" Clutching his harness with one hand, Jeid shoved Dorvin back with the other. "Stop that. Not now. We need this creature."

The demon began to laugh. It was a sound like bubbles rising in tar, like dead children crying from underwater, like fear rising in the night. It turned its many eyes toward Jeid.

"You will suffer, children of Requiem." Golgoloth hissed as it laughed, spewing out smoke and droplets of rot. "I have foreseen your future. One of you three will die today. You will die in pain. You will die screaming." It chuckled, body twitching. "There is nothing but failure in your future, nothing but agony."

Jeid clenched his jaw and leaned against his harness, shoving the creature across the floor. "And you will dig, Golgoloth. You will dig silently or we'll take another one of your eyes." He turned toward Dorvin and Bryn. "Help me. Let's shove him against the wall. He'll dig." Jeid nodded firmly. "It's time for the dragons of Requiem to return to the sky."

TANIN

Tanin sat in the tent, eating little, watching the famished young boy scarf down plate after plate of food.

"Chew," Tanin said. "Don't bolt it down."

But Fin didn't seem to hear. The young Vir Requis reached across the table with his one good arm and grabbed a bread roll. The other arm was no larger than a babe's, ending with a hand the size of a walnut, but it too clutched a chicken leg. Fin alternated between bread and chicken, taking a bite from each in turn. Before him, several emptied plates lay across the table, covered with the crumbs of meat pies, the bones of a roast duck, and a few last grains of rice cooked with pine nuts.

"The poor boy spent many days flying." Issari glared at Tanin. "Let him eat. The poor thing's half-starved."

"The poor thing just devoured my supper." Tanin lifted his own plate. Moments ago, it had been piled high with mutton skewers, flatbread soaked in olive oil, and spiced chickpeas. All that food now filled Fin's belly; the boy had snatched the plate before Tanin had taken a single bite.

Fin gulped down a mouthful of chicken. "I *am* chewing!" He grabbed a pear stewed in wine and stuffed the whole thing into his mouth. "It's just good."

The three sat in a tent of white canvas stretched over cedar poles. The place felt restrictive and hot. Tanin left the table, stepped to the tent door, and stared outside. He sighed.

Hundreds of thousands of souls . . . lost.

In the northern distance, he could see a cloud of dust upon the horizon--the ruin of Goshar, a city reduced to ash. Once a

great city-state, Goshar now lay among the mountains as a pile of
rubble and bones. Here, south of the mountains, three rivers
crossed the land; one flowed only a mark away from Tanin, the
setting sun gilding its surface. Plains of grass, golden farms, and
groves of trees stretched for marks--the great land of plenty Issari
had promised the children of Eteer.

"But more than Eteerians now cover this land," Tanin
muttered.

Thousands of Eteerians had survived the slaughter in the
mountains, but so had thousands of Gosharians. The two people
spread across the grasslands, some living in tents, others in the
open air. Scattered campfires burned, and the scents of cooking
meats wafted. Soldiers in ringed armor patrolled. And above . . .

Tanin raised his eyes, and finally some hope filled him.

"Dragons," he whispered.

A hundred dragons glided above, Gosharians blessed by the
Draco constellation. Two hundred had once hidden in the stone
labyrinth of Goshar; half had fallen to the nephilim's claws,
paving a path of fire and blood to this camp.

Like me in the north, they hid, Tanin thought. *Like Issari in
Eteer, they were hunted.* Pride welled up in him, inflating his chest.
*But now we fly free. Now Issari and I can return home, a hundred dragons
behind us, and save what we can of Requiem.*

As soon as it had risen, his chest deflated.

"Requiem . . . fallen."

He spun around and reentered the tent. Fin was now eating
honeyed cakes topped with sliced almonds. Issari sat beside him,
sipping wine but eating nothing.

"Fin," Tanin said, "tell me again. Tell me everything you
know."

The boy swallowed another bite and nodded solemnly.
"Sphinxes." He shuddered. "They have the bodies of lions, the
wings of vultures, and the heads of men. They work for Raem,

they said, and they're flying all over the north." He stared at the remaining cakes but seemed to have lost his appetite. He shoved the plate away. "We all escaped Requiem. Many of us died. Jeid and Laira flew north to hide but . . . I couldn't join them. I had to find you." He looked at Issari. "I had to tell you, my priestess."

The boy wrapped his arms around Issari and clung to her. She stroked his hair.

"Return to your tent, my sweet boy." Issari kissed Fin's forehead. "Lie down to sleep and do not worry about sphinxes or demons or any other monster. You are safe here in my camp. I'll visit your tent soon to tuck you into your bed."

Fin nodded. He grabbed a few honey cakes, stuffed them into his pockets, and left the tent.

Tanin placed his hands on the table, stared down at the empty plates, and felt as if he'd just eaten raw meat. His belly roiled and bile filled his throat.

"We have to return." He turned to look at Issari. "We must fly north to Requiem."

Seated in her cedar chair, Issari breathed deeply and folded her hands in her lap. She had replaced her harem silks with a white tunic and cloak. A string of coins hung around her brow, chinking as she shook her head.

"How can we return now?" she said. "We flew south to claim the throne of Eteer, to banish demons. Yet the children of demons now fly across the land, and Eteer lies in ruin, the gates of the Abyss open and spewing out evil." She caressed the amulet in her palm. "The people of the south need me--the people of Eteer, of Goshar, of the eleven other city-states of Terra. How can I abandon them?"

"Requiem needs us!" Tanin stepped toward her and clasped her hands. "Do you forget Requiem, our home? That home lies fallen now. Our people are fled, and enemies live in our marble hall. We must return to find Laira, to find Grizzly and Maev, to help them. To help our kingdom."

"And what of Eteer?" Issari's cheeks flushed. She rose to her feet and pulled her hands free. "Is Eteer not a kingdom? Is it not a home to me as much as Requiem? Its halls too have fallen, but its people still live. They live out here, in the wilderness, afraid, hurt. You cannot ask me to abandon them. And what of Goshar? I was the abina's wife. I slew him. By the laws of Goshar, its people too are mine; I am their queen, no less than I'm Queen of Eteer." She walked toward the tent's door, stepped outside, and swept her arm across the camp. "Multitudes are without homes, without hope. And they look to me, Tanin." She spun toward him. "They look to me for hope."

Tanin took a shaky breath, scarcely believing what he heard. "Issari . . ." He tried to hold her, but she stepped back. "Issari, this is not how I know you. Requiem needs us. You used to believe in Requiem. Where is the bright-eyed girl who wandered the streets of Eteer, sending dragons north to safety? Where is the girl who flew across the sea, bringing us a warning of demons? Where is the girl--"

"That girl is a queen now." Her eyes flashed. "Never call me a girl again. I am no longer the girl you knew, the girl you fell in love with, the girl you thought you could protect, that you could save." Her cheeks reddened. "I am Queen Issari Seran. I am the Priestess in White. I am the Lady of Eteer and Goshar. I am a savior to these people." She gestured at the rolling camp. "Saving dragons? Yes, Tanin. I saved dragons. I saved them in Eteer and in Goshar, and I will travel the great lands of Terra, city to city, saving whoever I can, uniting them under my banner." She raised her chin. "That is my task. Not in the north."

Tanin blinked. "By the stars . . . Issari!" He tried again to embrace her, but she squirmed away. "Issari, please. You're not some . . . some messiah, some savior, some prophet. You're . . . you're my Issari. My girl. My--"

"I told you." Her eyes blazed and she shoved him away. "Do not call me that. A savior? Yes, I am a savior. A messiah? A prophet?" She raised her voice to a shout, and she raised her palm, letting her amulet shine. "I am a daughter of Taal! I am bound to his light."

That light blazed out, washing over Tanin.

He shouted and fell to his knees.

The light burned him, searing his skin, driving into his eyeballs and through his veins, and--

She closed her fist, hiding the glow. She stared at him in shock, lips trembling, then spun and fled back into the tent.

Tanin remained on his knees on the hill, breathing raggedly. He stared at the closed tent door.

"Who are you?" he whispered.

He thought back to the Issari he had first met in the streets of Eteer--a kind, determined young woman, soft-spoken but strong. The woman he loved. The woman he had made love to on the beach. The woman who had become something more, become a figure too great, too distant, too wreathed in light for him to reach.

He looked to the north. Beyond the smoking ruin of Goshar, the desert, the sea, and the forests, lay the fallen Requiem and his family. He looked back toward the tent. The simple canvas wall suddenly seemed as great a distance as the northern wilderness, and beyond it lay Issari, a woman he loved and perhaps had lost.

He stood, torn, as the sun set beyond the horizon.

ISSARI

"What have I done?"

Issari stepped around the table and toward her bed. She knelt by the bedside, her breath ragged, and looked at the amulet embedded into her palm. Its glow had subsided with her anger. That hand now trembled.

"Who am I?" she whispered.

A priestess, a voice answered inside her. Was that the voice of Taal?

A queen, spoke another voice. Was it the voice of Eteer's children calling to her?

A Vir Requis, spoke yet another voice. Was it the voice of the Draco constellations?

A woman in love, said another voice. Was this Tanin speaking in her mind?

"I don't know." She lowered her head and tasted her tears. "I don't know who I am. I don't know who I should become."

Tanin saw her becoming some mythical figure, a savior, a messiah. He feared her. She had seen the fear in his eyes. And Issari feared herself, feared what she was turning into, no longer a mere princess but a figure of . . . of what? Of legend? Of piety or mythology? A woman who could destroy empires, raise nations, vanquish hosts of darkness? Perhaps her people saw her that way--the children of Eteer and Goshar. Perhaps Taal saw her that way, for he had blessed her with his amulet. Perhaps the Draco stars saw such greatness in her, for they had blessed her with their magic only last year.

"I'm scared," she whispered into her fist. "I'm scared, Taal. I'm scared, stars of Requiem. Myriads of people worship me; they call me the Lady in White, the Starkissed Queen, the Bane of Demons, the Light of the Gods, the Daughter of Shahazar, and many other names. But I'm only Issari, and I'm frightened, and I don't know what to do. Where do I go?"

A part of her longed to heed Tanin's advice, to fly north, to find Laira and the others and help them with their struggle. Yet how could she abandon the people of the south? How could she forsake all these lost souls in her camp? How could she fly north when other Vir Requis might be hiding in the south, needing to hear her roar, to see her wings upon the wind?

Perhaps that part of her wanted to be what she had railed against--a girl again. To be as she had been--an innocent child, following others. Following her father. Following King Aeternum of Requiem. Even following Tanin.

There's less fear when you follow another. To lead is to always feel fear and doubt, not only for yourself but for those who follow you, who seek comfort in your strength . . . strength you feel cracking in the night, whose fragility you hide like a mother might hide an illness from her children. She took a shuddering breath. *And I am as a mother to the people outside my tent. Though I'm afraid, I must be strong for them, and I must lead them as others have led me.*

The tent door rustled behind her. She turned to see Tanin walk inside.

Issari rose to her feet. "Tanin," she began, "I'm sorry. I didn't mean to become angry, to hurt you, I--"

He approached her and grabbed her arms. He stared down into her eyes, silent.

"Tanin?" she whispered.

He kissed her.

He had kissed her many times before, but this was something rougher, deeper, ablaze with passion. He placed a hand

133

on the small of her back and pulled her body against him, and still he kept kissing her. Issari's legs loosened. His arms wrapped around her, holding her close, and for the first time in many days, she felt soft, she felt a loss of control, no longer that cold, hard leader.

"Tanin," she breathed. "I guess that means you forgive me?"

She felt his manhood harden against her belly, and he ran his fingers along her back, from her nape down to her tailbone and up again. He kissed her again, then all but shoved her onto the bed.

"Tanin!" She gasped up at him. "Now it's like *I* don't know *you*. What--?"

She gasped as he grabbed her tunic and tore it off. His clothes came off next, and he stared at her, silent and naked, then gently pressed her down onto her back.

He made love to her then, but he was not his old gentle self. He took her, claimed her, almost roughly, thrusting into her again and again, and she gasped and moaned, and it felt good, maybe better than any other time he had loved her. She surrendered to him, to his expert hands, and she was helpless in those hands. All she could do was let him take her, and the pleasure of it tore across her and she cried out into his palm.

"Oh, Tanin," she whispered when they finally broke apart. She lay by his side, sweaty and panting, aching with goodness and relief. "You definitely forgive me." She leaned over and kissed his cheek. "I'm glad you came back. I love you." She looked deep into his eyes. "I truly love you. I--"

She squinted.

She leaned back and gasped.

His eyes were as windows, showing deep caverns full of coiling flames. Dead eyes. Demon eyes.

He sat up in bed. He slowly turned his head toward her, his spine creaking. When he opened his mouth, she saw that instead of teeth he had small, metal shards growing from his gums.

Issari screamed and leaped away.

Tanin rose from the bed, only it wasn't actually Tanin. The stranger's jaw unhinged, dropping halfway down his chest, revealing rows of those metal teeth. His eyes burst into flames. Hooks and horns sprouted across his body.

Taal. Oh Taal . . .

Issari raised her amulet and cast her light. "I banish you, demon of the Abyss!"

Inside she trembled. *Oh Taal, it made love to me . . . it cast its seed inside me . . .*

"Be gone, demon!" she shouted, eyes burning.

Her light crashed into the creature, but the demon only laughed. Smoke burst from its body, and it changed forms rapidly, shifting into a dripping slug, a scaly reptile, a twitching centipede ten feet tall, and then took familiar forms: a dying girl with entrails dangling, the one Issari had comforted in the north; Sena, her dear brother, hanging dead from a tree; and finally Laira, sweet Laira, sliced open as her insides spilled out.

"No!" Issari screamed. "Stop this! Leave! I am a Priestess of Taal and of Draco, I--"

"You cannot banish me." The demon laughed, still in Laira's form. "I am no lowly demon. I am not Angel, a daughter of Taal whom you can burn." The demon raised dripping red hands. "I am Sharael, the Deceiver. I met your father, Issari . . . and I made him a vow." The demon licked its chops with a dripping, translucent tongue. "I vowed to make you, his dear daughter, suffer. Enjoy my gift to you."

Issari leaped toward him, prepared to shove her blazing amulet against his head.

With a ripple in the air and a swirl of shadow, the demon vanished.

Issari spun from side to side, trembling, panting, barely able to breathe. Cold sweat washed her.

Oh Taal . . .

She reached for her water basin and almost knocked it over. With shaking hands, she drew water and splashed it between her legs, desperate to wash him off, to cleanse herself, and her heart beat madly and blackness spread across her eyes. She felt ready to faint, to collapse.

Breathe.

She drew a shaky breath.

Exhale.

She blew out the air.

Be strong. Be a leader.

She doubled over, and she fell to her knees, and she was sorry, she was so sorry, and she missed him.

"Come back to me, Tanin. I'm so afraid." She raised her voice to a hoarse cry. "Tanin!"

She opened her palm and stared at the amulet. It was cold and hard and emitted no light.

LAIRA

The sun rose and fell. Rain washed the world. For days they lingered, tied to the boulder in the valley of the Cured. For days they watched the sun and moon and stars, the grass swaying, the inuksuks upon the hills sending their shadows across the valley.

"Drink," Auberon said every day, offering them the jug.

Laira always shook her head. Maev always cursed and spat and thrashed.

"I will not force you," Auberon said, "for you must choose to be cured. I will return tomorrow."

The days went by.

They remained upon the boulder, the rain washing them, the sun baking them, the wind cutting into their skin.

On the sixth dawn, vultures began to circle above.

"We're going to die here," Maev said, voice hoarse.

Laira shook her head. "The druids will keep us alive. They offer us food and water." She sighed. "We'll grow old upon this boulder until we drink their elixir."

Maev managed to growl. "I won't grow old here. I'd sooner die."

As the sun rose, the druids emerged as always from their huts. They chanted in the valley, spears raised, praying to the inuksuks upon the hills. They tended to their campfires. They traveled into the forests to return with nuts and berries. And like every dawn, Auberon walked toward them.

As always, the old man wore his blue robes, the hems stained green from the grass. As always, mist floated around his feet, and the charms hanging from his staff chinked. As always, he held two vessels--one bowl of stew, one goblet full of the green elixir.

"Eat," he said, offering the clay bowl to Laira.

The smell of stew tickled her nostrils. Today the stew was thick with wild hare, mushrooms, and onions. She wanted to refuse him. She wanted to spit the meal at his face. But Laira's belly rumbled and her mouth watered, and she guzzled down half the bowl.

"Drink," Auberon said next, offering Laira the goblet. The tillvine swirled within, green like her eyes. "Drink and be cured."

She shook her head. "This drink I refuse. This is poison." She looked aside. "I will not drink."

Auberon nodded. "In time, you will learn that you are cursed. In time, you will join us, the Cured, and become one of our fellowship. I will pray for you, Laira."

Next the elderly druid turned toward Maev. He offered her the remaining stew.

Tied to the boulder, her limbs stretched out, Maev glowered.

"Eat," Auberon said, holding the bowl to her lips.

Maev swung her head, knocking the bowl aside, and spat on Auberon's face.

"Go rot in the Abyss, you wormy pile of buzzard dung." Maev snapped her teeth. "Try to feed me again and I'll bite your damn hand off."

Laira sighed. Maev had been refusing her meals for two days now.

And we might be here for a very long time.

"Maev, you should eat," Laira said.

The young woman glowered at Laira. "I'd sooner eat demon flesh. I'd rather starve to death than eat anything these goat-shaggers are cooking. Could be damn tillvine in the stew too."

Old Auberon wiped her spit off his face and shook his head. "The Cured Druids believe in honor, in truth. We would never deceive you. The true cure, our gods teach, must be voluntary, must come from within. You must willingly choose our elixir." He held the goblet up to Maev's lips. "Drink, daughter. Drink and--"

"Get shagged!" Maev shouted. She swung her head, trying to knock the goblet over, but Auberon pulled the vessel aside.

The old druid nodded. "I will return at dusk. I will pray for you, my daughters."

"Pray to save your arse once I'm free, bastard!" Maev shouted after him, thrashing in her bonds.

The old druid wandered off into his hut--a mere grassy mound with a stone archway for a door.

Laira turned to look at the struggling Maev. Her wrists and ankles were chafed and bleeding.

"You shouldn't struggle," Laira said. "You're only causing the vines to cut you. And you should eat. You need your strength."

Maev went limp and dropped her chin to her chest. She gazed at Laira between strands of scraggly hair. "For what? What do I need strength for anymore? Look at us, Laira. We defeated tribal warriors, rocs, demons, a southern king . . . to end up here. Tied up by a bunch of old druids." She snorted, blowing back a lock of hair. "Not quite the heroic death I imagined for myself."

Laira frowned. "We're not going to die here."

"I am." Maev sighed and her lips curled bitterly. "I'm not eating anymore of their food. Sooner or later I'll die here--maybe in a day, maybe in two, maybe three. If I don't eat or drink, it'll come." She raised her chin. "Live free or die. I will not linger here, tied to the boulder. And I will not drink their poison. I'd rather starve to death than lose my magic." She smiled wryly. "Funny. I always imagined my death would be in battle--fighting against the enemies of Requiem. But I'm glad, Laira. I'm glad because this means I'll die beside you." Her eyes watered. "And I love you, Laira. I love you as family, as a sister in arms, as a *dragon*."

Laira looked over the misty hills, the grassy valley, and the distant druids who were tending to their herb gardens. "I never imagined I'd end up like this either." Laira's voice was soft. "I always thought it would be Zerra who'd kill me--the Chieftain of Goldtusk. Whenever he beat me, I thought that I would die. I think I did come close to dying some of those times. When Grizzly found me, I was almost dead. I was burnt, cut, bruised, battered . . . every inch of me was covered with wounds. I weighed less than a leaf on the wind, and my mind was a storm. But I survived. I do not believe our journey ends here, Maev. Grizzly taught me that there's always hope. Always. Even when things seem darkest, so long as you breathe, so long as you can take that next breath, you can hope. And you can fight. We've overcome hunters, rocs, demons. We'll survive a few druids."

"Laira?" Maev said. "I'm . . . not quite sure you're right." She winced. "Not with sphinxes around."

Laira frowned. "What . . ." She looked up and felt the blood drain from her face.

Oh stars . . .

She raised her voice to a shout. "Sphinxes!" Laira tugged at her bonds. "Auberon! Druids! Sphinxes attack!"

The beasts shrieked among the clouds; Laira counted seven of them. The circling vultures fled. The sphinxes' stench wafted down--a stench of acid and stale urine and sulfur. The wind ruffled the fur on their lion bodies, and their human faces--bloated to an obscene size as if waterlogged--opened to reveal their teeth.

"Druids!" Laira shouted, tugging madly at her bonds. At her side, Maev was trying to shift, but whenever green scales flowed across her they vanished as the tillvine strands squeezed her.

Druids emerged from their huts, raced to the center of the valley, and pointed at the flying sphinxes. A few knelt and began to pray.

"Auberon, release us!" Laira shouted. "Release us or they'll kill us all!"

The bearded old druid emerged from his hut, gazed at the sphinxes that circled above, and raised his staff. His voice echoed across the valley.

"The sky gods visit us!" He shook his staff, letting its charms jingle. "Brothers and sisters, great blessed beings of the sky come to--"

The sphinxes shrieked, swooped, and blew blasts of foul smoke.

Laira winced. "Don't breath it, Maev!"

The smoke blasted across the valley, fetid and gray, full of specks--demonic grubs with human faces. Laira screwed her mouth shut and closed her eyes. She felt the tiny creatures land upon her, and she shook her head wildly, struggling to dislodge them. The smoke seared her skin, and her eyes--even when closed--watered and burned. Sickness rose in her throat. She struggled not to gag, and the stew churned in her belly. She felt the tiny demons patter across her, squirm along her skin, her lips, her eyelids, seeking a way into her body. Their voices chattered, calling to her, calling her name. She kept shaking her head wildly, knocking them off like a wolf shaking off droplets of water.

When finally she no longer felt the demons, and the heat wafted away, she opened her eyes and gulped down air.

Several druids lay dead in the valley, their faces bloated, their eyes and mouths leaking blood--victims of the unholy miasma. As Laira thrashed in her bonds, she watched the sphinxes land upon three living druids, drive down their claws, and tear the men apart. Blood spilled across the grass.

"Auberon!" Laira cried. "Free us!"

The old druid stood among the carnage, staring at the dead, lips twitching. Around him, druids raced forward with spears and bows--weapons used for hunting. They thrust the flint-tipped spears at the sphinxes. They fired their arrows of pointed wood. The beasts laughed as they swatted at the druids, knocking them down, tearing them open.

"Auberon, damn your hide, release us and we'll fight!" Maev shouted.

The old druid stared at them, then back at the sphinxes, seeming torn. The seven creatures were now racing between the burrows, tearing them down and biting the women and children they found within. Blood stained the beasts' jaws.

"I . . . I prayed to them," Auberon whispered.

"Free us!" Laira cried, knowing that as soon as the sphinxes were done slaying the druids, they'd turn toward her and Maev.

Auberon trembled, cheeks pale. A sphinx landed before him, opened its jaw wide, and shrieked, blowing back Auberon's hair.

The druid thrust his staff, hitting the creature's eye. Wood shoved through the eyeball, and the sphinx yowled. Several other druids leaped forth, spears jabbing at the sphinx. The beast screeched and turned toward them, snapping its teeth.

"Auberon," Laira said softly. "Auberon, you know what to do."

As blood spilled across the valley, Auberon met her gaze, raised his chin, and ran toward her. He drew a curved dagger from his belt and sliced at her bonds.

Laira stumbled to the grass, free from the boulder for the first time in days. She was so weak and dizzy she fell to her knees. The battle raged before her. More druids fell. Laira ground her teeth, clenched her fists, and shifted.

Wings thudded out of her back, and she rose with a roar, a golden dragon. She blew her fire.

The flames washed over the sphinxes like waves over seaside boulders.

Maev rose at her side, a green dragon, blasting out her dragonfire.

The inferno filled the valley like flames in a forge. The sphinxes shrieked as they burned. They fell and writhed in the grass. In their agony, their magic left them. They returned to human form--tattooed Widejaw warriors, their cheeks cut open.

Growling, Maev walked between the fallen warriors, driving down her claws, tearing through them. One man tried to flee; the green dragon pounced upon him, grabbed him between her jaws, and ripped him apart. The blood filled her mouth and leaked between her teeth.

Still in dragon form, Laira walked across the grass, beating her wings to part the smoke. One Widejaw was still alive. He lay on the ground in human form, coughing weakly. Burns covered his body. He struggled to his feet and began to shift.

Laira leaped, shoved him down, and knocked the magic out of him. She pressed her claws against the man's chest, pinning him against the grass.

"Try to shift," Laira hissed, "and I'll tear your throat out. That's it. Lie there. Nice and still and you'll live."

Maev came walking forward, still a dragon. Bits of flesh dangled between her teeth, and smoke wafted from her nostrils.

"Gut him," the green dragon said. "Let him die slowly."

Laira shook her head. Her scales chinked. "This one will live." Still pinning the man down, she looked over her shoulder. "Auberon, bring your goblet! Bring the elixir."

The druid was staring at her, face smeared with ash, robes covered in blood. Around him stood several other druids in the mist, and at their feet lay their dead.

"Bring me the drink," Laira repeated, blasting smoke from her mouth. "Auberon, I am not your enemy. Dragons saved your life today. Bring me the elixir, and let this man drink." She smiled wryly. "We'll see if it cures sphinxes."

Auberon stepped forward, silent and hesitant. His face remained blank but his eyes were a storm; in them, Laira saw herself reflected, a golden dragon, a creature the druid had always thought a monster. But he obeyed her. He held the elixir over the Widejaw's mouth. At first the man resisted, trying to spit it out, but his split cheeks--a deformity meant to frighten his enemies-- were now his bane. Auberon was able to tug the split cheek open and spill in the green liquid.

The Widejaw sputtered, convulsed, and then screamed. He howled and kicked the air.

No strands of starlight rose from him but rather a foul, murky smoke thick with insects. Laira grimaced and stepped away. Even freed from her claws, the Widejaw could not rise. He thrashed in the grass, screaming as the smoke rose from him, as the insects bustled out of his nostrils, his ears, his mouth, fleeing into the sky . . . and vanishing.

The Widejaw lay panting, thinned, ashen.

"Shift!" Laira said. "Shift into a sphinx. Shift and I will let you fly away."

The man struggled to his feet. He stared at her blankly. He closed his eyes, clenched his fists, and twisted his face . . . then fell to his knees.

"He is cured," Auberon whispered.

Maintaining her dragon form, Laira stepped closer to the Widejaw. She stared into his eyes. "You may leave. You may live."

The man stared at her, eyes wide with fear . . . and with gratitude. He nodded. He turned to walk away.

Green scales flashed.

Maev roared, leaped on the man, and drove her fangs through his armor and into his torso. The dragon swung her head, tossed the man high into the air, and torched him with dragonfire.

"Maev!" Laira shouted. "The battle was over! His back was turned."

The green dragon clawed the air, beat her wings, and howled. The inuksuks upon the hill shook. Wreathed in smoke, Maev spun toward Laira. Her eyes blazed, rimmed with red.

"The battle is never over." The green dragon sneered. "Not for us. Not for Requiem. Don't you understand, Laira? Don't you see?" Her voice sounded torn, close to tears. "They will always hunt us. Rocs. Sphinxes. Druids. A thousand other enemies. Ours will forever be a life of war. And I will fight this war. I will slay all my enemies." She howled to the sky, claws digging up grass, then beat her wings and soared. "Requiem! I find your sky! I fight for you. I kill for you, Requiem!"

Her wings blasted air, rippling the grass, as Maev soared higher and flew off into the wind. She vanished into the clouds.

Laira turned to look at the Cured Druids. Most lay dead. The survivors stared at her, some solemn, others trembling.

"You could have fought them," Laira whispered. "You were Vir Requis once. If you had kept your magic, you could have flown as dragons. You could have defended your wives, your children. Now they're dead, more victims in this world of cruelty, of bloodshed, of hatred. They didn't have to die." She tossed back her head and roared. "They didn't have to die!" She stared at Auberon, and rage flared in her, bursting out from her nostrils as hot smoke. "We are not cursed. We are not diseased or impure. We are dragons." Her voice dropped to a whisper. "We are beings of starlight."

Auberon approached her slowly. Tears drew lines down his ashy face. The old man embraced her scaly head.

"We are sorry," he whispered. "We are sorry. We are not cured. We are broken. We are bleeding, hurt, torn asunder." The druid stared into her eyes. "And we will have our revenge."

JEID

"Shove it left!" Jeid shouted. "To the left, damn you."

Dorvin grunted at his side. "I'm trying! The damn thing's got a mind of its own."

"Of course it does." Jeid growled. "And probably a brighter mind than yours."

The two men walked abreast, each holding a wooden staff ending with a leather harness. Golgoloth shrieked and struggled before them, trapped in the harnesses, scuttling madly. As the demon thrashed, its claws and teeth tore through granite and limestone as easily as a shovel through loose soil.

"I will slay dragons," hissed the burrowing demon. "I will snap your bones, suck out the marrow, and pop your organs in my mouth. I will--"

Jeid shoved the shaft forward, slamming the demon against the far wall and smothering its words. "You will keep digging."

The creature squealed, legs thrashing like a mad spider. Chips of stone flew, buffeting Jeid and Dorvin.

They'd been digging for a long time now--perhaps a full day--shoving Golgoloth forward through the stony innards of the mountain. The tunnel was narrow, just large enough for him and Dorvin to walk abreast, its walls jagged and chipped.

When Jeid gazed behind him, he saw the others walking there--dozens of Vir Requis stretching down the sloping tunnel. They were wounded. They were grieving. They were hungry and thirsty and afraid, but hope shone in their eyes.

We will find a way out, Jeid swore. *We will find our sky.*

He turned back forward. He shoved against the shaft, driving the demon against the stone. He clenched his jaw as he worked, and Dorvin leaned forward at his side. Sweat drenched them, and the flying chips of rock cut their skin, but they kept shoving the demon forward. With squeals, with showering dust and rock, they kept advancing--foot by foot--tunneling ever upward.

After so long in the caves, Jeid was desperate to find his way out, to fly again, to breathe the open air. But part of him never wanted to emerge. Part of him hoped they'd keep burrowing forever, never finding the edge of the mountain.

When we emerge, I might find a world without you, my family.

The thought was almost too much to bear. He loved the Vir Requis behind him--they were his people, and each soul was dear to him. Yet if he didn't find his wife and children, how could he go on? The pain of losing little Requiem, his daughter, still clawed at him; how would he survive if he lost Maev and Tanin too? Many nights, Jeid still dreamed of his first wife, of fair Keyla whom his own brother had slain. If Laira too was lost to him, the only woman he had loved since, how would he find reason to keep flying?

I will find you, Laira, he thought. *I will fly to the ends of the world. I will crumble empires to the ground, and I will boil lakes, and I will uproot forests, and I will watch this world burn to find you. Wherever you are, know that I'm coming for you.*

They kept tunneling. Foot by foot. Mark by mark. The demon dug through soil and granite alike, tearing boulders apart as easily as sickles cutting stalks of grain. Dorvin soon panted and had to step back, letting another man replaced him at the right-hand harness; soon that man too tired and allowed a third Vir Requis to hold the shaft. But Jeid kept to his post, his palms raw around the wood, always shoving the creature, grinding his jaw, thinking of his family. Tunneling up and up through the darkness, seeking the sky.

"Requiem," he said through the flying dust, through his dripping sweat. "May our wings forever find your sky."

After what felt like days, like marks and marks of tunneling, he smelled it ahead, and he closed his eyes and savored it.

Cold, fresh air.

He growled and leaned against the shaft, shoving the thrashing demon forward. Its claws lashed. Its teeth bit through stone. Rocks collapsed and dirt rained, and there Jeid saw it, and tears filled his eyes.

The sky.

The stars.

Freedom.

Golgoloth twitched and squealed. Bound to the edge of the harness like a chunk of meat on a skewer, the demon burst out into the open air.

Jeid looked at Dorvin; the young man was back holding the other shaft. The two shared a glance, then tightened their lips and stepped out of the tunnel and onto the mountaintop.

The wind blew across them, cold and wonderfully scented. The moon shone above, snow flurried around their feet, and distant pines spread below upon the mountainsides, sliding down into shadows.

Jeid turned to look south. Far in the distance, a mark away or more, he could see fire streaming out of the mountainside. Bryn, the last defender of the mountain, was blowing her dragonfire from the cave, keeping the sphinxes out. In the night, the distant sphinxes looked like fireflies, orange in the dragonfire; hundreds buzzed there.

The Vir Requis began to emerge from the tunnel, pale and weak, many of them wounded.

"Gather here. Come, make room." Jeid guided them across the mountaintop. "Keep silent and do not shift. The sphinxes can't see us."

They kept emerging from the burrow: an elder who leaned on his son; a mother who held her babe to her breast; a pair of sisters, only six years old; dour young men; pale young women. They gathered upon the rocky crest. Some glanced nervously down toward the distant sphinxes, and others looked longingly at the sky.

"Wait and don't fly yet," Jeid whispered. "Wait until we're all out. We'll fly together. We'll--"

The demon on the harness bucked and twitched. It began to dig another burrow, trying to reenter the mountain. Jeid ground his teeth and raised the shaft, holding the creature aboveground. Dorvin grunted at his side, clutching the creature's second harness.

"That's it, you dung-guzzling pile of maggot shite," Dorvin whispered. "Be a nice good demon."

Jeid looked back south. Dragonfire was still spurting out of the mountains, but it was growing smaller.

"Go on, Bryn," Jeid whispered. "Into the cave. We're ready."

Below, the firelight flickered . . . and was gone.

BRYN

She blasted out the last sparks of fire in her. The flames sputtered and died.

Bryn was so tired she could barely breathe. She had never blown fire for so long; she felt emptied of all her innards. Gasping for air, she stared outside the cave with narrowed eyes. The sphinxes--stars, hundreds of them were swarming in the night-- stared back, their eyes blazing white and cruel in their bloated human faces. The creatures hissed and raised their claws. With her fire gone, the beasts swooped toward the cave.

Bryn, an orange dragon, retreated from the cave opening and spun around in the cavern. She sucked in a raspy breath and released her magic, returning to human form. Locks of her hair clung to her face, damp with sweat. More sweat covered her body, and her fur tunic clung to her skin.

Not waiting for another breath, she ran.

For you, Requiem, she thought, racing across the cavern and toward the tunnel. *For you, Aeternum, my king.*

She glanced behind her and grimaced. The sphinxes were landing inside the cave, turning back into humans and drawing their swords. They wore rusted bits of ring mail, and tattoos covered their faces and bald heads.

"Find the weredragons!" one shouted, jaw opening from ear to ear. "Slay the scum!"

Bryn turned back forward, tightened her lips, and raced into the narrow tunnel--the natural cave the exiles of Requiem had been hiding in for so many days. Those exiles were gone now, fled through the exit the demon had dug.

"Fly away, Jeid," she whispered as she ran. "Fly with the others. Fly to safety." She raced around a corner just as Widejaw arrows flew; they slammed into the wall behind her. "Fly and find the sky."

Of all the Vir Requis, only she remained in these caves now, a last defender--she, Bryn of Stonemill, a daughter of Requiem. Her eyes dampened.

"Requiem," she whispered. She needed to say no more; in one word, she could speak of her dreams, of her hope, of her kind, of the magic inside her. It was a word itself imbued with magic, itself a prayer, itself the anchor of her soul and the beacon of her heart.

The Widejaws roared behind her. Their voices echoed. When Bryn looked behind her again, she saw them racing forward, carrying torches. Each man was twice her size, clad in metal, brawny arms covered in coiling lines. Rings of bronze pierced their brows, noses, and lips--those horrible lips cut and stretched across their entire jaws. Old blood encrusted their leaf-shaped swords. One man raised a bow and shot an arrow. Bryn raced around a corner, and the arrow missed her again, snapping against the cave wall.

She looked back forward. She raced as fast as she could. She was famished, weak from blowing so much fire, weak from days with barely any food or drink or sleep. But Bryn ran.

For Requiem. For my king.

Her eyes stung. Her fists clenched at her sides.

I will always run for you.

She found tears stinging her eyes, for she was no longer the simple girl from the village, a gatherer of berries. She was no longer a frightened child with a secret, so afraid of her curse, of the reptilian disease. For many years she had lingered in the shadows of her hut, the shadows of the forest outside their village, the shadows of her fear and shame.

But she had found a light.

She had found Requiem.

"And I found you, Jeid." She touched her lips, remembering the times she had kissed his cheek, wanting to kiss his mouth but daring not. "And I will always fight for you."

Jeid Blacksmith. King Aeternum. The lord of Requiem. A gruff man, perhaps a man she might have once been frightened of--a man tall, powerful, bearded, his hair shaggy and grizzled, his face so hard and his eyes full of shadows. A man she had come to see kindness in, the greatest kindness she had ever known. Eyes she had seem wisdom in. Hands--large, callused, rough hands--she had seen strength in and yet softness too.

"Grab the whore!" rose a shout behind.

Laughed echoed. Men cursed and jeered.

"Bring her here!"

"Strip off her clothes!"

"She will be ours."

A man roared out, "Come here, weredragon! I'm going to make you mine. We all are. And once you've borne our children, we're going to cook your babes on the fire."

The narrow cave sloped upward. Bryn clenched her jaw and ran as fast as she could. When she glanced over her shoulder, she saw the men following, their torches casting long shadows.

The archer licked his chops and fired.

An arrow whistled and slammed into Bryn's leg.

She howled with pain. She fell. She slammed against the floor.

The men roared with laughter.

"Drag her over!"

"We're going to bed her here in the caves!"

"Chop off her hands first. She won't need those and I'm famished."

Bryn screamed. Her eyes watered. Her blood gushed.

Get up.

She screamed again. Her hands balled into fists.

Get up!

She leaped to her feet. She ran again, the arrow still embedded in her. Every step blazed with agony. The archer fired again, and she winced and jumped, and the arrow clattered between her legs. The Widejaws laughed and she kept running, rounded a corner, and gritted her teeth. Tears of pain flowed down to her lips.

I'm going to find you, Jeid. I'm going to fly with you again.

"Where are all the others?" rose a voice behind her.

The other men spat and cursed. "Damn maggots hiding deep. We'll find 'em."

Bryn did not think she could keep running. Every step was too painful, and every breath shot an inferno through her lungs. Dorvin had wanted to stay behind, to guard the entrance while the others fled, but Bryn had insisted on this task. She wanted to do this for Jeid, for the man she loved, for her king.

I will not let you down.

She kept racing, step by step, until she saw it ahead--the crude, narrow tunnel the demon had carved, a burrow leading out of the caves and into the sky.

The Widejaws laughed behind her, taunting and jeering. Bryn ran, leaving a trail of blood.

JEID

The demon was growing restless, tugging at its harness, snapping its teeth, and clawing the air. Jeid dug his heels into the mountainside, clutching the wooden shaft which connected to the digger's harness. Dorvin stood across from him, grumbling as he tugged his own shaft.

"Free me . . ." hissed the demon. "I released you. Free me . . ."

Jeid shook his head. "So you can devour more of us? No. Not until we're all out of the mountain. Not until we shift as dragons and fly, scales protecting us from your claws."

Golgoloth hissed out its laughter. "My claws can cut through granite and metal. They can easily pierce the scales of a dragon." The creature licked its lips, and its tongue flailed, the blades upon it flashing.

Jeid looked back at the tunnel. The last few Vir Requis were emerging: a wounded man, his legs bandaged; an elderly woman wrapped in a thick cloak; and a mother and her young child.

"That's all of them," Dorvin said, grimacing as he struggled against the thrashing demon. "I counted."

The survivors huddled together--seventy-three in all, pale and thin, shivering in the cold night.

The demon gave a mighty tug, nearly lifting Jeid off his feet. Yanking the creature back, Jeid stared down the mountainside. Far below upon the slopes, a good mark away, the sphinxes hadn't

seen them yet. Most had already entered the cave in pursuit of
Bryn; perhaps only fifty still flew outside, awaiting their turn to fly
into the mountain.

Jeid glanced down to the hole at his feet, the tunnel the
demon had carved. It wouldn't be long before Bryn emerged.

"Remember, Dorvin," Jeid said. "As soon as Bryn's here, we
shift and blow fire into the hole. We'll roast the Widejaws chasing
her, then fly off."

Dorvin nodded. He glanced down the mountainside.
"Almost all the sphinxes are inside the mountain now." He tapped
his foot. "Where are you, Bryn?"

The demon hissed and tugged at its harness. "Free us . . .
free us . . ."

Dorvin spat. "Be quiet. Once we're done with you, I think
I'll roast you like the sphinxes. Nice cooked demon on a stick."

The demon squealed. Its tongue lashed out, and its legs
clawed the air. It gave such a mighty yank upward, both Jeid and
Dorvin were tugged onto their toes.

"Hush!" Jeid said. "The sphinxes will hear." He glanced
down below; a good forty-odd sphinxes were still outside the
mountain. One seemed to look up toward the mountaintop, and
Jeid's heart sank.

Oh stars . . . don't let them hear us. Not until Bryn's here.

But the demon on the harness kept struggling. Its voice rose
louder. It let out a shriek.

"Damn it!" Jeid tugged the creature down. "Dorvin, we
have to silence it."

The young man nodded, grinned, and drew his sword.
"With pleasure."

Tugging Golgoloth's harness with one hand, Dorvin swung
his blade with the other. The sword clanged against one of the
creature's legs, doing it no harm.

The demon yowled and gave such a mighty pull, the wooden shaft tore free from Dorvin's hand.

Jeid tried to hold the creature down himself, but alone he wasn't strong enough. Screeching madly, Golgoloth broke loose, flew into the air, and spun in the sky. Its scream rolled down the mountainsides.

Below, near the cave, sphinxes roared and began flying up the mountain.

The Vir Requis gasped, whispered, and pointed toward the approaching beasts.

Jeid looked down into the hole at his feet.

Bryn . . . come on,

"Scum on the mountains!" rose a hoarse cry from the sphinxes. "Weredragons on the peak! Widejaws, slay them!"

Jeid cursed, shifted, and rose as a dragon.

"Rise, dragons of Requiem!" he cried. "Rise and fly!"

He beat his wings, soaring higher. Below him, the other Vir Requis took dragon forms and rose too. A silver dragon, Dorvin blew fire, roasting the fleeing tunnel demon.

The sphinxes shrieked.

Do we flee? Jeid growled. No. The sphinxes would chase them, and their comrades in the mountain would join the pursuit. It was time to fight.

"Burn them, dragons of Requiem!" Jeid shouted. "Burn them down!"

He roared and flew down the mountainside toward the forty sphinxes. Dorvin flew at his side, and dozens of other dragons flew behind them.

We must burn them before hundreds more emerge behind Bryn.

"Requiem!" Dorvin howled. "Slay the enemy!"

The silver dragon blew his dragonfire. Jeid joined his flames to the blaze. Around them, a dozen other dragons blasted out their wrath.

Shooting up the mountainside, the sphinxes screeched and spewed their demonic miasma.

Fire and smoke crashed together.

The inferno blazed across the mountain. Jeid's fire tore through the smoke, roasting the tiny demons that buzzed within. At his side, Jeid saw the noxious cloud wrap around a lavender dragon, saw the demonic parasites flow into the dragon's nostrils and throat. The dragon screamed, her face bloated, and her scales cracked as the demons coursed through her. She fell against the mountainside, writhing, and lost her magic.

Jeid grimaced and blasted flames again. Two sphinxes ahead caught fire and shrieked. Two more swooped from above, and Jeid soared, goring one with his horns and lacerating one with his claws.

"Die, you toad-licking sons of sows!" Dorvin laughed as he fought, clawing, biting, burning. The silver dragon streaked across the battle, fangs dripping blood.

Dozens of sphinxes and dragons tumbled, spun, and shot across the night sky. Fire rose in pillars. Foul smoke blasted everywhere. A blue dragon breathed in the poison, twisted, and crashed down in human form. A blast of fire took down a sphinx; the creature became a man again and tumbled, his skin ablaze. Two sphinxes crashed into a dragon, ripping into her hide. The Vir Requis fell as a screaming girl, slammed onto Jeid's back, then rolled off and tumbled down to the mountain.

Corpses rained in the night.

Jeid refused to let the horror overwhelm him.

"Fight them! Don't breathe their smoke. Burn them dead!"

The battle swirled like a typhoon of red and black and blazing blue fire.

Jeid sliced open another sphinx; its blood and organs rained down, and Jeid roasted the sphinx as it screamed. He glanced back at the mountain. The hole still gaped open.

Where are you, Bryn? Jeid blasted out more fire, roasting more of the creatures.

The hole remained dark and empty.

Bryn, and hundreds of other sphinxes, still waited to emerge.

BRYN

She raced through the tunnel, stumbling, an arrow in her thigh. The Widejaws howled and hooted behind her, getting closer. Their torches crackled, and their shadows fell upon her. Bryn grimaced, sweat and blood covering her, and ran on, limping, dizzy, seeking the exit, seeking the sky.

"Requiem!" The words shook as she panted. "May our wings forever find your sky."

The tunnel sloped up steeply, forcing Bryn to climb on hands and knees. Her blood kept dripping. Her head spun. When she looked behind her, she saw the Widejaws climbing in pursuit, only feet away now. Their mouths opened with lurid grins, tongues licking their chops, their saliva dripping.

If they caught her, Bryn knew they would batter her, strip off her clothes, then slice off her limbs and devour her flesh. Tears stung in her eyes, and she was so weak; she could barely cling to the stone. She ground her teeth and kept climbing.

Another arrow flew from below.

She roared with pain. The flint head tore into her shoulder and emerged bloody from the other side.

She fell. She slid down several feet.

A Widejaw grabbed her ankle. His teeth drove into her calf.

It's over.

She closed her eyes.

I can't defeat them. They'll slay me. They'll emerge on the mountaintop, hundreds of beasts. Jeid and the others will fall.

The teeth kept biting, and the Widejaws laughed and jeered, and her blood spilled.

And she saw him again in the darkness.

Jeid.

She reached out. She could imagine his kind face in the shadows, an apparition, a dream before her death.

His eyes stared into hers. His voice cried out.

Fight them! Climb, Bryn! Flee them.

She shook. She could not. She was too weak, too hurt.

She sucked in air as the Widejaws tugged her down, as their teeth ripped into her, eating her alive.

For Requiem.

She reached up a shaking hand. She could see it above in the darkness--the stars of Requiem.

For you, Requiem. For our eternal halls.

She screamed and kicked madly, slamming her foot against the Widejaw's face. She felt his nose crush. She heard him scream. She scurried up the tunnel, leaving them behind, as her blood spurted.

Two arrows filled her. The Widejaw teeth had torn into her leg; she feared to see the wound, to find her foot gone, consumed down to the bone. She kept climbing, dragging herself forward, digging her fingers into the rock. They roared behind her, laughing.

"Stop playing with your food, Shog!" one voice cried out. Others laughed.

"The playful little minx is making this fun. Slick as a fish!"

She kept climbing, bleeding, gritting her teeth, until she felt the cold wind, and she smelled it above--the sky.

She laughed and wept.

She climbed a few more feet, and she saw them above--the true stars of Requiem, bright and beautiful in the sky, calling to her.

Bleeding, maybe dying, Bryn reached out and felt the wind upon her fingers. She saw him fly above, a great copper dragon limned in moonlight--Jeid, her king.

I'm going to live, she thought. *I'm going to fly with Jeid again.* She clutched the edge of the hole and began to climb. *I'm going to climb out, and we'll fill this hole with dragonfire. I--*

Pain blazed anew across her leg.

She turned her head and saw the Widejaw biting into her again, ripping into her flesh, eating her.

She screamed and reached up, struggling to climb out. She looked back at the stars . . . and could no longer see them. Fire and smoke washed across the sky.

Bryn gasped.

"Dragons of Requiem, fight them!" Jeid was crying above. Sphinxes mobbed him. Poisonous smoke enveloped him. Dozens of dragons and sphinxes flew above.

Bryn could barely breathe.

I must climb out! she thought. *I must join them!*

She looked behind her at the Widejaws biting into her feet, ripping off her flesh.

If I climb out, I'm too weak to blow fire, maybe too weak to shift into a dragon. The Widejaws will emerge. They'll become sphinxes--hundreds of them. They'll kill the others. They--

The jaws tightened, hitting her bone, and she screamed.

Climb!

"Flee, Jeid!" she tried to cry out. "They're going to slay me, to fly out, to overwhelm you, you have to flee."

But her words were only a whisper; she was too weak for anything louder.

Her fingers released the rim of the hole.

She slid down, and another Widejaw grabbed her, and teeth tore into her thighs, eating their way up, eating her alive.

Bryn closed her eyes.

"I love you, Requiem. I love you, Jeid."

With her last sparks of strength, she summoned her magic.

Still inside the tunnel, the sky hidden behind smoke and flame, Bryn became a dragon.

Wings burst out from her back. Her body grew, slamming against the tunnel walls. Her jaws rose toward the exit, puffing out smoke, trying to call out, to blow fire. Her tail lashed out from her back, slamming into the Widejaws.

As she kept growing, the pain cut through her like a thousand arrows.

The tunnel was too narrow for a dragon. The walls pressed against her, cracking her scales. She felt her ribs snap, driving into her organs.

She lashed her claws.

She swung her tail.

Keep shifting.

She slammed her head from side to side, banging the stone walls. Her tail thrashed. She dug madly. Chips of rock and clumps of soil fell. Below her, the Widejaws screamed. Around her, the walls crumbled.

Stones rained.

Dust flew.

The burrow collapsed.

The pain was too much. Bryn lost her magic and tumbled down, a human again, falling into endless darkness, into blood, into a sea of enemies, teeth, eyes, reaching fingers, pain that flowed into warmth and numbness.

Above her, the tunnel crumbled. The walls cracked and caved inward, and stones rained, and the mountain shook, and Bryn could no longer see the sky.

She closed her eyes. She smiled.

Farewell, Requiem.

As the mountain shook and closed in, burying her and the hundreds of Widejaws beneath her, Bryn smiled, for she had saved her king, her people, her kingdom. And then she saw them above--the halls of Requiem, woven of starlight, calling her home.

ISSARI

She glided upon the wind, a hundred dragons flying behind her, myriads of people walking below.

"A flock of them on the horizon." Flying at her side, Tanin narrowed his eyes and pointed his claws. "Looks like . . . maybe twenty. No more."

Issari nodded. "We fly out. We take them down."

She looked behind her. The dragons she had freed from Goshar flew there in several V formations. Their scales gleamed under the bright noon sun, and smoke trailed from their nostrils. Many had never flown before, too ashamed of their magic, and some still wobbled with every gust of wind.

But they're growing stronger, Issari thought. *They're growing proud.*

Below them, upon the grasslands, walked a great swarm-- the refugees of Eteer and Goshar, mingled together into one people, fled from their ravaged cities. They wore tunics of canvas and wool, white cloaks, and sandals, and they carried only staffs and sickles as weapons. Their cattle walked before them, a multitude of sheep and goats and pigs--their last belongings. Babes swayed in baskets strapped to mothers' breasts, and elders hobbled on canes. The nephilim had toppled their cities and ravaged their farms, and now they were Issari's to protect; they were her people just as much as the dragons who flew above.

"Dragons of Requiem!" she called out, for now these hundred were children of Requiem too. They had never seen King's Column, had never met King Aeternum, but the magic of the Draco constellation flowed through them. That made them

Vir Requis. That made them her kin. "Dragons of Requiem, nephilim in the west. Fly! Fly with me and burn them."

The dragons sounded their cry, flocked toward her, and raced across the sky.

They had been traveling south for days now, seeking the ancient city-state of Tur Kal, the largest and oldest of the thirteen. Nephilim had plagued their journey, emerging every hour--a cluster here, a scout there, sometimes as many as fifty flying together. Once Issari had even seen a great swarm of them-- perhaps a thousand together--upon the horizon, flowing south like a cloud of locust.

They're breeding, Issari thought. *Maybe with humans, maybe with one another, but there are more every day.*

She winced and fear washed her with ice, the same fear that hadn't left her since Goshar. Her belly twisted--whether with terror or with lurking life, she did not know.

A demon knew me in my tent, she thought and shivered. Her scales clattered. *A demon planted his seed within me.* Her belly twisted again, and Issari winced, wondering if the seed had quickened, if a nephil--one of these twisted, rotting creatures--now festered within her, growing larger, growing stronger, soon to--

"Burn them!" Tanin cried and blasted out his fire.

Issari shook her head, banishing her thoughts. The nephilim were close now, only moments away. She opened her jaw wide, and she blasted out flame, replacing her fear with the rage of the battle.

The nephilim screeched and attacked, claws outstretched. The dragons circled them, blew fire, and roasted the demon spawn. They had slain many before, and they slew these ones, sending their carcasses down toward the fields where they shattered, spilling rot.

But we cannot kill all the nephilim in the world, Issari thought as
the dragons cheered around her. *There are too many. They breed too
quickly.* Her belly gave a twist. *They breed inside me.*

"Kinat!" she said to one of the Gosharian dragons. "How
far is the city of Tur Kar?"

The bronze dragon glided at her side, old and creaky, his
wings peppered with holes. "I have not been there in many years,
White Priestess, but it does not lie much farther. The great Tur
Kal, the Jewel of Terra, lies beyond the hills upon the border of
grasslands and deserts. We'll be there soon."

Issari looked toward the distant tan hills.

I must find a home for the people of Eteer and Goshar, she thought.
I must find more dragons. And I must find a cure for whatever rots inside me.

As the sun set, they reached the hills, and the people cried
out and pointed and sang. Gliding high above the exodus, Issari
looked to the south and saw the city there.

"Tur Kal," she whispered.

The city sprawled across the horizon, many marks wide,
surrounded by ocher walls. A river flowed around it, feeding fields
of wheat and barley. Beyond the wall stretched many narrow
streets lined with tan, domed homes. In the city center rose three
pyramids, hundreds of feet tall, structures even taller than King's
Column in the north. All of Eteer and Goshar, Issari thought,
could fit within these walls.

And they might have to. She looked at the people traveling
below, leading their cattle, singing and dancing at the sight of the
city, of hope. They pointed, and they played timbrels and drums,
and they prayed--to Taal, to Shahazar, and to her. Could this be a
home for them?

As they drew closer, Issari's heart sank.

Gliding at her side, Tanin cursed. "Stars damn it."

Issari nodded. "More of them. Hundreds of them.
Nephilim."

The half-demons bustled above the city, their shrieks carrying on the wind. The sunset gleamed against thousands of arrows rising from the city walls. The cries of dying, and the scent of blood, reached Issari even here.

She looked behind her. She didn't even have to cry out; her dragons mustered, eyes bright, breath flaming, ready to fight.

They streamed across the hills.

They raced to the city of Tur Kal.

And there, as the night fell, Issari roared out her cry. "Dragons of Tur Kal, hear me! I am Issari, Queen of Dragons. Rise! Rise and fight with me!"

Nephilim buzzed toward her. Her fellow dragons flew around Issari, holding them back, burning and cutting and knocking them down. Below in the city, archers fired up at the half-demons, and swordsmen raced to hack at those nephilim who landed upon roofs and in streets.

Issari flew higher, circling above the pyramids, above the death and bloodshed. Her cry rang across the city.

"All in Tur Kal who can become dragons, fly with me! Your magic is a blessing, not a curse. Fly and fight with us, with the dragons of Requiem!"

And like in Goshar, here too they rose.

One by one. Hesitant but soon flying high. Metallic dragons. Green and blue and red dragons. Old clattering beasts and young supple dragons with eager eyes. A hundred or more rose from the city, joining her in the sky, and their fire lit the night.

When dawn finally rose upon Tur Kal, a thousand nephilim lay dead and stinking upon its streets, slashed with claws and charred with dragonfire. Buildings lay toppled, walls fallen, domes caved in. Holes peppered the ancient pyramids.

Among the fallen half-demons lay thousands of dead men, women, and children--the people of Tur Kal and two dozen Vir Requis.

Issari and Tanin glided above the devastation, two single dragons in the dawn.

"We've lost so many," Tanin whispered.

Issari nodded. "And we gained more."

The hundred dragons she had led here--risen from Eteer and Goshar--stood upon the walls below, bright in the sunrise, sentinels of scales. A hundred new dragons, children of Tur Kal, stood among them.

New dragons of Requiem. Our nation grows.

She turned to look north of the walls. The outcasts of Goshar and Eteer sprawled across the hills, gathered around smoldering campfires. These men, women, and children had no dragon magic, yet they too were her people. These too were nations she led, nations she had to protect.

She looked back at the city. A palace rose from the ruins upon a hill, built of limestone, its columns soaring--as tall as the columns of Requiem. A stairway stretched toward the palace gates, lined with statues shaped as jackals and falcons, crystals inlaid into their eyes. The corpses of nephilim lay strewn across those stairs, giants fallen from the sky, their black blood splattered. Soldiers of Tur Kal--so small compared to the massive size the nephilim had grown to--were racing about and pointing at the two dragons above.

"Come, Tanin," Issari said. "Here stands the Palace of Tur Kal, the home of its queen. We will speak with her."

The two dragons glided down and landed atop the staircase. The columns soared before them, their limestone engraved with scenes of soldiers, birds, and racing hinds. An archway rose ahead, leading into a hall, and the stench of dead nephilim wafted from the staircase behind her.

Issari and Tanin resumed human form: a woman clad in white robes, her black braid hanging across her shoulder; and a man in bronze armor, a fur cloak wrapped around him, his cheeks covered with thick stubble, his eyes dark, his frame tall.

The palace guards stood before them, their skin tanned deep bronze, their heads bald, their beards thin and pointed and wrapped with golden rings. They wore breastplates and sandals, and they carried curved blades.

"I am Issari Seran, Queen of Eteer," she told them, raising her chin. "Years ago, your queen visited our city upon the northern coast. Now, in this time of war that sweeps across all of Terra, I've come to speak with her again."

The guards stared down at the ruins that sprawled below: toppled buildings, crumbled walls, and thousands of dead, both beasts of the Abyss and people of the city. Numb horror filled their eyes, ghosts Issari knew would never leave them, as they would never leave her. The men stepped aside. She entered the hall of Tur Kal.

A mosaic of birds among reeds covered the floor, and bright murals of stars and suns lit the ceiling. Soldiers raced across the hall, servants bustled about, and messengers rushed in and out of rooms. Two wounded soldiers lay by a column, and priests prayed above them.

In the center of the hubbub, an elderly woman stood in a white robe. Golden links hung around her neck, and she held a gnarled wooden staff capped with silver. Though her face was deeply lined, and her hair was snowy white, her eyes were sharp and shrewd. She listened as soldiers spoke, as messengers raced forth, and as priests prayed. Her concentration never faltered as she turned from one man to another.

As Issari approached, the old woman's eyes flicked toward her. No hesitation filled them, no flicker of uncertainty.

"Issari Seran," the Queen of Tur Kal said. "New Queen of Eteer and savior of Goshar." She stepped closer and examined Issari, those shrewd eyes narrowing. "By the gods, child. Last time I saw you, you were an innocent youth. You have the eyes of an old monarch now. Hard as bronze and cold as a killer's. Your father has those eyes."

Issari shuddered. "Queen Rasha, my father has fallen to evil. The creatures who swarmed here were his creations. I've seen the evils rising from Eteer, and--"

"Wait." Queen Rasha took Issari by the hand. "Not in this hall. Come with me to the balcony. Eat and drink and speak to me there." The queen's eyes flicked toward Tanin. "And bring your companion, for I see strength in him too, and loyalty to you."

They stepped out from the hall and into a wide balcony. Porphyry tiles covered the floor, and flowers bloomed upon a stone railing. Stone tables stood here, set with dishes of fresh figs, dates, apricots, and grapes. The view faced west, and Issari could see marks of streets and houses leading to high walls. Beyond flowed a river, and in the hazy distance rolled the golden dunes of the desert.

Issari spoke to Queen Rasha for a long time, eating little. She spoke of Requiem in the north, of the Abyss gates open, of Eteer and Goshar falling, of the refugees in the hills, of the dragons who were joining her cause. She spoke for what seemed like hours, spilling all these words like a wound spilling its poison. A weight seemed to lift from her; it had been so long since she'd spoken to anyone who could help, anyone older, wiser, stronger. For a blessed short time, it seemed as if the burden of leadership, this yoke she had carried for so long, was shared--if only for a morning.

Only one thing she did not speak of. She dared not speak of Sharael, the Deceiver, the demon who had visited her in her tent. She had not spoken of him to Tanin; she would not to the queen of Tur Kal. That was a secret she would bury with her, a shame too painful to bring to her lips.

Finally, when all her words were spoken, she ended her speech. "And so, my queen, we must fight united. All the thirteen city-states of Terra. The soldiers of Eteer and Goshar who walk with me. The dragons of Requiem. And the armies of all standing cities, your own included." She took a shuddering breath. "We must march to Eteer, we must slay my father, and we must close the gates to the Abyss."

The queen rose to her feet. Her hand tightened around her staff. "My darling child, the south will rise. All of Terra will fight. I will find you a chamber in this palace. Sleep here. Rest here. Heal here. In the morning, you will fly again--and you will find more dragons."

"I will stay among my people tonight," Issari said. "I will walk among them and spend the night in the hills. I won't live in a palace while they sleep under the stars."

Night fell upon the land.

In the city, men still buried their dead. In the hills, tents rose and campfires crackled like a field of orange stars. Queen Rasha sent forth wagons of grains, and the refugees cooked flat breads upon metal sheets, and they fished in the river and hunted deer upon the hills. For the first time since leaving Goshar, bellies were filled.

Issari lay in her tent, in her bed, in her lover's arms. Tanin slept beside her, his chest rising and falling, his breath soft. She looked at him--his scruffy face, his shaggy brown hair, the lips she had once loved to kiss--and she saw *him*, the Deceiver. When Tanin mumbled in his sleep and tightened his arms around her, Issari winced and her belly twisted, and she remembered the demon making love to her, claiming her, and she remembered herself moaning with her passion, enjoying the creature's touch, loving it, craving it.

Finally she could stand it no more. She could no longer look at Tanin or feel his warm body beside her. Everything about him reminded her of that night, of her terror and shame. Silently, she rose from her bed and, without waking Tanin, left her tent. The camp sprawled around her across the hills: tents, campfires, tethered cattle. Above spread a field of stars. She breathed the cool air, took one step away from her tent, then doubled over as pain stabbed through her belly.

She gasped, arms wrapped around herself. Something inside her twitched, kicked, tugged. She grimaced, sweat flooded her, and she placed a hand upon her belly. She felt the thing inside kick, waking up, bulging, waiting to emerge.

A nephil grows inside me.

The creature within her--Sharael's son--gave another kick, and Issari could hear it now, hear the tiny, chattering sounds like rustling cockroaches.

She stumbled down the hill.

I have to kill it. I have to kill my child.

Hugging herself, trying to ignore the movement inside her, she walked between the tents, crossing several hills until she reached the tent she sought. It was a simple tent, smaller than her own, its walls formed of animal hides. The creature inside her gave such a twist that she nearly fell. Jaw locked, she stepped inside.

Teean was still awake, seated upon a wooden stool, drawing letters into a wet clay tablet. She turned around to face Issari, the candlelight upon her face. She was perhaps fifty years old, her long dark hair streaked with white. Her eyes were deep and green and wise, and bronze bracelets chinked around her arms. An amulet of Irishin, the god of healing, hung around her neck--a serpent coiling around a staff.

"Teean," Issari whispered. "I'm ill."

The midwife rose to her feet and rushed toward her. "Sweet Issari! Come. Lie down. Let me see."

Issari stumbled forward and lay down upon Teean's bed. Twenty years ago, Teean--then a healer in Eteer--had delivered Issari from her mother's womb.

And today she will remove my child from my womb, she thought. *And I will kill it.*

Issari gasped and screamed as the pain drove through her, knives inside her belly.

The midwife touched Issari's forehead; her fingers came back wet with Issari's sweat.

"You're feverish," Teean said. "I'll prepare you a drink of healing herbs. I--"

"Teean," Issari whispered and clutched the midwife's hand. "In Eteer, I heard unwed women whisper. They spoke of midwives helping them, pulling out early babes from their wombs, tiny things no larger than an apricot's pit. They . . . they said you helped them." She squeezed Teean's hand. "Please. Help me now. Help me remove the child inside me."

Teean stared down, eyes wide and cheeks pale. For a long moment, the midwife said nothing, simply stared into Issari's eyes.

She understands.

Finally Teean nodded. "I still have my tools."

The midwife opened a wooden box in the corner. Issari glimpsed tongs and metal tubes, and then the pain washed over her, and she shut her eyes and clenched her fists.

While Teean worked, Issari screamed.

Please, Taal, please, she prayed, clenching her fist so tightly the amulet hurt in her hand. *Please . . .*

Something large and smooth and wet slithered out of her.

A babe cried.

It was a beautiful sound--soft, tender, begging for a mother's love.

Issari took a shaky breath, her eyes still closed.

My son needs me.

"Oh blessed Irishin . . ." rose the midwife's voice. The clatter of falling bronze tools followed.

Issari opened her eyes and she wept. He stared at her from the edge of the bed, eyes wet and wide. Her son.

"My son," she whispered.

The nephil blinked, his eyelids making soft, wet sounds. Blood and amniotic fluid covered his wretched, twisted, rotting body, and his tiny jaws opened, lined with teeth, and he cried again. Cried for her, for his mother. His hands wrapped around her leg, clinging, drawing blood with his tiny claws.

"My son." She wept. "He needs me."

Face pale, Teean lifted a knife. She thrust the blade into the nephil's back.

"No!" Issari screamed, hoarse. "Teean, no!"

Her tears fell and she leaped from the bed. Her son screamed. A horrible sound. A betrayed sound. He gazed at her, the blade protruding out from his chest, and his mouth opened and closed.

Why? he seemed to ask her. *Why did you abort me? Why do you slay me?*

"My son. . ." Weeping, she reached toward him.

But the boy turned and leaped away. The little nephil, no larger than a newborn kitten, scuttled across the floor, leaving a wet trail, and fled the tent.

Bleeding and dizzy, Issari stumbled off the bed, shoved Teean aside, and raced outside.

"I'm sorry!" she cried out, for now that she had seen her son, she pitied him. She loved him.

And he was gone.

She searched the hills for hours, searched every tent, but she could not find him, and finally she stumbled out of the camp, and she fell to her knees in the wilderness. She lowered her head, and her body shook, and her tears fell.

"I'm sorry," she whispered.

She placed her hand upon her belly, and she felt empty. She had slain demons, had saved Vir Requis, had led an exodus from ruin to new life, but for the first time she had created life--even if it was a twisted, miserable life--and she had tried to extinguish that precious life, to kill her own son.

She lowered her head, and despair washed over her.

I can't do this, she thought. *I can't keep going. I don't know how to lead all these people, how to find them a new home, how to stop my father, how to seal the Abyss, how to become a leader, a savior, a mother, how to heal the pain inside me. It's too much, and I'm too small, too weak.*

She looked up at the sky, blinked her tears away, and saw them far above--the Draco stars, the dragon of the sky.

"Please, stars of Requiem. If you can hear me, and if your light truly blesses me, help me. I'm frightened." Her voice shook. "Help me."

The stars shone, distant and cold, unreachable as always. Issari stared, feeling as if they too had left her like her son. Both her belly and soul were hollow.

Light flashed above.

A comet streaked across the sky.

Issari gasped and rose to her feet.

The comet fell, blazed with blue fire, then thinned into a pale white line. It flashed down toward her, and a small stone, no larger than an egg, slammed down at her feet. It lay there, glowing white, a shard of star.

Her right hand closed around Taal's amulet. She reached down and, with her left hand, lifted the comet.

She gasped. It blazed against her skin, and she tried to drop it but could not. The light shone from her hand, silvery starlight, as the shard melted and reformed in her palm, embedding into her.

The light faded to a soft glow. Issari raised her left hand and stared at her palm. The star pulsed there, a twin to the amulet in her right hand.

She looked up at the sky.

"Thank you," she whispered.

She had been blessed by Taal, and now by the Draco stars. One hand connected her to the silver god, to Eteer, to her coastal home, and the other would forever bind her to Requiem. Forever would she be torn between two worlds, forever blessed.

She was no longer frightened. She no longer felt alone.

She returned to her tent. Tanin still slept, and Issari crept back into her bed, and she pulled his arm across her again, and she too slept.

JEID

"Bryn!" he shouted as the tunnel caved in below him. "Bryn!"

He had caught a last look at her eyes, a last flicker of her fire, and then the walls had caved in, burying her. Smoke blasted out. The mountain shifted and shook. Boulders tumbled and the slopes sank down, rearranging themselves, sealing most of the sphinxes in a tomb of stone--along with Bryn.

A handful of sphinxes still flew above the mountain. Jeid torched one and Dorvin took down another. A swarm of dragons flew toward the last few sphinxes, blasted their fire, and the creatures fell.

The battle was over.

Jeid landed on the mountaintop and stared around him. Corpses lay upon the slopes, shattered, ashen, their lights gone. A hundred Vir Requis had entered the mountain; fifty now stood around him.

Fifty beings alone in the world, our kingdom stolen, our friends and family fallen. Jeid lowered his head, smoke rising from his nostrils. They had defeated one group of sphinxes, but hundreds still lived in Requiem.

"Too many gone," he whispered. "Too many--"

"Yeah!" Dorvin shouted, interrupting him. The silver dragon flew above, blasting out fire. "Yeah, you see, sphinxes? You see, demons? That's what happens when you attack Requiem. That's what--"

"Dorvin!" Jeid reached up, caught the silver dragon's tail between his jaws, and yanked him down. "Silence."

Dorvin struggled at first, opened his mouth to say more, then looked around him. He seemed to notice the dead for the first time, then landed and lowered his scaly head. He said no more.

Jeid was about to speak to the crowd, to comfort the grieving, to offer prayer and hope, when dragonfire crackled in the distant sky.

He stared, eyes narrowed, then took flight.

Two dragons were flying through the night, heading toward the mountain. A distant voice carried on the wind.

"Grizzly! Grizzly!"

Jeid flew toward them, laughing, relief sweeping across him.

"Laira!" he cried out, and his eyes stung. "Maev!"

The two dragons, gold and green, flew toward him, laughing and crying. They slammed into him in the sky, wings beating madly, as they laughed and struggled to embrace in dragon forms.

"Land first!" Jeid said, grinning like a boy. "Oh, thank the stars."

They landed on the foothills, shifted into human form, and the two women crashed into his arms. He squeezed them both against him, tears in his eyes, and then a cry rose above, and Dorvin landed and shifted and joined the embrace. They stood together, talking all at once, telling stories of sphinxes, druids, fear, and triumph.

"I was so worried, Maev," Jeid finally said, holding his daughter at arm's length. "If I had lost you, the sky might as well have fallen. I love you, my daughter."

The wrestler stared at him, and her face hardened--chin raised, eyes narrowed, bottom lip thrust out--and she crossed her tattooed arms, the gruff warrior with no emotion in her heart. But as Jeid stared at her, the walls cracked, and her eyes dampened, and she pulled him back into an embrace.

"I love you," his daughter whispered. "I love so much, Papa. I was so scared."

Still holding her, Jeid reached out and clasped Laira's hand. Staring over Maev's shoulder, he looked at his wife. They gazed at each other silently. Her eyes were huge, green pools, and her lips-- those slanted lips in her crooked jaw--rose in a small, knowing smile. He saw her love for him, and her silence spoke more than any words could.

You are my stars, Laira, he thought. *You are my sky. You are the light that guides my flight.*

He did not need to speak those words; she knew and she felt the same, and Jeid swore to never part from her again.

Dawn rose around them, a dawn of some hope, some life. The other Vir Requis joined them, and they flew--perhaps the last dragons in the world--far from the mountains and across the plains. They hunted bison from a roaming herd, and they drank from a river, and they built campfires and tended to their wounds. They huddled together in the wilderness, ragged and famished and hurt, but ready to heal, ready to fight.

"We slew many sphinxes," Jeid said at length as the others gathered around him. "With Bryn's sacrifice, Requiem defeated the beasts who followed us north. But many of the Widejaws, perhaps hundreds, might still be living in Requiem. We survivors, only fifty Vir Requis, might be all that remains of our nation. Now the time has come to decide our path. Do we flee into the distance to find a new home? Or do we fly back to Requiem and fight?"

"Fight!" Dorvin leaped up and swung a bison rib like a sword. "I'm done hiding. We fly to war. Fifty dragons?" He blew out breath, fluttering his lips. "More than enough. We'll slay the lot of them."

Laira rose to her feet too. The young woman, clad in a shaggy fur cloak, stood no taller than Dorvin's shoulders, but she spoke with the authority of a great queen.

"We return to Requiem," Laira said. "Not with dragonfire and claws, but with a gift of meat . . . and a gift of herbs." She reached into her cloak and pulled out a rolled-up ball of vines. "Tillvine. Dragonfire won't save Requiem. These leaves will."

TANIN

When dawn rose, he found her changed.

Tanin woke with her in his arms, but she was a different Issari, more fragile, stronger, paler, colder, warmer. Hurt.

"Issari?" he whispered.

She rose from the bed and stood before him, only a sheet draped across her body. Two lights gleamed upon her hands--her amulet of the south and a new light, brighter, softer, the glow of a star. She had been transfigured, grown mightier overnight, yet her eyes seemed haunted, filled with more pain than he'd ever seen in them. She placed a hand upon her belly and whispered softly, but he could not hear the words.

"Issari, what's wrong?" He rose and stood before her, then gasped to see blood on her sheet. It dripped between her legs.

"We must find more dragons," she whispered.

He touched her cheek. Her skin was burning hot. "Issari! What happened? Your hand . . ."

"Please." She looked away. "Never ask me. Never speak to me of what happened this night. Just . . . be with me."

He pulled her into his arms. "Always. No matter what happened or will happen. No matter how much pain we suffered or will suffer." He held her close and kissed her feverish forehead. "I swear to you. We might still bleed, and we might face wars and horrors, but no matter what the world tosses our way, I'm here with you. I would fight all the demons of the Abyss for you."

She raised her chin. "Then fly with me. Fly now. Fly for our stars--for dragons."

They flew.

They flew over fields and deserts, over mountains and rivers, from city to city. They crossed the vast southern land of Terra, a realm of ancient civilizations, of thirteen city-states crumbling under the nephilim. A city on a mountain, towering and pale. A city in a vale, lush and green. A city upon the water, rivers forming its streets, thick with boats. A desert city of sandstone and caves, its towers tall, its dungeons deep. A city carved into a canyon, its hundred gateways leading to a hundred labyrinths. Cities of soldiers, cities of poets and singers, cities of learning, cities of might. And wherever they flew, they found them--more dragons.

"I raise this nation for you, my stars," Issari would say in the night, lifting her eyes to the Draco constellation.

"For Requiem," Tanin would always add. For his home. For his fallen sister. For a dream of peace.

A thousand dragons of every color flew behind them, covering the sky, a dragon nation risen from the south, a nation of starlight.

As the full moon shone, the thousand mustered in a vale, and they lit many fires, and Tanin and Issari looked north at the distant darkness.

He held her hand. "It's time to go home. It's time to go to Requiem."

She looked at him, her eyes reflecting the firelight. "Not yet. Not before I return to my other home . . . to Eteer. And to my father."

LAIRA

They trudged through the snowy forest, fifty men and women wrapped in fur, seeking the lost halls of Requiem.

Laira looked around her at her fellow Vir Requis, and she barely recognized them. Their heads were all clean-shaven, even the women's, and tribal paints covered their scalps and faces. They all carried sharpened wooden sticks and shields of leather stretched across wooden frames. If not for her constant cursing, Laira would never have recognized Maev; green and black stripes covered the wrestler's bald head and hard face. If not for his wide, lumbering form, Laira doubted she'd even recognize her husband; for the first time in many years, Jeid wore no beard, and his long shaggy hair was also gone. Red and white paint covered him, and without his wild mane, he seemed smaller to Laira, thinner, more fragile. When she looked across the rest of their group, she saw no Vir Requis; she saw a new tribe.

Laira caressed her own shaved head. Where once black hair had grown now coiled lines of black and green paint.

"Do you think it'll work?" she asked Dorvin.

The young man walked at her side, bare-chested even in the cold. He too had shaved his head, and his scalp, torso, and face sported coiling lines in silver and black. He twisted his lips and spat. "It better work. I'm bloody freezing."

"Where's your cloak?" Laira asked. She tightened her own fur pelt; snow clung to it.

Dorvin shivered and stuck his hands under his armpits. "I spent all morning painting my chest. I'm not going to hide the dragon I painted. It's a masterpiece."

Laira glanced at his chest. A melting, dripping figure seemed to have been painted onto him, surrounded by spirals and lightning bolts. "It looks more like a worm."

"It's a dragon." He growled and thumped his chest. "A vicious, fire-breathing, man-eating, killer dra--" He glanced down at his chest and bit his lip. "Stars damn it. It melted. Well, maybe it's a worm." He shook his fist. "Worms are vicious too, you know."

Maev approached them and slapped the back of Dorvin's head. "It was a damn stupid idea to paint a dragon anyway. We don't want the enemy thinking about dragons today. To them we must be the Sharpspear tribe, come to pay tribute." Maev passed her hand over her bald head and sighed. "Though I still don't know why we had to shave our damn heads."

"The illusion must be complete," said Laira. "If they recognize even one of us, it's over." She shuddered. "Hundreds of Widejaws might still live in Requiem, more than enough to slay us all. They must suspect nothing. No more talk of dragons. No more talk of disguises. Become Sharpspears."

They walked on through the snow, the last survivors of Requi-- *No.* Laira shook her head wildly. *The last Sharpspears,* she reminded herself. A few children. Three mothers holding babies. A few haggard men and women, their wounds still bandaged. All bald. All painted. Clad in furs, holding spears, moving onward through the forest, seeking the halls of Requiem.

In the afternoon, Laira finally saw it in the distance, rising from the forest like a beacon--King's Column. Her eyes dampened, and she had to pause from walking. The others gathered around her and stared silently. The pillar was still marks away, so tall it called her even from the horizon, a beam of light rising toward the sky. Even in the day, it seemed to shine with starlight.

"The heart of Requiem," Laira whispered. "The beacon of a nation."

She raised her chin and kept walking, her steps faster now. The others walked silently around her, staring ahead at the column, at their home that had been stolen, the home they must reclaim.

Laira hefted her pack across her back. Within she held the hope of Requiem. She raised her eyes and stared at the sky. The sun shone behind clouds. She could not see the stars, but she prayed to them silently.

Please, stars of Requiem, if you shine behind sunlight and clouds, and if you can hear me, grant me courage today. Grant me the wisdom and strength I need.

She heard no reply, felt no warmth in her heart, only fear in her belly. She tightened her lips and walked on. Perhaps this day she would have to rely on herself alone, on her own strength, not the strength of starlight. Her strength had brought her this far, had carried her through slavery and war; she would need to draw a little bit more.

The sun was low in the sky when, weary and covered with frost, the travelers reached the halls of Requiem.

King's Column rose before them among the trees, and several other columns rose around it, twins to the original pillar. Most of the birches here had burned in the battle; they rose charred and black and barren. The sound of crude songs, curses, and laughter rose from the hall. Smoke plumed skyward from campfires, and the smell of cooking meat--stars, it might be human meat--invaded Laira's nostrils.

"Halt!"

The voice rose from between the burnt trees. A sphinx padded toward them through the snow. Its lion body was large as a dragon's, and its matted wings lay pressed against its flanks. The creature's human face stared down at them, ballooned to thrice the normal size. The jaws opened from ear to ear, revealing rows of sharpened teeth.

Laira raised two open, emptied hands. "Greetings, sphinx of the Widejaw tribe! I am Kelafi of the Sharpspear tribe. Tales of your glory have traveled across the land. We've come to pay tribute to your might, Widejaw, and we bring gifts."

Wings thudded and three more sphinxes dived down, crashed through the forest canopy, and landed in the snow. Large as dragons, the fetid creatures stared at the Sharpspears with narrowed eyes. Laira's heart thrashed. She glanced at her sides. The other Vir Requis--no, only Sharpspears now!--stared back with hard, determined eyes, but Laira saw their nervousness. Jeid's hand strayed near the spear strapped to his back. Dorvin was clenching his fists, and Maev bared her teeth. But none made a move to attack nor shift into dragons. Laira herself struggled to curb the urge to shift, to blow fire, to attack.

We cannot win here with might, she thought. *There are too many enemies. We will win this battle not with dragonfire but with wisdom.*

At her side, Jeid took a step closer. He opened his pack, revealing salted deer flanks. The burly man, unrecognizable without his shaggy beard and hair, spoke in his deep voice. "We bring tribute! Salted deer. Mammoth flanks. Wild boar. The meat is fresh from today, fatty and rich. Our gift to the new masters of Requiem." Jeid's painted face twisted in a show of disgust. "The cruel dragons hunted our tribe down to only fifty souls. We welcome our Widejaw masters!"

The other Vir Requis opened their own packs, revealing their gifts. Laira's pack contained fresh boar flanks, the meat marbled and packed with salt and wild herbs.

And with a special spice, she thought. Her heart hammered. *With a special ingredient these men must eat.*

The sphinxes ahead released their demonic magic, returning to human form. Even as men they were beastly. Each Widejaw stood as tall and wide as Jeid. Ring mail covered their bodies, and swords and spears hung across their backs. Their heads were bald and tattooed, their earlobes stretched with rings, their eyebrows pierced with many pins, but worst of all were their cheeks--slashed open from mouth to ear, revealing all their teeth. More Widejaws approached, and soon dozens stood among the burnt birches, staring at the strangers who had come to pay tribute.

"What are you louts doing over there?" rose a deep cry. "You useless pieces of shite! Who's there? Bring 'em over."

Laira glanced over at Jeid. He stared back, eyes dark.

We will do this, she thought, staring into his eyes, trying to transmit her thoughts into his mind.

He gave her a nearly imperceptible nod. *We will do this.*

The Widejaw soldiers nodded and moved aside, clearing a path between them.

"Go," said the Widejaw who had first spoken to them. "Bring your meat to our king. Kneel before him. Worship him. And we will let you serve us." His eyes flicked toward Laira and lust filled them. "We will take all your gifts."

Suppressing a shudder, Laira walked through the snow between the charred trees and leering Widejaws. For the first time in many days, she stepped into the hall of Requiem.

Once this had been a place of glory and beauty. A dozen columns had risen here, carved of purest marble, white and glittering in both sunlight and starlight. Once marble tiles had spread across the forest floor, polished and reflecting the sky. Once many birches had rustled beyond the columns, and the proud Oak Throne of Requiem had risen with its back to the mountains. The Vir Requis had never completed their palace--they had not yet installed a roof nor living chambers--but what they had built had shone with light and nobility.

The place was now a hive of ruin.

Several of the columns had fallen and lay smashed between the birches and across the tiled floor. The Widejaws had draped bloody fur pelts across one toppled column to dry. One Widejaw stood by another fallen column, pissing against it. Most of the marble tiles were cracked and shattered. Two Widejaws stood over a pit dug right into the palace floor, gutting a boar. Horses stood tethered to the trees, and dogs roamed across the hall, relieving themselves upon the floor without any master to stop them. Campfires burned upon some tiles, staining the marble with soot; human limbs roasted over the flames. The hall of starlight had become a hall of blood and filth.

"Stars damn it--" Dorvin began, but Laira hushed him with a glare. The young man glowered, clenched and unclenched his fists, and bit down on his words.

The Oak Throne of Requiem still rose in the hall, its back to the mountains, but a new man now sat here. He was massively built, large as a wild boar, even larger than Jeid. Tattoos coiled across his head, and cruelty shone in his eyes. His mouth opened wide, stretching open from ear to ear, revealing sharp teeth.

Slyn, Laira knew. Ruler of the Widejaw tribe. She had met him only briefly--the day he had conquered this hall. She prayed that with her bald head and painted face, he would not recognize her.

She glanced at her companions, and she saw the hatred in their eyes. Maev was grinding her teeth, and Dorvin looked ready to race forward and attack. Behind them, the other Vir Requis exchanged dark looks. Only Jeid seemed calm, staring forward with expressionless eyes.

Laira took a step closer to the throne, her feet padding over snow and blood.

"Slyn of Widejaw!" she called out. "I am Kelafi, chieftain of the Sharpspear tribe. I've brought my tribe here to pay tribute to

Widejaw, and to bring you gifts." She knelt. "I kneel before you, Slyn, chieftain of Widejaw."

She knew that if Jeid, Maev, or Dorvin--tall and proud warriors--had claimed to be chieftains, they'd be slaughtered as a threat. But Laira was small and slim, no more threatening than an ant. Perhaps they would allow her to bend the knee.

But Slyn rose to his feet and drew his sword. His face twisted with rage, and his cheeks reddened. Laira's heart pounded. *He knows!* she thought. *He recognizes me! He remembers my crooked mouth, even with my face all painted!*

Slyn took a step closer and snarled. "Chieftain of Widejaw?" He spat on her. "I am no mere chieftain. I am King of Requiem!"

Across the hall, his fellow Widejaws cheered. Men raised bloody hands in triumph. One Widejaw approached King's Column--the only pillar not scratched or cracked--and began to hump the marble.

Dorvin growled and reached for his spear. Jeid had to grab his arm to hold him back.

Her innards swirling with rage, Laira nodded. She bowed her head to Slyn. "King of Requiem! Defeater of dragons!" She upended her pack, spilling the boar flanks onto the floor. "We of Sharpspear suffered under the dragons' yoke. I praise you! I bring you these gifts of gratitude, of tribute. Allow my humble tribe to serve you, oh great king."

Across the hall, the Widejaws drew nearer and sniffed.

"That's good meat," said one man, his face pierced with a hundred bronze rings. "Shame it ain't human, but boar'll fill the belly too." His nostrils flared. "Seasoned and fatty and still leaking blood. Just how I like it."

Another Widejaw approached, wide of belly, and saliva dripped from his enlarged mouth. He reached for the meat, grabbed a piece, and took it back to a campfire. When Slyn did not object, a dozen more Widejaws raced forward to grab their own meat.

Laira turned and nodded toward Jeid and the others. They too upended their packs, spilling out legs of goat, boar ribs, deer hides, mammoth steaks, and plucked geese. The Widejaws howled and hooted, grabbed the rich pieces, and brought them to the campfires.

"Wait!" Slyn howled.

At once the hall fell silent.

Widejaws froze and stared. The only sound came from the crackling fires and the wind among the birches.

Slyn turned toward Laira and leaned down. His eyes narrowed as he scrutinized her. Suspicion and lust for her flesh filled his eyes. He turned toward his men.

"Why should we fill ourselves on the meat of deer and boars?" he called out. "We have here dozens of nice, juicy men and women to feast upon." He drew his bronze *apa* sword. "Why don't we carve up this sorry lot for our meal?"

Maev growled, took a step forward, and raised her fist. Jeid had to grab her and tug her back. Dorvin cursed under his breath. Luckily, the Widejaws were focusing on Laira and did not seem to notice.

Laira stared into Slyn's eyes. The man was thrice her size, and his hands could easily snap her bones, but she refused to break the stare.

"Dead, we are a single meal to you. Alive, we can hunt for you. Gather berries for you. Serve you in any way you please." She allowed the edge of her cloak to fall off her shoulder. "We are not your enemies, King Slyn. We are not your meals. We will be your servants, catering to your every desire--for flesh to eat, and for flesh to claim." She took a step closer to him and placed a hand on his chest. "You slew the dragons, our tormentors. We ask only that you let us serve."

His eyes flicked down to her bare shoulders. She let the cloak fall further, revealing the top of her breasts.

I tempted Zerra this way, she thought, *and I got what I wanted from him. I'm too weak to defeat these men with swords or spears, but I can deceive them. I can turn their need to conquer, their lust for blood and for body, against them.* She gave Slyn a deep stare, letting him imagine all that she offered.

The brute licked his lips and turned back toward his men. "Roast us a feast!"

The Widejaws cheered and returned to their fires, tending to the meat. The scents of the meal filled the air: the fresh meat, the dripping fat, the spices, and the secret herb Laira had added.

The smell of tillvine. Her heart quickened. *The smell of our victory.*

She thought back to her captivity by the Cured Druids. She remembered watching the poor Vir Requis man swallow the tillvine juice, writhe and scream, and how his dragon magic had risen from him in strands of starlight. The memory still chilled her. But she also remembered feeding the tillvine to the Widejaw she had captured in the valley, watching him thrash, watching his own foul magic leave in a cloud of demon-infested smoke. Now the tillvine filled the meat. Now she would watch hundreds of Widejaws scream in agony as their magic tore from their bodies.

The Vir Requis crowded together in the center of the hall. All around them, the meat roasted and the Widejaws laughed, sang, and drank from wineskins. Slyn returned to his throne and stared at his domain, his eyes never straying far from Laira.

Laira inched closer to Jeid and glanced at him. He looked back, expressionless, but she saw the fear and hope in his eyes.

"The meat is cooked, my king!" said one Widejaw. He rushed toward the throne with a slab of roast boar. "Eat first, King Slyn, as is your right."

The meat steamed and its delicious aroma wafted, mixed with the tangy hint of tillvine. Laira could see green flecks of the crushed leaves on the meat.

Sitting on his throne, Slyn snatched the meat. The Widejaws all stared, drooling and sniffing, awaiting their own turn to feast. But Slyn would not eat. He held the hot slab, sniffed once, and stared over the steaming meal at Laira. His eyes narrowed.

Eat, Laira thought, staring up at him. *Please, stars, let him eat.* He simply stared, not taking a bite.

Laira wanted to scream. There he was--the man who had slain so many Vir Requis, who had stolen their throne, who had defiled their hall. There was Slyn, a servant of Raem, the destroyer of Requiem, so close to losing his power . . . and he would not eat. He only stared. Laira's innards shook with hatred for the man, with a desire to shift, to blow her fire, to see his body burn.

"Eat, my king!" she said, struggling to keep her voice calm. It seemed that none of the Vir Requis behind her so much as dared to breathe. "Enjoy our gift."

The meat steamed in his hand, flecked with tillvine. He lowered the slab.

"I smell a strange smell," Slyn said. "This meat is strangely spiced."

Laira nodded. "We've dusted the meat with herbs, my king, giving it a delicious flavor you will enjoy."

Please eat, she thought. *Please, stars, let them all eat.*

"I'm hungry!" shouted a Widejaw from across the hall. "Let us feast."

But Slyn only stared at Laira. He rose again from his throne, walked toward her, and held out the steaming meat.

"Take a bite," he said to Laira. "The great kings in the south have slaves taste their meals, testing them for poison. Eat, chieftain of Sharpspear. Take a big bite."

She stared at the meat, hesitating.

What do I do?

She felt everyone stare at her--the Widejaws around her and the Vir Requis behind her. They all waited.

"Eat." Slyn's voice dropped, turning dangerous. He reached for his sword. "Is there a reason why you're not taking a bite?" He gripped her arm, his fingers digging into her. "Do you bring bad meat into my hall?"

Laira trembled. She looked over her shoulder at the other Vir Requis. Jeid took a step closer and shook his head.

No, his eyes told her. *No. Don't.*

Behind Jeid, Dorvin and Maev glanced at each other, then back at Laira. They placed their index fingers against their thighs, pointing downward, a predetermined symbol.

We fly as dragons, they were telling her. *We attack.*

She shook her head. "No," she whispered to them. She looked back at Slyn. "It is your right, my king, to eat first. Who am I to steal that right?"

Slyn's nostrils flared as the scent of poisoned meat filled them. "Eat now or we will feast upon your flesh instead." Slyn licked his massive chops. He twisted her arm painfully, nearly dislocating it. "I will enjoy crunching your bones between my teeth."

Laira closed her eyes.

In her mind, she was a child again, a mere girl of only several years, flying with her mother through the night. She was a young woman fleeing her tribe, flying through the open sky, no longer a beaten wretch but a proud dragon. She was flying with her husband, a queen of many other dragons, a queen of Requiem. She was free. She was strong. The wind flowed across her, and her stars shone above, and her fire lit the darkness.

How would she live without the magic of dragons? How would she go on, powerless, lacking the one gift that had always given her strength?

Jeid stepped closer. He placed a hand on her shoulder, prepared to pull her back, to shift, to attack, to die. And Laira knew that he would die this day. They were fifty Vir Requis, and five hundred Widejaws stood here, each capable of becoming a sphinx.

A tear streamed down Laira's cheek.

If I cling to my stars, I'll lose my husband. Like I lost my mother, my brother, maybe my sister. She looked at Jeid through a veil of tears.

She loved her magic. But she loved Jeid more.

"I love you," she whispered . . . and took a bite.

Jeid stared, eyes wide. His hands dropped to his sides and he took a step back. But within an instant, the King of Requiem steeled himself and turned back toward Slyn, his clenched fists his only sign of distress.

Laira stared ahead, chewing, maintaining eye contact with Slyn. He stared at her greedily. Saliva dripped down his chin. Laira swallowed her bite and pushed the meat back toward him.

He stared at her, eyes narrowed, perhaps waiting for her to collapse.

She stared back. She felt nothing. She felt hollow. She felt dead.

Slowly, Slyn's face split into a grin. He bit deeply into the meat.

Across the shattered halls of Requiem, five hundred Widejaws roared with approval and began to feast. Teeth sank into the meat. Bones crunched. Gravy dripped down chins.

Laira lowered her head.

Maev stepped closer and grabbed Laira. She leaned down, scrutinizing her. "Laira," she whispered. "Laira, are you . . .?"

As the Widejaws feasted, Dorvin and Jeid stepped close too, staring at her, talking to her, but she couldn't see them, couldn't hear them. The world blurred. All was starlight, silvery and cold and beautiful, flowing around her. All sounds faded into a hum, a song of dragons.

"It's beautiful," she whispered. She wept. "I can see the stars."

She realized that she was lying down, that Jeid was holding her, calling to her. She realized that the Widejaws had fallen around her, that they were writhing, kicking, screaming, that smoke rose from them. The strands of starlight thickened around her, flowing upward, taking the forms of many dragons of silver and white, and Laira smiled.

"Requiem," she whispered. "May our wings forever find your sky."

Her head tilted back, and she looked up and tried to find that sky, but she could see nothing but smoke and silvery strands, and she knew that the sky was lost to her forever.

JEID

All across the hall of Requiem, Widejaws thrashed and screamed as smoke rose from them. The miasma flowed on the wind, thick with countless buzzing demons the size of maggots. The foul magic of the Abyss was leaving the Widejaws, but Jeid barely spared them a glance.

"Laira!" he cried, holding her small frame. "Laira, can you hear me?"

The strands of starlight rose from her, coalescing into the form of a great, glowing dragon with gleaming eyes. The astral figure seemed to stare at Jeid, to smile sadly, to weep tears like diamonds . . . and then the dragon ascended in many strands, streaming skyward until it vanished.

Laira fell limp in his arms.

"Laira!" He touched her cheek. "Laira, can you hear?"

She lay still.

Jeid shook her. "Wake up, Laira. Wake up." He shook her. "Laira!"

Dorvin, Maev, and the other Vir Requis crowded near, silent and staring.

"Laira?" Dorvin whispered.

She felt so light in Jeid's arms. Her head, bald and painted, hung limply on her neck.

"I can't lose you, Laira," Jeid whispered. "Wake up. I can't lose you too. I--"

Her eyes fluttered open, and she coughed and gasped for air. She blinked and tears streamed down her painted cheeks.

"It's gone," she whispered to Jeid. She squeezed his hand and stared up. "The sky. The call of the stars. Gone." She looked at him, and horror filled her eyes. "I'm no longer Vir Requis."

Jeid's eyes stung, and he pulled her close against him. "You are alive. You are Laira. You are my wife. That's what matters. You are--"

". . . a filthy weredragon." The voice rose from behind. "You all are. Maggoty, disgusting weredragons."

Kneeling over Laira, Jeid slowly turned his head around.

Most of the Widejaws still twitched on the floor, the last blasts of unholy smoke leaving them. But Slyn still stood, glaring down at Jeid. The towering, burly man stepped closer, his ring mail chinking, and spat out a chunk of uneaten meat.

Jeid snarled and shifted into a dragon.

With a roar, Slyn leaped into the air and became a sphinx.

The two beasts--one scaled, one furred--slammed together with snapping teeth and slashing claws.

Hundreds of Widejaws still lay across the hall, their magic lost. But dozens more emerged from between the trees--those who had not yet eaten--and rose into the sky as sphinxes, blasting out their miasma.

Dorvin and Maev roared and soared as dragons. An instant later, the rest of Requiem rose into the sky, blowing fire and crying out for their kingdom. Dragons and sphinxes crashed together.

Jeid beat his wings, shoving against Slyn. The sphinx's jaws snapped open and closed, tearing at Jeid's scales, ripping through flesh. The creature's claws dug into the dragon's flanks.

"I will feed upon the girl," Slyn hissed, blood on his teeth, and laughed. "Limb by limb, as I keep her alive, as she screams, as she begs me. I will force her to eat her own flesh."

His body shaking with laughter, Slyn blasted out his smoke.

Jeid roared and blew his flames.

Demon smoke and dragonfire washed across them.

The flames burned Jeid. The stench of Slyn's burning fur filled his nostrils. Tiny demons filled the smoke blasting from Slyn's mouth. Most of the creatures roasted in the dragonfire, screaming as they died, but a few invaded Jeid's mouth and ran down his throat. He felt them clawing inside him, moving through his gut, cutting him from within.

He roared and swiped his claws, knocking off the burning sphinx. Slyn crashed down, a ball of fire.

Jeid tried to fly, to rise higher, but pain filled his gut, and the tiny demons swarmed with him. He fell and hit the marble tiles, nearly losing his dragon magic. He leaned over and gagged, vomiting up fire and a stream of the small demons. Vaguely, he was aware of the others fighting around him. Maev flew overhead, roaring fire against sphinxes, while Dorvin raced between columns, a silver dragon lashing his claws against more of the creatures.

Where was Laira? Jeid struggled to his feet and looked from side to side, seeking her.

"Laira!" he called out. "Lai--"

Still ablaze, Slyn beat his flaming wings and crashed into Jeid.

The feathers had burned off the sphinx's wings, leaving dark membranes stretched over bones. The fur across Slyn's lion body still smoldered, falling off to reveal raw, red skin. Worst of all was Slyn's face. When shifting into a sphinx, it had bloated to three times its size. In the dragonfire, it had burst like a boil under a needle. Shreds of flesh hung loosely, revealing a skull rustling with worms. One eye was gone, burned away. Little more than the jaw remained, open wide, laughing, snapping its teeth. Those teeth closed around Jeid's neck.

The two beasts slammed against the floor, cracking tiles beneath them. Slyn dug his teeth deep, laughing even with his face burned away.

"I am the king!" the burning sphinx shrieked. "I will vanquish all. I am Lord of Requiem!" He tugged his head back with a spurt of blood, tearing a scale off Jeid's neck.

Jeid struggled to rise. His head spun. He managed to shove himself up, but Slyn's claws lashed out, cutting into Jeid's snout, knocking him back down.

"Dragonfire cannot hurt me!" the creature shouted as it burned. "The power of demons fills me!" A chunk of his face fell off like fat from a cooking roast. It slapped against the floor, but still Slyn laughed. "The power of my lord Raem will forever give me the strength to slay dragons. To--"

Slyn gasped.

The spear burst through his throat, emerging bloody and jagged.

Laira snarled as she twisted the wood, splintering it inside the sphinx's neck. The young woman stood in human form, her magic gone, but with the spear in her hands, with her bared teeth, she looked as fierce as any dragon.

"Raem is my father." She snapped the spear inside Slyn's neck. "And his darkness will vanish before the light of Requiem."

Slyn screamed, spraying blood from his mouth. The creature beat his crumbling wings, rising higher. His body was burnt, his face crumbled, his neck spurted blood, but still he rose, still he laughed, and his screech tore across Requiem.

"You will all bow before me! I am Slyn of Widejaw! I am King of Requiem!"

As all around dragons and sphinxes battled, the mutilated Slyn blasted out his demonic smoke.

Jeid blew his dragonfire. The stream crashed through the smoke and showered against Slyn. Roaring, Jeid beat his wings, rammed into the burning sphinx, and slammed the creature against King's Column. The forest seemed to shake. Light blazed out.

"Now die against the marble you desecrated." Jeid growled, leaned in, and bit through Slyn's neck. He tugged his head back, spat out flesh, and watched Slyn's severed head slam down against the tiles. The burning body followed with a thump.

Jeid landed back on the tiles, panting, and looked around him. Dorvin and Maev blasted out dragonfire, slew the last two sphinxes, then landed too. Hundreds of Widejaw corpses lay across the hall and forest, torn apart and burnt. Among them lay a dozen Vir Requis bodies.

The survivors stood, their scales covered in soot and blood. Among them stood one woman, bald and painted, small and frail, her magic lost.

Jeid released his own magic and ran toward her.

"Laira."

He pulled her into his arms, and she laid her head against his chest, and he held her for a long time as ash rained.

LAIRA

She walked alone through the snowy forest, and though she knew every birch here, and though the columns of her home rose behind her, Laira felt lost.

Ice coated the naked branches of the trees, and snow piled upon them; every tree was a three-layered painting of brown wood, silvery ice, and white snow, the tricolor strands spreading across the blue sky like cobwebs. The snow lay glittering in blankets, rising halfway to her knees, a field of stars marred only by the footprints of scurrying coyotes whom Laira only glimpsed from a distance, their eyes shining between trees. The sounds of Requiem still rose behind her: the flapping of dragon wings, the song of survivors, the music of a harp. Laira kept walking, moving away from the warmth and song of her hall.

For Requiem is no longer my home. She placed a hand against her chest. *My heart was ripped from me. My magic is gone.* She paused and closed her eyes, too overcome with pain to continue. *I am no longer Vir Requis.*

Since eating the tillvine, a hollowness had filled Laira. It felt as if an unseen force had ripped out her innards, leaving nothing behind her ribs, only an empty cavern. All her life, Laira had suffered. She had fled the cruelty of her father in Eteer. She had suffered the fists of Zerra, cruel chieftain of Goldtusk. She had fought demons and watched those she loved die in fire. And throughout all her nightmares, she had clung to a dream of beauty, to a pillar of light within her, a twin to King's Column--to her magic. The magic of dragons.

"And now that magic is gone." She raised her chin, tightened her lips, and tasted her tears. "And so I will leave."

She took another step, her tears freezing on her cheeks. She turned around only once and gazed across the forest. The pillars of Requiem rose there, dwarfing the trees, white columns against a blue sky.

"Requiem," Laira whispered. "I leave your sky."

And my story ends here, she thought. *After all my heartache, all the blood I spilled, all those I loved and hated . . . I am again alone.*

She turned around. She took another step.

Farewell, Requiem.

"Laira."

The voice rose behind her, soft and deep. She turned around again and she saw him there. Jeid emerged from behind snowy birches, walking toward her. He wore thick bear pelts, and his hair and beard were growing back, still short, snow clinging to them.

"Why have you come here?" Laira said, voice hoarse. "Don't try to convince me to return. Don't even say goodbye, because parting from you will shatter what remains of my soul. Let me leave."

But he stepped closer to her, trudging through the snow. "I won't let you leave."

Her eyes stung with fresh tears. Her body shook. Her voice was barely a whisper. "I am broken."

She tried to keep walking, to escape him, but his stride was longer than hers, and he caught her, and he pulled her into his arms.

"Laira, where would you go?"

She tried to free herself from his embrace, but she felt too weak--too weak physically, too weak emotionally. "I don't know. Away. I'll travel north as far as I can go, into new exile."

His eyes softened. "You saved Requiem. And now you would leave it?"

She touched his cheek. "Jeid, don't you understand? All my life I searched for a home, for a place to belong. When I found Requiem, I found that home. I found kindred souls. And for the past year, I fought for Requiem with every fiber of my body, every drop of my blood, every horror that still claws inside my skull. The nightmares of the Abyss and the beauty of Requiem's columns will never leave me. Yes, I saved Requiem. I saved her for you. For Dorvin. For Maev. For Issari and Tanin. For every lost weredragon who is afraid, who is alone, who seeks a home. Requiem is saved. But not for me." She trembled. "My magic is gone, and I feel so hollow, so cold, but I gave the others a home. That will comfort me in my exile."

"Laira," Jeid said slowly, "when I first met you, I found a strong, wise woman. And for this year of war, I learned that your wisdom is greater than any I've known. But right now, you are speaking like a fool. By the stars, Laira. You're still Vir Requis."

"Even without the magic? Even without being able to shift into a dragon?" She snorted, tears in her eyes. "I'll never fly again, Jeid. I'll never feel the wind around me. I'll never see the forest from above. I'll never find our sky."

Jeid laughed softly. "Of course you will."

He took a step back and shifted.

The copper dragon stood in the snow, staring at Laira, the largest dragon in Requiem, his scales frosted, his eyes deep brown. Wordlessly, he lowered his wing, forming a ramp. He nodded.

Laira sniffed. She wanted to run. She wanted to forget him. But she found herself climbing his wing and straddling his back. Jeid kicked off, scattering snow, and beat his wings. Branches cracked and rained snow around them. With a few massive strokes, bending the trees and blowing back snow, Jeid cleared the treetops. He soared higher, caught a wind current, and glided.

Laira sat on the dragon's back, clinging on. The wind streamed across her, cold and fresh. The forests rolled below them, an endless painting all in white and silver, and Laira laughed and wept, for it was beautiful, and she was happy, and she was at peace.

"You will always fly, Laira," the dragon said. "We will always fly together. We will always find the sky."

The dragon turned in the sky, and they glided over the columns of Requiem. The grand hall seemed so small from up here, a mere toy, as if Laira could reach down and pluck the columns like a child lifting sticks. From up here, the palace seemed small but the sky was endless, blue, cold, and beautiful. Other dragons rose from below, and they all flew around her.

"Queen Laira!" they called. "May the stars bless our queen."

The wind blew her tears away, and Laira's voice rose in song. "As the leaves fall upon our marble tiles, as the breeze rustles the birches beyond our columns, as the sun gilds the mountains above our halls--know, young child of the woods, you are home, you are home." The others joined her song, and Requiem's prayer rose from many throats. "Requiem! May our wings forever find your sky."

She would always find this sky, she knew. And Requiem would always be her home.

JEID

Snow coated the graves of war, and new light and life filled the hall of Requiem, by the time the young blue dragon returned.

Fin glided on the wind, a small dragon with three normal legs and one leg shrunken. Jeid sat on the Oak Throne, staring up. The azure dragon circled the hall once, then glided down. Three of his feet clattered against the marble tiles; the fourth foot hung loosely, no larger than an apple. Smoke plumed from the dragon's nostrils, and he shifted back into human form, becoming a boy clad in rags, his left arm only several inches long. Face tanned and eyes wide, Fin stepped closer and knelt before Jeid.

"King Aeternum!" he said. "I bring news of Issari and Tanin."

Jeid rose from his throne so fast his head spun. His heart burst into a gallop. Laira, who stood by his side, rushed with him toward the boy.

"Tell me everything you know," Jeid said. "Where are they? Are they well? Are they--"

But Fin's eyes rolled back and he swayed. Jeid had to catch the poor boy before he collapsed.

I told the damn boy not to fly for days straight, Jeid thought as he cried out for food and water.

Fin lay on the floor, mumbling, only half-awake. Vir Requis rushed forth with a meal: wild berries, mushrooms, venison, and water infused with sweet leaves. The scrawny boy nibbled the food at first, gained some strength, then bolted down the rest. He spoke between mouthfuls.

The Vir Requis crowded around the boy, and for a long time, they listened. Whenever Dorvin interrupted with a question, Jeid cuffed the young man's nape, silencing him, and Fin spoke on. The boy spoke of Issari and Tanin traveling across the southern realms from city to city, gathering an army. He spoke of nephilim--the winged children of demons and mortal women--infesting the south and mustering for war. He spoke of Raem descending into the pit of darkness, of naming himself King of the Abyss, of wedding Angel in the shadows.

"Thousands of nephilim still fly in the south," Fin said, stuffing more mulberries into his mouth. "And real demons too! I saw some while flying north. Nasty creatures. They're all flowing out of Eteer. There's a gaping hole where the palace was, a pit leading right down into the Abyss. I flew over it." He shuddered. "And I looked down and . . . the Abyss seemed to look into me. Like a great black eye." His skin paled and he clutched Jeid's hand. "My king, she's going to fight him. Issari. She told me! She and Tanin and all the other dragons--they're going to fly right into that pit. Right into the Abyss. Issari said that's the only way to stop Raem." He wrapped his arms around Jeid and clung to him. "I told her not to. I told her it's too dangerous. But she won't listen. I had to come tell you so that maybe you can stop them." The boy's eyes gleamed with tears. "You can't let them fly into the Abyss. It would kill them."

The boy closed his eyes and fell silent, his cheek pressed against Jeid's chest.

Everyone else started talking at once.

"I'll fly into the Abyss right away!" Dorvin shouted and punched the air. "I'll slay a thousand demons while Tanin and Issari are wetting themselves with fear."

"Dorvin, you go fly into a gopher hole; that's more at your level." Maev flexed her muscles. "And Tanin wouldn't even be able to face gophers. I'll fly there to save my lump of a brother. We burn demons!"

Laira, meanwhile, was urging calm. The young queen leaped onto the throne and cried out, "Silence, everyone! This is foolishness. We must seal the Abyss, not fly into it. That's flying into a trap. We must travel south and stop Issari."

Other Vir Requis spoke too. Some called for an end to war. Others demanded vengeance against Raem. A few spoke of digging new tunnels and spending their lives hidden away from the evils in the world.

Throughout it all, Jeid remained silent, listening.

Finally all eyes turned toward him, and the Vir Requis fell silent--souls weary from war, thin, clad in only ragged furs, the seedlings of a kingdom.

Jeid spoke to them, his voice slow and deep. "For many years I thought that my family was alone--the only weredragons in the world, cursed, outcast souls. For many years I sought others--others with the same curse, others to stand proud and strong, to unite, to forge a kingdom. And we found others; others here in the north, and now others muster in the south across the sea. Now we call ourselves Vir Requis, and we call our magic a gift, not a curse. And we stand within the hall of a kingdom named Requiem, and we are proud. But we're not yet strong. Not while Raem, King of the Abyss, still lives."

Some Vir Requis stared with dark eyes. Others cried out in approval, fists rising.

Jeid continued speaking. "It was Raem who sent the Goldtusk tribe to attack our old home in the escarpment. It was Raem who drove us to Two Skull Mountain and slew many of us upon the slope. It was Raem who sent the Widejaw tribe to shatter our columns. So long as Raem lives, we will never have peace in Requiem. So long as Raem lives, he will hunt us. We can no longer hide from him, no longer sit and wait for him to attack again." Jeid raised his chin. "We must join the southern dragons, and we must fly into the Abyss, and we must slay its lord."

A few Vir Requis stared at one another fearfully. But most stared back at Jeid, shoulders squared, eyes proud.

"We fight," Dorvin said. He stepped forward and stood at Jeid's side. "I will always fly with you, my king."

Maev nodded, eyes stern. Her dragon tattoos danced as she clenched her fists. "We fight." She came to stand at Jeid's other side. "I will always fight for Requiem."

Laira joined them--smaller, shorter, her magic gone--but she stood proudly, head held high. She spoke in only a whisper, but her voice carried the gravity of a great battle cry. "I've been fleeing my father my whole life. If you would let me ride upon you, King Aeternum, I would fly with you into the very pit of the Abyss, and I would face my father again. And I would tell him: My magic is gone, but forever I am a daughter of Requiem, and I will not let you defile her hall again."

The others stepped forward one by one--a few dozen people, all that remained of their kingdom.

But we're not alone, Jeid thought as they gathered around him. He turned his head and stared south between the trees. *My son lives. Issari lives. And they found others, a great nation of dragons in the south. We will fly together.*

208

RAEM

The craving filled him, overwhelming, maddening, tearing at his insides. He was a starving man. Dying of desire. The curse clawed inside him, begging for release.

The curse of dragons.

He gripped the arms of his throne--the wriggling, wet throne of the Abyss, a towering seat woven of thousands of living tongues. His fingers dug into the fleshy, wet armrests.

"Bring me another!" Raem shouted. "Another!"

Demons filled his hall. They clattered across the floor. They clung to the great ribs forming the chamber walls. They hung from the ceiling, dangling sacks of blood. Some creatures were furred, others scaled, some skinless. Some towered in the hall, globs of ooze, bony creatures with horned heads, living trees with branches of fingers. Other demons were small, scuttling underfoot, leaving trails of pus and slime. Some played musical instruments made from bones. Others babbled unintelligibly. A few rutted in puddles, screaming out in their lust. Some fed upon blood and bones, while others fought, tearing one another apart, and feasting upon severed limbs.

"Another!" Raem shouted from his throne.

The demons scurried aside, forming a path between them across the hall, leading from the throne to the tunnel that led into the hall. Two gray, pot-bellied demons framed the entrance. They began to beat drums made from human skin, and across the hall, demons joined the chant, thumping their feet and chests. Eyes lit up in the tunnel, and a demon clattered into the hall, a great isopod the size of a bull. Many tentacles and claws grew from its mouth, the tendrils wrapped around a struggling young man.

Daniel Arenson

"Bring him here!" Raem cried, delight filling him. Good. Good! This would quell the desire.

The isopod clattered forward on its many legs, snorted, and dumped down its captive. The man struggled to rise, only to fall again. Blood dripped from many wounds across him. He was a man of Eteer, perhaps a fisherman, perhaps a farmer, one of the few souls who had stayed in the ravaged city.

Raem stepped toward the wounded wretch.

"Please, my king." The man bowed before Raem. "Please, great lord. Spare my life."

Raem's blood boiled. He stretched out his tentacle--his new left arm--and lifted the man's chin. "Look me in the eyes, my son." His voice was soft, barely containing his glee. "Keep looking into my eyes."

The man stared up, trembling, his eyes rimmed with red. With a sudden jerk, Raem thrust out his right arm--his lobster claw--and grabbed the man's neck.

Just as he squeezed the claw shut, severing the head, the man looked away.

Demons cheered.

"Gods damn it!" Raem shouted and kicked the head aside with his hoof. "Why did the fool disobey?"

As demons leaped onto the body and began to feed, Raem stomped away, moving on his hoof and talon. It was worthless this way. Why even bother to kill a man if he looked away? Killing was the most intimate connection one could make with another living soul. To gaze into the eyes of a man or woman, to take their life as they stared into you, as you stared into them, as you formed a bond just as the life slipped away . . . it was perhaps the only emotion that could quell the fire inside him, the need for the dragon magic.

"Fetch me another one!" Raem shouted, blood on his claw. "Another human!"

The demons bowed before him, quivering. One dared approach, a bloated red thing like a living boil with legs. "But my lord!" The creature bowed. "There are no more humans. All have fled. They hide in holes, or they hide in the desert, or they fled to find your daughter, the Priestess Issari, or--"

"You will not mention my daughter here!" Raem roared, swiped his claw, and tore into the demon. Blood spurted and entrails spilled. As the hall erupted with screams, Raem looked toward the others. "Fetch me another human to kill. Dig through the ruins of Eteer and find me a coward who hides. Trawl the coast for fishermen. Comb the desert for exiles. Whoever fetches me a mortal will feed upon his heart!"

The demons clawed over one another in their race toward the tunnel. Several dozen blasted out from the hall, traveling the darkness toward the great crack in the earth, the crack leading up into Eteer, his fallen kingdom.

Eteer was a ruin now, of course. A cesspool. A broken toy. Raem gazed around him as his hall. *Now I am king of a greater realm. Of a--*

The craving flared inside him so powerfully he nearly doubled over. The damn disease was growing stronger. It had been moons since Raem had shifted into a dragon. Back in Eteer, he would travel into the cisterns, he would shift in the shadows, would release the tension. But here in the Abyss there was no privacy, and the magic ached for release.

He stormed out of his hall, walked down a corridor carved into the living stone, and entered the nursery. Veined membranes coated the walls like tapestries, quivering and pumping with blood. A dozen of Raem's children sat here, curled up, sucking from fleshy tubes that ran from the walls to their mouths. The nephilim's throats bobbed as they drank, and the red light gleamed upon their warty skin, long jaws, and gleaming green eyes.

My children, Raem thought, looking at the half-demons. *My legacy.*

Among them lay Angel, Queen of the Abyss, and she held a nephil to her bosom, nursing the rotting creature. Raem marched toward her, tore the nephil off her breast, and tossed the child aside.

Angel sneered at him and snapped her teeth. Smoke rose from her nostrils. Since feeding upon human flesh in Eteer, she had grown to monstrous size, a woman twenty feet tall, her wings wide as sails. Lava leaked from cracks in her stone body.

"We make more," Raem said. He gripped her arms. "Now."

She growled. "I am feeding your children now, my husband. I--"

He didn't let her finish her sentence. He grabbed her with his tentacle, and he shoved her onto her back, and he mated with her here in the nursery as their children squealed around them. He screamed as he released himself into her, seeking relief from his magic, from the pain inside him, the pain of betrayal, of his children flying against him, of the disease that would not leave him, of Requiem that still stood in the north. He screamed and Angel howled and the overflowing desire nearly blinded Raem. Yet when he was spent, and his seed was planted, he found the curse still aching.

I need to shift. I need to become a dragon. I need to fly.

He shoved Angel away and left the chamber.

He walked through the Abyss, traveling through tunnels where skinned creatures screamed on the walls, hanging from meat hooks, where mountains of quivering bodies rose from chasms, where great birds dug their beaks into screaming meals, where all the nightmares of existence twisted and screeched and worshiped him. He was King of the Underworld, but he would have no peace--no peace while the dragon clawed inside him.

"I will find no peace," he said into the darkness, "while dragons live."

He stepped down a tunnel and entered a great chasm, a hall larger than all of Eteer. His new army mustered here, thousands of humanoid insects with hard shells like armor, with red eyes, with serrated claws, with venom that dripped from coiling tongues. An army to crawl over the world, to crush every city, to slay every living being.

"You will destroy all life!" he cried. "You will turn the world aboveground into more of the Abyss!"

They roared with approval, their cries echoing, and Raem gnashed his teeth so powerfully they cracked. Soon all dragons would die. Soon even the starlight would vanish from the sky. And then, finally, he would find peace, an end to the eternal torture that coiled inside him like a parasite.

ISSARI

The dragons of the south flew.

A thousand beasts of scales, claws, fangs, and fire, they dived across the sky. Their tails streamed like banners. Their wings stretched wide. Metallic dragons of silver, gold, copper, bronze. Colorful dragons with scales of green, blue, red, lavender. Small dragons, barely more than children. Old beasts, their fangs long fallen, their wings perforated with holes. All flew this day. The dragons had risen from the city-states of the south--from the ruins of Eteer, from the inferno at Goshar, from the devastation of Tur Kal, from the civilizations that sprawled between sea and desert. For years, they had hidden, ashamed, the outcasts of thirteen cities. Now they flew united. Now they were no longer afraid; they were dragons of Requiem.

Issari and Tanin flew at their lead: a slim white dragon, her horns small and her eyes green, and a long red dragon, his eyes dark, a hole in his wing. A Princess of Eteer and a Prince of Requiem. A southern woman and a northern wanderer. White and red fire. Twin rulers of a motley nation. Behind them flew the multitude, the greatest flight of dragons the world had seen.

Below stretched the open plains of wild grass. The shadows of the thousand dragons raced across the land like a herd of astral bison. They flew over the city of Tur Kal where scaffolding covered walls and towers, where workers bustled to rebuild after the nephil attack. They flew across hills, valleys, a river, and fallow fields until they reached the mountains. There they flew over Goshar, a ruined city nestled in the mountain range, guardian of the northern desert--the place of Issari and Tanin's captivity, now a place of dust and fallen bricks. They flew over the desert, the lifeless realm where once they had wandered, hungry and afraid, leading the Eteerian exodus. They flew without rest until finally, in the sunset, they saw it ahead.

"A shadow upon the land," Issari whispered. "A stain of evil." She shuddered, feeling that evil emanate from the darkness ahead like strands of nightmares rising from one's deepest fears at night. "A pit of terror."

Flying at her side, Tanin grunted and flexed his claws. "The ruins of Eteer."

Once a proud city had stood here, an oasis of civilization. Over the past hundred years, the humble seaside tribe of Eteer had risen to a great nation. Thousands of homes had sprawled along cobbled streets, gardens flowering upon their roofs. A canal had driven into the city, thick with ships from distant lands bringing in fabrics, sweet wines, exotic fruit, and toys of wood and clay. A palace had risen upon the hill, home to Issari, its blue columns capped with gold, its hanging gardens a marvel whose beauty spread in tales across the world. This had been a place of splendor, of learning, of culture--the first civilization to develop writing in clay, to build boats, to map the lands north of the sea.

Eteer--Jewel of the Coast. Fair Daughter of Taal. Kingdom of Light.

Today Eteer was a stain of ruin and shadow.

Little more than the walls surrounding the city remained standing, and even they were cracked and punched full of holes. Within this crumbling shell lay ruin. The houses had fallen. The gardens had burned. The temple to Taal had collapsed, as had the fortress of the city garrison. No more ships sailed in the canal; great boulders and piles of bricks filled the water now, rising like cairns.

Issari lowered her head. *My home.*

But the city was not lifeless. Nephilim still lived here. The half-mortals nested like hives of disease upon ruined flesh. They had raised huts of leather, bone, and the rotting flesh of their human victims. They dug through piles of bricks and peered from hovels. They danced upon the crumbled walls and they rutted on the beach north of the city. The city was still distant, but even from across the marks, the stench hit Issari's nostrils.

Her belly cramped and her eyes stung. *Is my son among them? Is the child I birthed one of the city's new denizens?*

Her throat constricted and her belly twisted as she remembered that night, remembered the creature leaving her womb, fleeing her, darting off into the night, an aborted child who needed her, whom she had betrayed. A monster. Her son. Issari did not know anything about his father, the deceiver who had visited her in her tent, but if she found his son here, would she be able to burn him?

She focused her attention back toward her task. She pointed.

"Do you see the hole upon the hill?" she said to Tanin. "That's where the palace once stood. That is the crack of the Abyss. Through that hole is where we'll find him."

Little of the palace remained, only the broken stems of a few columns; they rose like shattered teeth from the hill. The walls, the roof, the balcony where Issari had stood so often--all had fallen and lay strewn across the hillside. The memories of her home stung her, more powerful than the jabs of arrows.

Only a couple of years ago, she had stood upon her balcony in this palace, and she had gazed upon the sea, and she had imagined adventures in distant lands. She had been only a child then, a soft youth clad in cotton, a golden headdress resting upon her hair. Innocent. A child who dreamed of heroes and legends, who had never heard of the evil of the world.

My own adventure showed me this evil, she thought. *And the distant lands I found were full of more terrors than heroes and legends.*

She returned now to Eteer, but she was not the same child. She had grown into a woman, hardened, emptied, something missing from inside her, a child lost. An innocence lost. And she knew that even should the palace rise here anew, she would nevermore be able to gaze upon the sea again, nevermore imagine adventures, never more feel that innocent joy, nevermore dream like a child dreams, full of wonder.

Behind Issari, the other dragons grumbled, prayed, and blasted out smoke. They all saw the pit now. As they flew closer, Issari got a clearer view. The hole gaped open between the shattered columns of the palace--a chasm that seemed to delve down eternally. It was not merely dark. Darkness was only the absence of light. It was not merely black. Black was only the lack of color. This pit was an emptiness, a despair, a sinkhole crafted from the nightmares and anguish that tugged at the soul in the middle of the most silent, lonely night. Smoky tendrils rose from the deep, twisting like the tentacles of some subterranean creature reaching up to the sky. Evil itself seemed to be rising from the underground, a pain that clutched at the heart, that Issari felt deep inside her. It was the emptiness of her life, of her womb.

The nephilim upon the walls seemed to notice the dragons. They screeched. A few cowered. Others took flight and hovered over the city. Soon hundreds rose like flies from a disturbed carcass, yet they did not yet swarm to attack.

Issari darted ahead, then spun around, the city to her back, and faced the army of dragons.

"Hear me, Requiem!" she cried. "Hear me, dragons! The creatures of the Abyss crushed our homes. They swarm across all thirteen city-states of Terra, devouring, destroying. Their king lurks in darkness, festering in his pit. We will find him. We will slay him. For dragonfire, for justice, for Requiem!"

The dragon army returned her call, a thousand voices rising. Issari turned back toward the city and beat her wings, flying toward the ruins, gaining speed. Behind her, the thousand dragons streamed forward, roaring, smoke blasting from them. They hid the sky behind their wings. Their shadow covered the land.

In the city, the nephilim screeched, took flight, and flew toward them. The rotting creatures stretched out their lanky limbs, and their fangs shone. Their flesh was shriveled like that of mummified corpses, but their eyes blazed with hatred. They beat their insect wings, crying out for blood to drink, for bones to snap, for flesh to eat.

Which one of you is my son? Issari thought.

She blasted out her dragonfire.

The two hosts slammed together above the ruins.

"Slay them all!" Tanin shouted at her side. He blew his fire, torching two nephilim, and clubbed a third with his tail. Blood rained around the red dragon. "Slay every nephil you see!"

Suddenly Issari wanted to turn back. She wanted to stop Tanin, wanted to stop this assault. Slaying demons--as lurked inside that hole--was one thing. But suddenly she could not bear to kill nephilim. Here were the sons of mortal women! Here somewhere was her own brother, the creature Ishnafel, born to her father and the Demon Queen. Here somewhere might fly her own son. How could she slay them?

And yet Issari slew them.

She fought with tears in her eyes.

As the cackling, snapping creatures flew toward her, she burned them. She ripped out rotted flesh with her claws. She snapped their bones between her jaws. She slammed her tail against them. Their black blood rained upon the ruins.

Around her, the other dragons of Requiem fought with fang and fire. They bellowed as they fought, torching enemies, clawing nephilim apart. Even the old, the young, the weak fought under the setting sun, their fire bright. They slew many . . . but their blood too spilled.

Three nephilim landed on a young green dragon. The half-demons cackled as they disemboweled the beast, tugging their claws along the dragon's belly. With a scream, the Vir Requis returned to human form and tumbled down, a gutted woman. Several other nephilim landed on an old gray dragon, tore off cracked scales, and drove claws into flesh. The dragon lost his magic and fell, a screaming graybeard. The body thumped down onto the ruins, shattering against the piles of bricks. More bodies rained--men, women, children, their magic gone, their human forms shattering across the ruins.

"To the pit!" Tanin cried. He blasted forward a path of fire. "Dragons of Requiem, cut through them! Into the Abyss!"

The red dragon roared, scattered dragonfire every which way, and slashed with his claws. The dragons rallied behind him, driving through the enemy, making way toward the pit on the hill. Bodies fell before them. Issari flew at Tanin's side, burning nephilim, moving closer to the pit. She could see it gaping open ahead between shattered columns, a mouth with broken teeth, a chasm leading into the underworld.

"Fly, dragons of Requiem!" she cried. "Into the darkness! Into--"

Her words died.

He rose before her from the ruins, large as a dragon, a rotting man with black wings, a toothy jaw, and piercing green eyes. He had grown to monstrous size, but Issari knew him. Her son.

The creature rose in the sky, wings outstretched, ringed with fire. His long, serrated jaw opened wide, revealing rows of fangs. His flesh was so rotted it hung loosely, revealing ribs and a beating heart. A halo of unholy fire crackled to life around its brow. The nephil cackled.

"I am son of Sharael the Deceiver, rightful King of the Abyss!" he cried. "I was born from the womb of Issari Seran, a Queen of Eteer, the Priestess in White. I will lead you, nephilim. I am Legion! Slay the dragons for my glory."

The dragons roared and blasted fire.

"Kill it!" Tanin shouted. "Kill the creature!"

Blasting out their dragonfire, the dragons flew toward the nephil.

Issari hovered in midair, staring at Legion. He met her gaze. His eyes seemed so human to her; they were her own eyes.

"I'm sorry," she whispered, then raised her voice to a shout. "Tanin, no! Dragons, to me! Leave him!"

But the other dragons seemed not to hear her. Nephilim rallied around Legion, cackling, grinning, licking their chops; a few were gnawing on Vir Requis limbs. Their wings raised a buzz like a swarm of locust. Tanin and the other dragons flew toward them, and their jets of flame blasted forward. The fire washed over the nephilim, and Legion screamed, wreathed in the inferno.

"No!" Issari cried. She darted forward, soared, and placed herself between the combatants. Dragonfire washed over her, and she screamed and closed her eyes against the horrifying heat. She heard her scales crack.

"Dragons, hold your fire!" Tanin shouted somewhere beyond the inferno. "Issari!"

The flames died, and Issari coughed and shuddered but kept beating her wings. Her silver scales were black with soot.

"Into the Abyss!" she shouted to Tanin and the others. "Leave the nephilim to me. Go! I order you, by the light of Taal and the stars!"

She raised both front feet, and light blasted out from them-- the white light of Taal from the amulet embedded into one foot, and the light of Requiem from the star-shard embedded into the other.

"I'll hold them back!" Issari shouted. "Go!"

She spun back toward the nephilim, and her twin lights blazed over them, starlight and godlight. The unholy horde screamed. They covered their eyes. They buzzed and tried to attack but could not fly through the light.

"Go!" Issari shouted over her shoulder.

Tanin nodded and spun back toward the pit. He flew down toward the darkness, and the other dragons followed. One by one, they plunged into the pit, heading into the Abyss.

Issari returned her gaze to the nephilim. The creatures were screaming in pain as her light bathed them. She beat her wings, flew closer, washing them with the light of the gods.

"Back, nephilim!" she shouted. "Leave this place. Away! Away or I'll burn you." Her tears streamed as her son wailed in pain. "Away! Leave!"

Legion screamed, the light washing over him, and his voice sounded almost human to Issari, almost begging, pleading with her for mercy. She thought she could hear words in his cry. *Why, Mother? Why do you hurt me?* Issari wept but she flew closer, blasting him with the light of Taal and the light of stars. His skin burned.

"Leave, nephilim! Leave this place, Legion!"

They screamed as she herded them away, burning them, burning her son. She drove them from the city, but she could no longer kill them, and when finally the nephilim had fled over the walls, Issari wailed in pain, for she had hurt her son, and she had driven him away from her once more.

JEID

They flew over the sea, twenty dragons carrying men and women on their backs, heading toward the demonic hive.

Jeid's wings stretched wide, gliding on the wind. Laira and Maev slept upon his back, both in human form. Around Jeid, the other nineteen dragons also carried sleepers. The last survivors of Requiem had been traveling across the sea for days now, taking turns flying, the dragons carrying the humans upon their backs.

Now, after so long aflight, Jeid saw the distant shore of Eteer.

The sun touched the horizon, casting last flickers of red light like blood spurting from a dying man's mouth. But the ruins of Eteer burned with their own light. Scattered fires blazed among piles of bricks, cracked columns, and fallen walls. The city must have once been massive--truly a place to dwarf every village in the north combined. A white dragon flew above the ruins, and two beams of light blasted out from the beast, one white and the other silver. Thousands of demonic creatures shaped like giant, desiccated men fled from the rays, screeching until they vanished into darkness.

Those in human form woke up upon the dragons. They stared toward the distant ruins.

"Issari!" Laira cried, clinging to Jeid's neck. "It's Issari!"

The Vir Requis who were in human form leaped off the dragons' backs and shifted. The dragons' numbers swelled to fifty. All but Laira shifted; the queen remained in human form, her magic gone, clinging to Jeid's horns.

"Issari!" Laira cried again, rising to stand on Jeid's nape.

Hovering over the ruined city, the white dragon turned toward them. She lowered her feet, and her two beams faded.

The northern dragons reached the coast and shot over the beach. Below lay the corpses of many nephilim and men, and blood stained the toppled city walls. Beyond lay hills of rubble. The sun dipped below the horizon, leaving them in darkness.

"The others have gone into the pit!" Issari said when they reached her. The white dragon pointed at a hill that rose from the ruins. Shattered columns rose here in a ring like broken teeth, surrounding a chasm like a black mouth. Dark light seemed to emanate from the pit; though black as tar, Jeid could clearly see the columns, the ruins around them, and the chasm, as if staring at an astral world, a painting in many shades of darkness. He did not need to ask to know; here was the pit of the Abyss. A sickening, gut-twisting energy rose from it, palpable evil like smoke that invaded his nostrils. He was reminded of the demonic miasmas the sphinxes could spew; the same unholy aura clung to this place, invisible but just as sickening.

"Where's Tanin?" Jeid said, looking around for the red dragon, praying his son was not among the dead on the beach.

"Leading the assault into the Abyss," said Issari, beating her wings in front of him. "I remained behind to drive off the nephilim, the spawn of demons and mortal women. Let us follow into the darkness." The white dragon's eyes flicked up toward Laira. "Sister, shift too! Into a dragon!"

Laira said nothing, perhaps lost for words. Jeid answered for her. "Laira will ride me into battle, firing arrows from my back." He looked over his shoulder at her; his wife stared back, her eyes determined, and reached for her bow. Jeid cried out, his voice ringing across her and billowing her cloak. "Dragons of Requiem, follow! Follow into darkness and fear no demons. We fight for Requiem!"

He pulled his wings close together and swooped toward the hill. The columns shook and tilted below like teeth in a widening mouth, and it seemed to Jeid as if the hill were a great beast eager to swallow him whole. He narrowed his eyes, blasted down dragonfire, and shot into the darkness.

Silence engulfed him.

His dragonfire could not pierce the darkness.

As he dived down, Jeid looked over his shoulder. The other dragons had faded into smudges, shadows flecked with shards of light, figures beyond a dream. They too were blowing fire, short blasts of white and blue that flickered more like lightning than flames. Strands of blackness coiled everywhere, a soup of a foul, invisible smoke. The world had changed, time stretched and slowed and quickened, a world of muffled sounds, of blotches of darkness and light, of distant screams.

"Jeid!" rose a distant echo of a voice, a voice from worlds away. "Can you see anything?"

It was Laira's voice. Jeid couldn't even feel her weight anymore. Did she still ride him? He kept gliding down into the darkness; it seemed an endless pit.

"Nothing!" he shouted. "Can you hear me, Laira?"

His voice seemed to vanish into the nothingness. She did not reply. White scales flashed beside him, and he glimpsed Issari flying near, shouting to him, but he couldn't hear her words, and soon the white dragon vanished. Other dragons appeared and disappeared around him, ghosts flickering in and out of existence, only snippets of their voices reaching his ears.

"Papa!" rose a voice. "Papa, please. My stomach hurts. Help me. Please."

Jeid narrowed his eyes.

He gasped, then roared with pain and rage.

A small, fragile dragon was flying toward him, a mere toddler.

"Requiem!" he cried.

She flew, wobbling, trying to reach him. Her little claws stretched out. Blood dripped from her mouth.

"Father!"

Jeid's eyes watered. "My daughter!"

The little dragon kept flying his way, reaching out to him but never getting closer. The blood gushed from her mouth, and her eyes dampened.

"Papa, my stomach hurts. It hurts! I ate something bad. Help me." She beat her wings mightily but only seemed to be growing more distant. "Help me. They locked me here in the darkness. I'm scared."

"Requiem!" he shouted. "Fly to me. Fly!"

He beat his own wings, flying as fast as he could, streaming forward, shouting for her.

"Father, they have me! They're dragging me back. Father, help!"

Jeid watched in anguish as bloated, laughing, crimson demons emerged from the darkness, each several times Requiem's size. They grabbed the little dragon, wrapped their claws around her, and tugged her away. She screamed.

Jeid roared, the horror pulsing through him. Little Requiem, dead all these years, was here--his daughter was here! Being tortured, afraid, needing him.

"Requiem!" He tried to reach the demons grabbing his daughter, but they vanished into shadows, taking the little dragon with them.

"Jeid, what do you see?" Laira shouted somewhere; her voice sounded marks away.

Jeid kept roaring, kept flying into the darkness, trying to find her, to save his daughter. Did he see her soul here, trapped and cursed in an afterlife underground? He cried her name again, but she wouldn't answer, and all he heard was the demonic laughter that echoed all around him.

"Jeid," said another voice, frail and weak. "Help me . . ."

She materialized in the darkness. His beautiful Keyla. His first wife.

"Keyla!" he cried.

She hovered before him as a woman; she had never possessed the magic of Requiem. Her cheeks were sunken, her skin white and brittle, and instead of teeth, maggots filled her mouth. Her hair had grown wispy, and her fingernails had grown into claws. She was nothing but a corpse here, rotted away, rustling with worms, naked and shriveled, but her voice was the same. And she pleaded with him.

"Help me, my husband. Save me, Jeid. Save me. It hurts so much. They're clawing inside me . . . the creatures . . . they've been clawing for so many years."

Keyla tossed her head back and screamed. Demon claws reached out from the shadows, grabbed her, dug into her. Jeid howled as he flew, but he couldn't reach her either, even as the demons tugged her back, casting out cloud of blood.

The voices of his fellow Vir Requis echoed around him. Laira and Issari were crying out to Sena, begging demons to release their brother. Dorvin was screaming and cursing at other demons, demanding they release his sister Alina. Other dragons cried out names of their own lost ones. Were the souls of the dead truly trapped here, tortured eternally, or were these only visions?

"I can't see the other fallen," Jeid whispered. He heard Issari and Laira still crying out to Sena, but he couldn't see the dead prince. He couldn't see the fallen Alina, even as Dorvin screamed at the demons supposedly torturing her.

"It's a vision!" Jeid shouted. "Dragons of Requiem, hear me. Follow my voice! Follow my fire!" He blasted out flame. "You see only dreams. Only illusions the demons cast to torment us. Fly with me! Blow your fire with mine."

He blasted flames forward, a great shrieking jet. Maev emerged from shadows to fly beside him, his living daughter. The sight of her shot pride and comfort through Jeid. Requiem had fallen but Maev still lived, and she roared her fire with him. Red scales streaked above, and Tanin came flying to join them. It was the first time Jeid had seen his son in moons. The red dragon roared too and added his flames to theirs. The three pillars of dragonfire wreathed together, carving a path through the darkness. Other dragons joined their fire to the inferno, and the great stream crashed forward, lighting the darkness.

Shadowy demons shrieked and fell back from the blaze. Their voices cried out in terror. Some burned and crashed down. Others dispersed into smoke. The firelight revealed craggy walls around them, full of clinging demons who screamed and burned and died. The visions were gone. The darkness was lit. The fire of Requiem carved their way, slaying all in its path. A thousand dragons flew together, lighting the darkness.

DORVIN

Alina. Oh stars, Alina.

Dorvin shuddered as he flew through the darkness. His silver scales clattered madly like a suit of armor. He blasted out fire, and his eyes stung with the heat and rage. The dragonfire had banished the visions, but Dorvin couldn't shake the terror, couldn't stop seeing it.

Alina. His dear sister. Dead and gutted, her lacerated belly rustling with ants, worms in her eyes, her fingerless hands reaching out to him, begging him.

Please, Dorvin! she had cried. *Please save me. It hurts. It hurts so bad . . . they're hurting me . . .*

Dorvin paused from blowing dragonfire long enough to bellow with rage. He sucked in breath and blew flames again, adding his fire to the others' jets.

"It's only a vision!" Jeid was shouting, but the pain felt too real to Dorvin. Her voice had sounded too real.

I should have saved you on the mountain, Dorvin thought, remembering how Ciana had killed her, how he'd held Alina in his arms as she died. *I have to save you now.*

"Alina!" he cried out. "Alina, where are you--"

"Dung Beetle!" Maev growled at his side. The green dragon slammed her tail against his cheek. "Shut your jaw. It was only a dream, damn it. Like in Bar Luan. Now fly straight and blow your fire."

Dorvin winced but nodded. He kept flying with the others, kept roaring his flames. He was a warrior. He was a protector of Requiem. He would allow no fear or weakness to fill him.

Only a dream, he told himself. *Only a lie.*

The tunnel finally opened into a great cavern, a cave the size of a mountain. Dorvin thought that all of King's Forest, the woods surrounding the palace of Requiem, could easily fit into this place; the ceiling seemed as distant as the stars themselves. But this was no mere cave; the walls were not made of stone but fleshy membranes, veined and wriggling. They pulsed with blood and cast out a red glow. A sea flowed below, the water yellow and foul.

"We're inside the belly of some great beast," Dorvin said, flying with the others. Even a thousand dragons seemed small in this place, like a flock of bats in a cave.

Maev grumbled at his side. "Maybe the Abyss itself is a living creature, some great demon the size of a world, lurking underground."

Dorvin nodded and pointed ahead. "And all demons are parasites living inside it."

As if to confirm his words, a cloud of demons came flying their way, a thousand strong. Here flew creatures different than the ones that had swarmed to Two Skull Mountain. Here was not an unorganized mass but an army. Each demon was a soldier, a great insect coated with a metallic exoskeleton. Their claws reached out, embers filled their mouths, and red flames burned in their eyes. When Dorvin was young, he used to collect little roly polies--armored insects that would curl into a ball at his touch-- and toss them on his sister. These demons reminded him of those creatures but a thousand times the size, unholy and screeching for his blood, come to demand revenge for his torment of their little cousins.

At their lead flew a towering woman, large as a dragon, with stony skin that leaked lava through many fissures. Bat wings spread out from her back, and a ring of fire haloed her head. Her claws shone like swords, and her fangs gleamed with dripping saliva. Her eyes blazed white like smelters of molten metal, piercing Dorvin. He screamed under their gaze. The woman seemed to stare into him, to tear through his innards with those eyes, to peel back all his layers of skin, bone, organs, and the innermost secrets of his soul, leaving him bare, barren, a boy, frightened and alone.

Hello, Dorvin. The demon spoke in his mind. *Do you know who I am?*

He howled. He knew.

Angel, he thought. *Queen of the Abyss.*

She licked her lips and smiled at him. Her voice spoke again in his mind, high pitched like shattering metal, the shards of sound slamming against the inside of his skull.

Yes, I know you . . . her brother. Alina spoke of you. She screamed your name as I tortured her soul.

Dorvin roared with rage, beat his wings mightily, and shot toward the demon host.

"You lie, Angel!" he screamed. "I'll rip your damn tongue out, demon!"

He heard Maev roaring behind him, flying with him. Jeid bellowed above, Laira upon his back. Hundreds of other dragons shot forward too, and Dorvin flew at their lead, screaming, torn with agony and hatred. Angel's eyes bored into him, and her fire blasted out in rings, slamming against him. The shock waves knocked dragons into tailspin, but Dorvin righted himself and kept flying.

Angel smirked before him, churning smoke and fire with her bat wings.

Let's see how you like dragonfire, Dorvin thought and blasted out his flames.

The jet blazed forward, shrieking like a storm, white-hot in the center, expanding out to blue and roaring red. The inferno crashed against Angel and sprayed out, an explosion of dragonfire.

The Demon Queen only laughed. She flew across the cavern, swung her arm, and backhanded Dorvin like a parent cuffing a child.

The blow cracked scales on Dorvin's cheek and slammed his head sideways so powerfully his neck felt close to snapping. White pain washed over him, strewn with golden flecks of light, and his ears rang.

"Dorvin, damn it!"

Maev's voice rose from somewhere above; it sounded marks away. Dorvin shook his head wildly, tugging the world back into focus. The other dragons, an army of a thousand, were fighting around him in the cavern. Wave after wave of armored, insect-like demons flew toward them. Claws and fangs sparked against their exoskeletons, and dragonfire washed uselessly over their shells. Jeid grabbed one creature's leg and yanked it off with a shower of green blood. Laira, her dragon form lost, rode upon Jeid's back, firing arrows at the demons. Beyond them, Tanin and Issari fought back-to-back, lashing their tails at demons, punching holes through the thick armor. A thousand other dragons fought above and below, killing and dying.

"Dorvin, down, damn you!" Maev shouted.

Angel's hand swung again. Dorvin dipped in the air, and the demon's second blow thrust over his head. Maev came swooping down, fire raining on the Demon Queen. Angel laughed as the flames cascaded across her.

"Back, Mammoth Arse!" Dorvin shouted. "This one's mine. Go kill some smaller demon."

"Shut up and help me, Dung Beetle!"

Maev growled and swung her tail into Angel. The spikes drove through the demon's stone flesh. Lava spurted out from the wound, sizzling across Maev's tail. The green dragon screamed, tore her blazing tail free, and tumbled in the sky.

"All right," Dorvin muttered. "She's fireproof and her blood is lava. Fantastic."

He shot closer, braced himself, and swiped his paw, aiming at Angel's eyes. The Demon Queen raised her own claws so quickly Dorvin barely saw them. She blocked the blow, then thrust out her tongue. The wriggling muscle shot forward like a whip, wrapped around Dorvin's throat, and squeezed.

He sputtered, swinging his claws, Angel just beyond his reach. The tongue squeezed tighter. Dorvin tried to blow fire but he couldn't even breathe.

"Maev!" he managed to whisper. "Help!"

She flew above, flicking droplets of lava off her tail; the tip was red and raw. "I thought you said she was yours!" Maev shouted down. "Go on, warrior, slay her!"

Angel sneered, teeth gleaming. The tongue began pulling Dorvin closer to the waiting jaws. He thrust his paws, close enough to reach her now. His claws sparked against Angel's stone body. Only one claw tore through, and lava spurted out, burning Dorvin, and he couldn't even scream. Above, he saw Maev finally trying to swoop and help, but a crowd of flying demons, their armor dark with soot, crashed against the green dragon and tossed her back.

Soon you'll be with her, boy, the Demon Queen said in his mind. *Soon you and Alina will scream together.*

Rage pounded through Dorvin. Before he could pass out from lack of air, he raised his claws, gripped the demon's tongue, and twisted madly. The digit was elastic, wet, impossible to claw open, but Dorvin squeezed and tugged, and Angel screamed. He was hurting her. Good. The grip loosened around his neck, and finally he was able to blow fire.

The blaze slammed into Angel's face, entering her mouth, her nostrils, her eyes, and the Demon Queen screamed again.

It was no human scream. It was the sound of shattering souls, of crashing cities, of a million spines snapping together. The sound slammed against Dorvin so powerfully it ripped the tongue free and tossed him into a spin. His ears thrummed.

He blew fire again.

Maev swooped from above, raining down her own flames.

Scales flashed below, and Tanin and Issari both soared, blasting out two new jets of dragonfire.

Angel screeched, engulfed in the holocaust like a woman trapped within a sun. Within the flames, she writhed, kicked, struggled to fly, but her wings burned.

With a deep bellow and thudding wings, Jeid flew toward the battle and blasted out his own dragonfire, the widest of the pillars. Upon his back, Laira stood up, tugged back her bowstring, and fired. The arrow sailed through the flames and slammed into Angel's eye.

The Demon Queen tumbled down.

She crashed through lesser demons, tearing them apart, and finally struck the cavern floor. Cracks raced across the stone. She lay, twitching, struggling to rise.

"Burn her dead!" Dorvin shouted. "Dragons, slay the queen!"

He swooped, blowing his fire. A dozen dragons joined him, and soon a hundred descended, blasting down streams of fire. The jets crashed against the Demon Queen, knocking her back down, an inferno of heat and smoke and death. Her stone body melted. Lava spilled in rivers. As the outer layers peeled back, they revealed the Demon Queen's inner organs. Within the melting stone pulsed three hearts, squirming entrails, maggoty lungs, and blue veins. Faces twisted between the organs, human heads sewn along the spine, their mouths sucking air.

Dorvin hit the ground, claws clattering. Trickles of lava streamed between his feet. Angel writhed beneath him, still alive, her three exposed hearts pumping.

The demon tried to speak, but her throat had melted, revealing tendons bustling with insects. The other dragons landed around her, staring down at the dying creature.

Issari approached the demon. Blood coated her white scales. The dragon raised her head, then released her magic. Issari returned to human form--a woman clad in white, two lights upon her palms, her raven braid hanging across her shoulder. She stared down at Angel, her eyes hard.

"This is for Eteer," Issari whispered, drew her dagger, and slammed the blade down.

The dagger drove into one of Angel's three hearts.

Even with her ravaged throat, the Demon Queen screamed. The heart burst, showering blood. Issari stepped back, painted red, staring with cold eyes.

Laira stared down from Jeid's back, her face twisted with disgust. She nocked an arrow and tugged back her bowstring.

"This is for Sena," said the Queen of Requiem. Her arrow flew downward and slammed into another one of Angel's exposed hearts.

Blood showered. Angel convulsed. Red tears flowed from her eyes.

"Please," the Demon Queen whispered. "Please. I am Taal's daughter. Show me mercy as he would."

Dorvin too released his magic, returning to human form. He unstrapped his spear from across his back.

"I know nothing of gods," the hunter said. "But my sister did. She worshiped the stars, and she was the kindest, bravest, noblest soul I knew. Your army killed her." He raised the spear high, and he roared with his rage. "This is for Alina!"

He slammed the spear down, piercing Angel's last heart.

The demon bucked and screamed. Her legs thrashed. The faces sewn into her innards cried out in agony . . . and fell silent.

Angel's head tilted sideways, her stony flesh melting, running along the cavern floor in streams, until the Queen of the Abyss faded into nothing but a puddle of magma.

Across the cavern, the thousands of demons screeched with fear. Panting, Dorvin raised his head. Many dragons had died, but hundreds still flew above, battling the minions of the Abyss. The demons, seeing the death of their queen, turned to flee. They fluttered into burrows and halls. They dug through rock, vanishing into the floor and walls. Many willingly bit into their own flesh, slaying themselves and falling dead to the floor. Within moments they were gone.

The dragons of Requiem roared for victory and sang the songs of Requiem.

Dorvin glanced at his friends. They stared back.

"This isn't over yet," Dorvin said. "Where's that bastard Raem?"

The cavern began to tremble.

Light blasted out.

Dorvin turned and saw a great tunnel gaping open like a cervix, leading into a womb of crimson light. Laughter rose from within, deep and cruel.

"We will seek the hall of the underworld's king," Issari said softly. She shifted back into a dragon and took flight. "Follow! For Requiem!"

They rose as dragons, roared together, and flew toward the sickly light.

ISSARI

She flew through the pulsing, veined tunnel, feeling like a babe sliding out of the womb. The others flew behind her: Jeid, a massive copper dragon; Laira, riding on his back in human form, her magic gone; Tanin, the man she loved, a red dragon; and a thousand others, dragons who had united for their final battle--the battle against her father.

The tunnel narrowed, forcing the dragons to fly in single file. Issari flew at their lead. She drew up her paws, keeping them pressed against her belly as her wings flapped. She could feel the shards embedded there--her mother's amulet and the gift from the stars.

Finally Issari saw the tunnel's end, a circle of white and red light. She shot forward and emerged into a towering chamber, feeling like her son must have felt when emerging from within her.

She reared and tilted her wings, forcing herself to hover in midair. Fire sparked between her teeth.

A network of fleshy strands stretched across the chamber from ceiling to floor, crisscrossing, gleaming, pulsing with internal blood. They seemed organic, like hanging entrails or umbilical cords, forming a great web. The spaces between the strands were too small for Issari to fly through. Between them, Issari saw a great throne rising ahead; it seemed constructed of many small flaps of flesh--tongues, she realized.

Upon the throne sat Raem, King of the Abyss.

"Hello, daughter!" he cried out to her.

Issari could barely breathe.

The man she saw looked nothing like the father she remembered. In the battle of Two Skull Mountain, he had lost all four limbs. Demonic limbs now grew from his torso: a great bird's talon, a horse's hoof, a wriggling tentacle lined with suckers, and a great lobster claw. Leathery, bat-like wings grew from his back. His face too had changed, shriveled away, the cheeks sunken and gray, the eyes bloodshot and mad.

As the other dragons emerged into the chamber behind her, Issari blasted forth her flames.

The dragonfire blazed through the network of fleshy strands. The demonic web was dozens of feet deep, strand after strand all woven together. The veins shook in the dragonfire but did not burn. The fiery pillar broke apart into a fountain, dispersing into a cloud of flame, fading to sparks by the time it reached Raem's throne.

Most of the dragons still flew in the tunnel, but a dozen others came to hover by Issari's side, too large to fly through the fleshy web. They too blasted forth their dragonfire. The jets slammed against the pulsing strands. The web shook madly, scattering the flames, dispersing the inferno before it could reach the throne.

"The Abyss itself protects me, dragons!" Raem shouted from his throne. He laughed. His tentacle writhed and his lobster claw clattered. "You will have to face me as humans. Come, step through my web and face me."

It was Dorvin who reacted first. The silver dragon released his magic and raced forward in human form. He hopped between the fleshy strands, swinging his sword. An instant later, Tanin followed, then Laira, and soon many others were leaping between the strands. As humans, they were all armed with spears and blades, and they carried shields of wood and bronze. They cried out for Requiem as they ran toward the Demon King.

Issari still hovered as a white dragon, staring through the web at her father. He met her eyes across the distance and smiled.

May the stars protect me, Issari thought, landed on the floor, and released her magic. Unlike the others, she carried no shield, wore no armor; her faith would be her armor. Armed with only a dagger, she raced forward, moving between the strands; each was as thick as her wrist. Whenever she brushed against the dangling veins, they smeared her with sticky ooze. The other Vir Requis all raced around her, weapons raised, and more kept joining from the tunnel. They raised spears, swords, and shields. Tanin ran ahead, clad in bronze plates, holding shield and sword before him. The strands dangled madly whenever they bumped into them, and even swords could not break them.

"Stay with me, Issari!" Tanin shouted, running by her side. "We'll slay him together. We'll--"

A gasp swallowed his words. Issari stared ahead and felt the blood drain from her face.

Standing before his throne, Raem was shifting into a dragon.

The King of the Abyss ballooned in size, stretching like a boil, looking ready to burst. Black scales rose across him, clattering like a suit of armor. Horns grew from his head, fangs from his mouth, and fire burned in his gullet. His demon limbs too stretched out, the tentacle growing large as a tree, the hoof and talon kicking, the claw snapping like another set of jaws. The demonic dragon soared above the throne.

"Yes, weredragons!" Raem boomed. "I too am cursed with your disease. Now your own curse will be your undoing."

Issari paled and tried to shift too. She began to grow into a dragon, only for the clammy web to slam against her growing body, shoving her back into human form. Throughout the web, other Vir Requis too were trying to shift, but they had no room; the strands kept them humans.

"Tanin, your shield!" she screamed . . . and then the fire engulfed them.

Raem blasted out his flames. It was a massive jet of black fire, larger than any a dragon of Requiem could blow. Here was dragonfire tainted with a demonic curse, fire that danced like demons, cackled, and shone with many red eyes. The inferno slammed through the web, roaring, shrieking, cackling, a demon fire to burn all flesh.

Tanin shouted and held his shield before them. Issari crouched, pressed against him, hidden behind the bronze disk. The flames roared around them, reached around the shield, and burned across her leg. Tanin grimaced as the flames licked at his armor. Across the chamber, men and women screamed, and the smell of burning flesh filled Issari's nostrils.

When the fire finally died, Issari's heart sank. Dozens of Vir Requis lay dead between the strands, some propped up against the web. Their flesh was charred black and dripping blood; many were still burning. The flesh of some had melted, fusing with the demonic strands. A few victims still lived, screaming and rolling as the fire clung to them.

Issari leaped to her feet and ran again.

"Slay him!" Jeid shouted, running several feet away. Flames clung to his fur cloak; he tossed the garment aside. "Slay the beast!"

As more dragons entered the chamber, the survivors kept running through the web, moving closer to Raem. Only several more strands now separated them from the black dragon. Once past the web, they'd be able to shift again, to blow fire, to--

Raem rose higher, his belly swelled, and he blasted out new flames.

The jet crashed forward. Issari and Tanin hid behind the shield again. More Vir Requis screamed, skin peeling, flesh burning. When the flames finally died, dozens more lay dead, and the wounded ran screaming, fire clutching them.

Issari growled, raced between the last strands, and shifted into a dragon.

She soared toward her father. The demonic dragon loomed above her, thrice her size, tentacle writhing madly, eyes red and burning. Issari roared and blasted out her flames. Her white jet spun and crashed against Raem.

Other Vir Requis emerged from the web, some charred, some burning. They too shifted into dragons and soared. Their flames blasted out, bathing Raem.

The black dragon only laughed. The fire kindled his furred horse's leg, but the rest of him seemed unharmed. Raem lashed out his demonic limbs. The tentacle slammed against Issari, knocking her down onto the chamber floor. She groaned with pain, and through narrowed eyes, she saw Raem's lobster claw grab a young dragon and sever his neck.

"Cut him dead!" Jeid was roaring, leading a group of dragons. "Bite and claw!"

The copper dragon swooped, claws outstretched. Sitting upon his back, Laira fired arrows. Dorvin and Maev dived with their king, growling, reaching out their claws.

But the King of the Abyss only laughed, a massive creature to dwarf even the largest of Requiem's dragons. He blasted out more fire--a black, foul, shrieking storm. The stream blazed with the heat of a shattering star, with the rage of a typhoon, and crashed against the dragons. Laira screamed and hid behind her shield, but the blast knocked her off Jeid; she tumbled down into shadows. Dorvin and Maev slammed against the floor, their scales cracking with the heat. Raem's lobster claw swung and tore into Jeid's wing, ripping through it, and the copper dragon bellowed and fell.

Issari struggled onto her feet, coughing, burnt, bleeding. Tanin struggled to rise beside her. The two dragons glanced at each other, then rose again, flew toward Raem, and blasted out twins jets of fire.

The flames cascaded harmlessly off Raem. The demonic dragon only cackled, opened his jaws wide, and spewed out a cloud of buzzing demons the size of human babes. The creatures flew forward, shaped as maggots, isopods, centipedes, and clattering crayfish, all with human faces and cruel white eyes. Issari and Tanin managed to roast some of the creatures with dragonfire, but hundreds swarmed around the jet to land upon their backs, their wings, their tails. The little demons bustled across them, ripping holes into wings, yanking scales free. Issari screamed, the pain driving through her. When she looked at Tanin, she saw the demons tearing through him, pulling down his wings, tugging his horns.

"Tanin, shift!" Issari shouted . . . and released her magic.

She tumbled down, a human, leaving the demons in the empty air. Tanin followed her lead. Before they could hit the cavern floor, they shifted back into dragons and blasted fire skyward, roasting the swooping creatures.

Issari rose higher, bleeding and panting, her flames running low. Only a dozen dragons seemed to have made it this far; they were assaulting Raem, but their dragonfire flowed uselessly across the demonic dragon, and their claws and fangs did Raem's black scales no harm. The unholy beast laughed as he fought, grabbing and crushing dragons with his tentacle, snapping them apart with his claw, and roasting them with fire.

Dorvin lay moaning on the floor, bleeding from many cuts. Maev swooped toward Raem, but the black dragon's tail slammed against her, tossing her against the wall. The green dragon slumped down and lost her magic; Maev lay unconscious, perhaps dead. Jeid knelt on the floor over Laira; she lay with eyes closed, covered in blood. Other dragons flew toward Raem, only to die and crash down as lacerated, burnt humans.

"He's too strong," Issari whispered to Tanin. "We can't beat him."

Tanin panted, blood leaking across his scales. He tried to blow more fire, but only sparks left his mouth.

Towering above them, ringed with black smoke, rose the King of the Abyss, and Issari could barely see any dragon in him anymore. Raem had become not a Vir Requis but fully demon, a twisted thing, lava pulsing between his scales. His horns stretched out longer and longer, scraping across the ceiling and curling downward. His eyes leaked fire. Parasites scuttled in and out of his nostrils, ears, mouth, eyes. The Abyss had infested him, changed him, turned him into the greatest demon underground. No dragonfire could hurt him, Issari knew, no swords, no claws, no fangs.

"Only starlight," Issari whispered.

The creature who had once been her father turned toward her. The demon's chest puffed out, its wings spread wide, and it blasted out its unholy fire.

Still in dragon form, Issari reared in the air and held out her left paw, the one with the shard of starlight.

Only pale light glowed.

The demonfire flowed across Issari, and she screamed, fell, and burned.

"Issari!" Tanin cried.

She cried out in the inferno, and when the black flames finally died, she crashed to the floor, panting, burnt. Several of her scales fell and clattered against the floor. Tanin tried to reach her, but more of the small demons spewed out from Raem and crashed against Tanin's wings, holding him back.

Raem whipped his tail and tentacle, tossing dragons aside. He came clattering toward Issari, laughing. He loomed above, a hundred feet tall, and his eyes swirled like pits of molten rock.

"My daughter . . ." His smoke puffed down onto her, thick with flies. "Now finally I slay you. Now, in the pit of your despair, I will allow you to die."

Issari couldn't even rise. She was too hurt. Blood poured from her, and she tried to cling to her magic, but she was too weak. The dragon magic left her, and she knelt before the Demon King, a human again. The other dragons fell, cracked, burning; she faced her father alone. She stared up at him, a single woman, no larger than a mouse facing a wolf. She met the creature's gaze.

"I am not your daughter," she whispered. "You are no longer the man who was my father. You are nothing but an echo now, a shell of evil, emptied of all morality. You fought for Taal all your life, fought for the purity of humanity, but you let that humanity leave you." She struggled to her feet and opened her right palm. "But I still worship Taal. I still bear my mother's amulet, the woman you sent to exile and death."

She raised her palm, and Taal's amulet blazed out a pillar of white light. The beam slammed against Raem's eyes, and the demon bucked and squealed. Smoke rose from him. The light slammed Raem back against the wall.

Yet still Raem laughed. "I spit upon Taal. He has no power here. I am greater than Taal himself. I will kill the silver god."

Still holding the beam against her father, Issari took a deep, shaky breath. Her blood dripped. Her legs shook. But still she stood, shining her light.

"I worship more than Taal," she whispered. "I worship the stars of Requiem. I'm no longer your daughter, Raem, but I'm still--am always--a daughter of starlight."

She opened her left palm.

Please, stars of Requiem, she prayed silently. *Find me even here, even underground, even in darkness. Shine your light through me.*

Her hand thrummed, and a light began to glow there, growing stronger, not the pure light of Taal but a soft light of stars. Strands of starlight flowed out from that hand, wispy, forming dancing mottles no larger than doves.

Raem laughed above her. His wings spread out to crash against the cavern walls. His horns cracked the ceiling. Stones rained. "Do you think just a few strands of starlight can hurt me?"

He blasted down his fire again.

Issari raised her palm higher.

Flow through me, starlight. Flow through me, light of Requiem.

The light blasted out from her left palm, a great glow of starlight, forming a shield before her. The demonic fire cascaded against the disk of light, washing aside like waves around a boulder. Raem screamed, blinded by the light, and fell a step backward. He crashed against a wall, cracking it, and more bricks fell.

"Dragons of Requiem, slay him!" Jeid's cry rose somewhere in the distance. Issari thought she could glimpse the forms of dragons--they seemed so small next to Raem--blowing their fire, lashing their claws, cutting the Demon King. Raem's blood spilled, but still he fought, slamming the dragons aside.

"Send more light through me," Issari prayed. "Stars of Requiem, send all your might through the shard in my palm."

A voice seemed to speak in her mind, an angelic voice, kind and soft. *Child of Requiem! Too much light would sear through all flesh. We cannot give you more.*

"Send more light!" she cried out. "Send out the light of the constellation. Let me be a conduit to the stars."

The voice inside her seemed to weep. But the stars answered her prayer. The light grew, blasting out. It slammed against Raem, cracking the demon's scales, burning into the flesh.

The strands of starlight climbed up Issari's arm, turning her all to silvery light. She hovered in the air, lifted upon the stars, consumed with radiance, until all her body became nothing but starlight. The beam now moved not through the shard on her palm but through all of her; she rose as a star herself, casting her beam, lighting the Abyss.

Requiem, she thought and wept. *I have found your stars.*

The light coalesced and blasted out from her chest. It shot forward with new vigor, brilliant and blue and silver, and drove into Raem, shattering the demon's chest, crashing through the rotted heart within, and burning out the unholiness like heated metal cauterizing a wound.

His magic left him.

His demonic limbs detached and shriveled up like worms on a hot stone.

Raem Seran, King of the Abyss, once her father, slammed down against the floor, a mere man again . . . glowing with starlight, fading, burning, dwindling away . . . until he was gone.

Issari fell to her knees. The starlight still thrummed through her; she glowed, a figure of light, burning up.

"Issari, let it go!" Tanin was shouting. She could barely see him through the silvery veil. "Release the starlight!"

But she could not; she had taken on too much. She trembled, smiled, wept. She was one with the stars.

"Issari!" He reached into the light, grabbed her, and shook her. "Issari, enough!" He grabbed her hand and forced it shut, sealing the shard behind her fingers.

She gasped.

The beam of starlight pulled into her, sucked up. She felt it driving into her chest, coiling inside her. The glow faded. She fell into his arms, feeling so light, and the world spun.

"Is he dead?" she whispered. She looked to where Raem had stood and saw only charred bones.

"It's over," Tanin said, tears on his cheeks. He lifted her in his arms. "It's over, Issari. Now let's get you out of here."

The starlight glowed inside her head, overflowing, hiding everything behind silver haze. She saw nothing more.

LAIRA

She rode on Jeid's back, holding her sister in her arms.

"I'm with you, Issari," she whispered. "You'll be all right. It's over." Laira smiled through her tears. "We won."

The copper dragon flew beneath them, rising through the tunnels of the Abyss, heading back toward the good world above. King Raem had fallen. Their father--the man who had tortured Issari and Laira, who had driven Sena to take his own life, who had become a demon worse than any imaginary monster he had fought--had burned away, leaving but a memory for their nightmares.

"It's over," Laira whispered again, holding Issari close as the dragon glided beneath her.

She did not just mean the battle in the Abyss. She did not just mean the war against the demons and their hosts. She did not just mean Requiem's struggle to rise from scattered refugees into a kingdom. The great pain of their life had ended. Laira's longer struggle--from exile, to slavery in the Goldtusk tribe, to war and fear, to losing her magic in the shattered hall of Requiem--was over. Issari's own war--against a cruel father, against the nephilim in the south, against the deeper pain in her eyes of which her lips would not speak--too had ended.

"Our family is healed," she whispered. "Do you hear me, Issari?"

Her younger sister lay upon Jeid's coppery scales, smiling softly, held in Laira's embrace. Blood and ash stained Issari's robes, and dragonfire had burned the hems and sleeves. If the fire had burned Issari's skin too, the stars had healed it. Indeed Issari's skin seemed to glow with inner light, as if the strands of starlight still filled her. Threads of light glowed around Issari's fingernails, between the lines of her palms, through the slits of her closed eyelids, and between her lips, as if the starlight filled her to the brim, aching to spill out.

"Laira," she whispered softly, and luminous wisps fled her lips like frost on a cold day. "I'm so glad I met you again. I love you, Laira. I always have." She opened her eyes--they shone like two stars--and caressed Laira's cheek. "My sister. I will always look after you. Always."

Laira frowned and squeezed Issari's hand. "I'll look after *you*. I'm your older sister. We're going to Requiem now, and we'll live together again. A new family. Tanin can live with us too if he likes." Her eyes dampened. "We'll build a little hut, and we'll spend our lives among the birches, in the shadow of Requiem's columns." Tears rolled down her cheeks to splash against Issari. "We'll finally have the life we always should have lived--together."

Though even as she spoke those words, Laira knew they were a lie.

Life is not like that, she thought. *Tragedies and hardships fill life, and one can always fight against them, always hope to defeat them, but victory leaves one changed. Triumph, after so much pain and heartache, leaves one broken, scarred, sometimes too hurt to ever feel peace. Perhaps peace earned with blood and tears is forever stained.*

Thus were they hurt. Laira had saved Requiem, but not without sacrificing her magic; she could live in the hall among the columns, but she could nevermore fly above them as a dragon. Sena had overcome an army of demons, only to find that the true demons lurked within him, even in the peace of Requiem's forest, and those demons of the soul had overcome him. Issari had defeated their father, but she too was changed, soaked with

starlight, burning up in Laira's arms. Three children of starlight
and of evil. Three children too hurt, too haunted, too broken.
They had found victory but Laira knew that they would never find
peace.

*War leaves us all dead, some dead underground and others dead
inside. Some remain upon the killing fields. Others forever carry those ashes
inside them.*

Laira smelled fresh air above. The tunnel ended, leading up
into the ruins of Eteer. The dragons of Requiem emerged into the
night. Stars covered the firmaments. The Draco constellation
shone over the sea, but its light seemed faded despite the clear
night. The dragons flew across the toppled city and landed on the
beach, claws sinking into the wet sand. The waves whispered
ahead, their crests limned with moonlight. Of the thousand
dragons who had entered the Abyss, perhaps only five hundred
remained; the rest had fallen to the horrors of the underworld.

Laira climbed off Jeid's back and laid Issari down upon the
sand. The young woman smiled up at her, eyelids fluttering, and
ten beams of light flowed out from her fingertips and toes.

A red dragon landed beside them and released his magic.
Tanin ran up to Issari and clutched her hand, the one which
contained the amulet. Laira held her other hand, the one
embedded with a star.

"Issari," Tanin whispered. "Can you hear me? You have to
let it go. Let out the starlight." He looked up at Laira and barely
forced the words past his lips. "She's burning up."

The others gathered around: Jeid, his fur cloak gone to the
fire, his bare chest covered with welts and cuts; Maev, blood
staining the dragon tattoos along her arms, her eyes hard but her
trembling lips revealing her fear; Dorvin, his stubbly hair caked
with ash and blood, his eyes wide with horror. All stared down at
Issari.

"Is she dying?" Dorvin whispered. "She's lit up like a bloody lantern."

The strands of light began to flee Issari, flowing out from her body and coiling around her, wrapping her in a cocoon.

"The light of Draco shines within me," Issari whispered, and her voice thrummed, high, harp-like. "I've taken the light into me, a conduit for the stars, and now those stars call me home." Tears like diamonds fell from her eyes. "I will find Requiem's sky. Do you see it, Laira? Do you see?"

"What?" Laira whispered, holding her sister's hand. "What should I see?"

Issari smiled tremulously. "The palace of Requiem. The halls of our kingdom. All silvery, rising from the forest, hundreds of columns and Vir Requis in white robes, playing harps, and leaves upon the tiles. I see them above. The celestial halls." She squeezed Laira's hand. "You will build them, Laira Aeternum, Mother of Requiem. Your descendants will grow into a great nation that will rise in their light." She looked at Tanin. "And you will forever fly with her, Tanin, Prince of Requiem, the light of my heart, the love of my soul. You will build these halls together, and I'll watch over you. Always. Always."

Tears dampened Tanin's cheeks. He pulled Issari into his arms and kissed her lips. "Don't speak like that. As if you won't be there with us." His chest shook. "Don't you leave us, Issari Seran. Don't you dare."

She cupped his cheek in her hand and kissed his forehead. "Never, Tanin. Never. I love you." She turned toward Laira. "I love you, sister." She turned to look at the others, and her smile became warm, deep, a smile of pure joy. "I love you all, children of Requiem."

"Issari, no!" Tanin cried as the starlight intensified, spinning around her.

He cried out as Issari began to rise, and he tried to hold her back, but she broke apart in his arms into a thousand strands of light that rose higher, coiling and singing, a great white pillar that spun, rising higher, singing with the song of harps.

The Vir Requis stood in the sand, watching as the astral light ascended, taking the form of a white dragon in the sky, a spirit of Requiem. The dragon let out her cry, a song of dragons, a prayer of Requiem, an angelic choir. The spirit rose higher, growing smaller, flying toward the Draco constellation. There in the sky, the light coalesced into a single point, a silver star, and settled into the constellation, forming the eye of the celestial dragon.

"She became a star in the Draco constellation," Dorvin whispered. "Bloody barnacles." He whistled appreciatively. "Never knew the girl had it in her."

Laira stared up at the constellation, and she laughed through her tears. Jeid approached her and placed his arm around her.

"A new star shines in the sky," said the King of Requiem. "The eye of the Draco constellation will always watch over us, always guide us, always remind us of our war, of our victory, and of those we lost."

Tanin walked up to them, his eyes damp, and hugged them with a crushing urgency. Dorvin and Maev looked at one another, then held hands, approached the others, and joined the embrace. All across the beach, the dragons of Requiem whispered, prayed, sang, and pointed at the new star.

We begin an era of peace, Laira thought, holding her family close. The pain and joy mingled inside her, and she knew that both emotions would never leave her. She knew that this loss would forever be an emptiness within her, greater even than her missing magic. *I found a home. But I lost you, Mother. I lost you, Sena. I lost you, Issari. How can I, the last of my family, still feel joy?*

Jeid was looking at her, and she met his gaze. She saw the compassion there, the pain he too felt, and he held her tightly. Laira laid her head against her husband's chest, and the song of the sea and the prayers of Requiem flowed around her.

JEID

He had flown south with fewer than fifty dragons, the last survivors of the northern wars. He flew back with five hundred. They crossed the sea in three days and nights, sometimes flying as dragons, sometimes resting as humans on the backs of their comrades. On a rainy evening they reached the coast, then flew over the forests and plains, heading home. Heading to Requiem.

On a cold dawn, they finally saw them in the distance: the columns of Requiem rising from charred trees, calling them home.

Only King's Column still shone, unmarred and pure. Several other columns had fallen and cracked. Some still rose, but their marble was chipped, their capitals shattered. But unlike the ruins of Eteer, a portal to darkness, here was a glimmer of hope, Jeid thought. A place not of death but of dreams, of seeds that could still sprout even through the ashes.

The dragons flew toward Requiem. They spoke different tongues. They came from distant lands: from Bar Luan in the west, from the city-states of the south, from wandering tribes in the north. Some were tall and fair and blond, others smaller and darker, some old, some only children. They were hunters, scribes, masons, farmers, mothers, fathers, orphans. But flying as dragons on the wind, they were all the same. Their scales all shone in the dawn, and their wings all beat together. Here they were all Vir Requis.

They landed among the columns, and at once their work began. They pulled aside fallen stones. They cleared out gardens and collected seeds. They flew to the mountains to carve out new marble. They cooked, they sang, they wove fabric, they prayed. They built a home.

As Jeid bustled from garden to hut, from quarry to campfire, an absence gnawed on him.

"Have you seen Tanin?" he asked, approaching a campfire.

Turning a spit of venison, Maev shook her head. "Not since we arrived. I thought he was at the quarry. I-- Dorvin!" Maev leaped to her feet. "Stars dammit, you're burning it."

The dark-haired young man was kneeling by another campfire, holding a spit. The chunk of meat upon it was smoking. "It's not my fault! Dammit, I'm a hunter, not a cook. Back in my tribe, only women did the cooking."

Maev smacked the back of his head. "Well, you're not back with your tribe. You're in Requiem now. Move over." She shoved him. "Damn good meal and you ruined it."

Jeid left the two, seeking his son, but could not find Tanin at the quarry in the mountains, nor the gardens, nor the work sites where men and women were building houses of stone. Finally it was deep in the forest, as the sun set, that Jeid found his son.

Tanin sat on a hill, staring up at the sky as the stars emerged. If the young man heard Jeid approach, he gave no note of it. Tanin simply stared up at the stars, silent, leaning back. Jeid approached his son, sat down beside him with creaking joints, and stared up at the sky with him. For a long time the two men said nothing.

Finally it was Tanin who broke the silence. "I know I'll see her again someday, but the wait seems so long. The years ahead seem so empty without her."

Jeid thought back to his own years of grief. For over a decade after his wife had died, Jeid had hidden in the escarpment, wasting away, imprisoned not only within walls of stone but by his grief. That time now seemed a haze to him. An entire decade--just a blur, just missing time, for he had barely been a man in those years, only a shell. He looked at Tanin, and he refused to let the same happen to his son.

He spoke slowly. "The pain never really leaves you. Loss is an eternal emptiness inside us, and time does not heal all wounds. But that doesn't mean we should let the grief claim us. That doesn't mean we cannot go on. And you will go on, Tanin. You will build. You will plant gardens and raise walls of stone. You will help build our kingdom, and you will build a new life for yourself. With me. With Laira. With Maev and Dorvin. With all those who love you."

Tanin nodded. "But it hurts. And I miss her."

"It always will hurt. And you always will miss Issari. Pain is like that. Sometimes comfort, time, even love cannot banish it. Sometimes pain is like a scar, forever with you. But that doesn't mean you can't feel joy too. Old pain doesn't chill the warmth of new happiness. Old shadows cannot extinguish new light. Saplings still rise from burnt forests; thus can new happiness rise in a broken soul. We'll find new happiness, all of us. Together."

They sat together in silence then for a long time, watching the stars, and the Draco constellation seemed to gaze back down at them, its eye shining.

LAIRA

Spring bloomed in Requiem--a spring for a charred forest, for a united people, for shards of scattered life.

Many of the birches were still black with soot, but some still lived; leaves sprouted from their tips and birds fluttered between their branches. Saplings grew between them from ash. And beyond them, past where the battles had raged, older birches shrugged off the cloak of winter and gave forth new leaves, fresh and sweetly scented. The song of birds rose across the land, and bluebells bloomed upon the forest floor, a lavender carpet that hid the soil.

The palace of Requiem too found new life in the spring. The dragons of Requiem toiled, clearing the rubble of those columns that had fallen in the war. They raised new columns, and they mended the broken tiles, and a dozen columns soon rose in two proud palisades. Several masons from Eteer now lived here as Vir Requis, men and women with the wisdom to raise great halls. Laira spent much time among them, and she found herself adept at building, gradually mastering the art of balancing stones, of understanding their weight and pressures, of understanding the secrets of raising great halls like those in Eteer. Into clay tablets she etched the plans for a great palace, a roof resting upon its columns and halls leading to many chambers.

Across the rest of the forest, other buildings were sprouting--a foundation here, a wall there, homes of stone. The Vir Requis would no longer live in caves, in huts, in tents, but in permanent dwellings like those in the south. In Requiem they would build their own kingdom, a kingdom to last for eternity.

"It will take many years to complete," Laira said, pointing at her clay tablets. She tapped her engraving stick against one drawing; it showed many halls and homes rising from the forest. "But once this city is complete--when we are old and gray--it will be a wonder to the world."

Dorvin chewed his lip. "Which one's my house?"

Laira raised her stick to point at the true columns that rose ahead, the skeleton of their palace. "In there. In the palace. With us." She smiled. "You're to marry Maev, I presume, the princess of Requiem. You're going to be a prince."

He thrust out his bottom lip and nodded appreciatively. "A prince. I could tolerate that." He glanced over his shoulder. "I only need to get the old mammoth arse to agree to marry me now."

Maev came walking toward them, clad in furs and a bronze breastplate. "We better get married. I'm not raising our child without a husband."

Dorvin tilted his head. "Our . . . what now?"

The golden-haired warrior nodded. "You didn't think you could poke into me so often and not put a little baby inside me, did you?"

Dorvin looked at Laira, then back at Maev. His eyes widened, and he began to hop around. "Bloody dragon shite! I mean-- I can't curse anymore, can I? A baby. A little Dorvin." He shifted into a dragon, rose into the sky, and roared.

Laira stared up, smiling softly, and placed her hand upon her own belly.

Spring brought new life to Requiem, and when those leaves finally turned orange and gold and glided upon the marble tiles, more light lit the halls of Requiem. Maev walked across the tiles of the palace, holding her son, and came to present him to the king.

"I name him Eranor," Maev said, and for the first time in many years, there was softness to her eyes and voice, a deep love and compassion she let emerge through the brick walls that had always guarded her soul. "Eranor Eleison, a noble prince of Requiem."

The baby slept in her arms, his hair dark like his father's. Dorvin gazed at his son with pride.

"A future warrior," he said.

Maev shook her head. "May he never know war. May Eranor become a man of peace and wisdom, and may he never swing a sword, and may he never blow fire in rage or fear." She kissed her son. "May he know nothing but the song of wind in birches and the light of our halls."

The carpet of dry leaves was thicker, and the branches of trees almost bare, when Laira too entered the palace, holding her own babe. The little girl gurgled, her hair black like her mother's, but her eyes were large and brown like her father's.

Laira placed the newborn in Jeid's arms. "Your daughter. Issari Aeternum, Princess of Requiem. May she forever be blessed." Laira raised her eyes and gazed up at the stars that emerged in the sunset. "May those we lost forever protect her. May they look down upon us now from our celestial halls, and may they feel blessed."

Jeid rose from his throne and held his newborn daughter to his chest. The King of Requiem beamed with pride, and a smile rose on his lips, but sadness filled his eyes too. Laira stepped closer and placed her hand upon his chest.

"I see grief in you," she whispered.

King Aeternum nodded. "As new life rises, I think about those we lost. As the laughter of babes rings through our halls, I remember my tears for those who fell. But I know they're up there. That they watch over us." Holding his daughter with one arm, he wrapped his other arm around Laira. "We lost families, but we found new life, and we build new homes. Together, Laira. Always."

That evening, all the people of Requiem stepped into the hall of their king. They wore white tunics, and many held scarves of silver and green, the new colors of their kingdom. Above the hall fluttered a great standard of cloth, green like spring leaves, and silver stars were sewn in the shape of the Draco constellation. The largest among them was the dragon's eye, which they called Issari's Star. The true constellation shone above, its light falling upon King's Column and the children of Requiem.

A girl named Tilai played a harp, and men and women lit many clay lanterns. With light and song, Jeid and Laira, King and queen of Requiem, presented their daughter to their people.

Jeid spoke in a deep, clear voice that filled the hall, soothing as distant thunder in a fading storm. "For many years we hid. In northern caves. In southern cities. In forests and in deserts, in tribes and towns, in the wilderness and in the hives of great civilizations. All our lives, the people of the world hunted us, called us cursed, diseased, weredragons to be hunted and killed. But we united. Together we stood strong. Together we told the world: You cannot hunt us. We are not monsters. We are Vir Requis, and we have a kingdom."

The people raised their lanterns and cried out their approval.

Laira spoke next, her voice higher and softer but no less clear. "We've all suffered great losses in our war. We lost friends. We lost family. We lost something inside us; we will forever carry those scars. I lost a sister, a brother, a mother. I lost even the magic of starlight. But I gained a home. This home is precious. Requiem is a gift to always cherish, protect, and nurture. We will keep building our humble kingdom. For thousands of years, generations will look back upon us. They will remember us as those who kindled the fire, who first stood together, who set our ship upon its course." She raised her child in her arms, holding the girl up for all to see. "We will pass this torch of starlight to a new generation. May our children find peace. May they know only a Requiem of light."

Jeid spoke again, and now he lowered his head, and his voice was softer. "I am humbled that you've chosen me to be your king, that you followed me in war, that you follow me now in peace. I stand here thanks to the sacrifices of others. Of your brothers, sisters, mothers, fathers. Of my own daughter whose name lives on in our kingdom. Of Issari who shines in our sky. Of hundreds who sing in the starlit halls above, a twin to our palace below. I will not forget their sacrifice, and I vow to you, Requiem: I will lead you on a path of starlight, and I will not stray from it to the left or right." He shifted into a dragon. "Requiem! May our wings forever find your sky."

Holding their child, Laira climbed onto his back, and Jeid took flight. Around him, five hundred other dragons soared. They flew above the halls and shadowy forest, and their stars shone above. When Laira looked up, she imagined that she could see them there: her mother, her brother, her sister, smiling and at peace. She knew they were proud of her.

As the wind streamed around them, and as Jeid glided beneath her, Laira held her daughter close to her breast.

May you never know the pain I knew, little Issari, she thought and kissed the babe. *May you never feel so alone, so afraid, so hurt. May you always know a home, loving parents, a world of beauty.* A tear streamed down Laira's cheek. *Because I will never know peace, and I will never know beauty. The pain is too deep, the scars inside me too real, too raw, wounds that will never heal.*

When she closed her eyes, she saw them again--the demons of the Abyss, the cruel face of Chieftain Zerra, and her mother burning at the stake. She still heard so many screams, and Laira knew they would forever echo in her nightmares.

It's too late for me to know beauty and joy, she thought. *But not for my daughter. Not for our children. May my life be a sacrifice to them, and may my pain be the foundation upon which I can build them a joyous life.* She kissed her daughter's head. *That will comfort me in the long, cold nights when the memories do not leave. That will bring some peace for a soul too torn to fully heal.*

And that, she thought, was not a bad future. Her life so far had been of pain, of terror, of loneliness, but many years still lay ahead--years of of healing, of family, of starlight.

The dragons sang as they flew in the night, and riding her husband, Laira added her voice to theirs. "Requiem! May our wings forever find your sky."

Laira had no more wings, but she knew that the sky would forever be hers, forever be their children's, forever be the true kingdom of Requiem.

LACRIMOSA

She walked among the birches, holding her daughters' hands.

"Mama, I'm bored." Agnus Dei stamped her feet. A girl of three years, she had inherited her father's olive skin, curly black hair, and fiery temper. "I want to go home. I want to go." She struggled to break free from Lacrimosa's grip.

"Hush now!" Lacrimosa said. "It's the Night of Requiem. Three thousand years ago, our first king raised our column in the forest. We must go pray."

"But I hate praying." Agnus Dei pouted. "I hate it I hate it I hate it. I want to go home and play with our new puppy."

Lacrimosa sighed. The girl was a handful, a wild little beast, a ball of endless tears, passion, anger, love, and laughter. Lacrimosa loved the little devil more than the stars above and the ground beneath her feet.

"I like praying," said Gloriae, her voice soft.

Lacrimosa turned toward her other daughter. While Agnus Dei kicked and tugged mightily at Lacrimosa's right hand, little Gloriae walked primly, holding Lacrimosa's left hand with a firm grip. Though twins, the girls looked nothing alike. Gloriae had inherited her mother's pale skin, silvery-blond hair, and light eyes. While Agnus Dei was angry and strong like her father, Gloriae was like Lacrimosa--reserved, proper, always a little sad.

"I know you do," Lacrimosa said, squeezing Gloriae's hand. "You're a little gem of starlight."

"I'm a little bit of fire!" Agnus Dei said, tugging again and struggling to break free.

They kept walking through the forest. Other Vir Requis walked around them, clad all in flowing white. Priests played silver harps, and knights wore burnished armor. All bowed their heads as Lacrimosa Aeternum walked forth with her daughters, the two princesses of Requiem.

Soon Lacrimosa saw it ahead: the palace of Requiem. Many columns soared here, hundreds of feet tall, pale marble that glittered like starlight. A roof rose overhead, engraved with flying dragons of marble and gold. Hundreds of Vir Requis gathered here, all in white, many holding orchids and silver harps. Lacrimosa and her daughters walked among them and entered the hall of Requiem.

The marble tiles stretched between the columns, leading toward the Oak Throne. Upon it sat the old king, his beard long and white, a crown upon his head. At his side stood Lacrimosa's husband: Prince Benedictus Aeternum.

He walked toward her, a tall man, handsome but haggard, many years her senior. His black curls fell across his brow, and warmth filled his dark eyes. He wore garments of green and silver, the colors of Requiem, the Draco constellation embroidered on his doublet.

"Papa!" cried Agnus Dei. She tore free from Lacrimosa, ran across the hall, and leaped on Benedictus. He smiled and scooped her up, and the little girl rained kisses upon his tanned, stubbly face. Gloriae approached her father more slowly but with no less love; he lifted her in his other arm.

"Papa, I want to go home and play with the puppy," Agnus Dei said. "Please. Please! It's so boring here in the palace."

Benedictus smiled and mussed Agnus Dei's curly black hair. "It's the Night of Requiem, Agnus Dei. A special time. Over three thousand years ago, this column was first raised."

Benedictus walked toward one of the hall's columns. It looked much like every other column here, but legend said this one was special. They said that Aeternum himself, the founder of Requiem, had raised this pillar, creating a home for a lost people, a palace for a new nation.

Lacrimosa walked over to stand by her husband and daughters. She placed her hand against the marble. "According to legend, so long as Vir Requis live, this column will stand. Swords have tried to cut it down. The claws of sphinxes tried to scratch it." She imitated a sphinx's swipe, making Agnus Dei and Gloriae squeal. "But the stars protect it. Look." She pointed between the columns. "Those stars are appearing."

As the sun set and the sky deepened to indigo, the stars shone and Lacrimosa smiled, for they soothed her, warmed her, gave her hope. Many people were gathering in the palace now, standing between the columns.

"It's time, my husband," she whispered. "Our dance."

Prince Benedictus nodded. He walked toward a knight and his family who stood in the hall.

"Would you watch my daughters for a few moments, Lord Eleison?"

The knight ruled a noble family descended from Dorvin Eleison himself, the Great Hunter said to have slain the Queen of the Abyss thousands of years ago. The knight bowed his head. "Of course, my prince."

Lord Eleison's wife held her own child, a babe with golden hair. Benedictus smiled down at the boy.

"How is little Kyrie doing?" Benedictus asked.

"No more trouble than a turnip," said Lady Eleison and kissed her sleeping son.

Seeing the baby, Agnus Dei's eyes widened. "A little pup!"

Benedictus laughed, leaving his twins with the Eleisons, and walked back toward Lacrimosa. He took her hand in his, then led her to the center of the hall. There they danced, a prince and his wife, as the columns rose around them and the priests played their harps. Lacrimosa knew that Benedictus hated dancing, knew that he hated so many eyes upon him, but thus were the ways of the court, and Benedictus always did his duty. Still, she heard his sigh of relief as the first dance ended, as others joined the hall in dance and song.

Lacrimosa glanced over toward her children. Gloriae was standing quietly with the Eleisons, and Agnus Dei was hopping about, patting little Kyrie and planting kisses on his cheek, talking about how she'd marry him someday.

"I think they'll be all right for another moment or two," Lacrimosa said to her husband. "Will you fly with me? Under the stars of Requiem's Night?"

He nodded. She knew he preferred the sky to the busyness of the court. They walked together, her hand upon his arm, and stepped out into the forest. Here they summoned their magic. Lacrimosa rose into the sky as a silver dragon, slim and small, while Benedictus rose as a burly black beast, among the greatest dragons in Requiem, his scales darker than the space between stars but his eyes warm as hearths.

They rose together, she only half his size, silver and black, until they soared high above Requiem. Looking down in the night, Lacrimosa could see the palace, many homes of pale bricks, a domed temple to the stars, courtyards, statues, and everywhere the birches. Far beyond rose the indigo shadows of the mountains. Lacrimosa tried to imagine this land three thousand years ago--only a few wild Vir Requis living in the forest and caves, alone in the dark, a scattered people without a home. Lacrimosa had married into royalty, and Requiem was now her charge. She vowed to keep this torch of starlight forever burning.

"Now we can truly dance," she said.

Smiling, Lacrimosa stretched out her wings and glided through the night sky. Benetictus flew with her, rising and falling, and they spun languidly together, their scales bright in the moonlight. She sang with a high, pure voice like a harp, and he added his deep rumble, a sound like rolling thunder. They danced above Requiem, coiling in lazy swirls of silver and black, and their voices rose together in a song of dragons.

THE END

NOVELS BY DANIEL ARENSON

Dawn of Dragons:
Requiem's Song
Requiem's Hope
Requiem's Prayer

Song of Dragons:
Blood of Requiem
Tears of Requiem
Light of Requiem

Dragonlore:
A Dawn of Dragonfire
A Day of Dragon Blood
A Night of Dragon Wings

The Dragon War:
A Legacy of Light
A Birthright of Blood
A Memory of Fire

The Moth Saga:
Moth
Empires of Moth
Secrets of Moth
Daughter of Moth
Shadows of Moth
Legacy of Moth

KEEP IN TOUCH

www.DanielArenson.com
Daniel@DanielArenson.com
Facebook.com/DanielArenson
Twitter.com/DanielArenson